Heartsong Cottage

HEARTSONG COTTAGE

For information address St. Martin's Press, 175 Fifth Avenue, New York, NY 10010.

ISBN: 978-1-62953-754-2

Printed in the United States of America

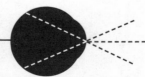

**This Large Print Book carries the
Seal of Approval of N.A.V.H**

Heartsong Cottage

EMILY MARCH

St. Martin's Press

Doubleday Large Print Home Library Edition

To Christina Dodd

For helping me so much on this ongoing #AuthorAdventure.

Anchors aweigh!

Heartsong Cottage

Chapter One

TEN YEARS AGO
SUBURBAN BOSTON

Daniel Garrett's eyes flew open to darkness and an unholy sensation of dread slithering in the pit of his stomach. He'd like to think it was due to the greasy plate of ribs he'd eaten with his dad last night at the Patriots game, but he knew better.

Something was off. His universe just wasn't right. The feeling had plagued him for the better part of a week.

So what was it? What had yanked him out of a sound sleep at—he glanced at the bedside clock—4:57 in the morning, a full hour before the alarm was due to go off?

He took stock of his surroundings. Beside him, his wife lay sleeping peacefully, smelling of the rose-scented lotion she'd lathered on after her shower, the blocks of ice that doubled as her feet burrowed beneath his legs. Lifting his head from his pillow, he turned his ear toward the doorway and listened intently for any sound coming from the bedroom down the hall.

No. Nothing from Justin. Nothing from the puppy who slept in his son's room. No creaks from the staircase or chime from the clock downstairs in the living room. No howl of wind or ping of sleet outside. The winter storm that had chewed its way across the Eastern seaboard last night as they went to bed had moved on as evidenced by the stars visible through the sliver of space between the white eyelet window curtains of the master bedroom.

No, nothing external had disturbed his sleep. The trouble was in his mind…his intuition…his gut.

He'd seen something. Sensed something. But what?

He lifted his arms, laced his fingers behind his head, and stared up toward the ceiling. Maybe it was work. Maybe he was about to be laid off. Rumors of budget cuts abounded, and he was the youngest detective with the fewest years on the force. Last in, first out would get him. Or at least get him bumped back to patrol.

He hadn't helped himself by failing to hide

his disdain for department politics, either. Daniel didn't play games. He didn't like people who did. As a result, he didn't get along with his boss or his boss's boss. They put up with him because he was good at his job, which made them look better at theirs.

But if heads had to roll...

Wonder where his old uniforms were stored? Guest room closet, maybe? He hoped his wife hadn't gotten rid of them. He tried to recall the last time Gail had gone into one of her closet-cleaning frenzies. If she'd done it since his promotion, the everyday uniforms were likely history.

I don't want to go back to patrol.

He loved the job. Maybe he could get on as a detective somewhere else. They didn't have to live near Boston. Gail's family was spread all over creation. His parents would miss their regular Wednesday-night dinner with their only grandson, but they'd come to visit. They could fly free—one of the advantages of his mom having worked for an airline all these years. And his brothers...well...it might be good to put some distance between himself and those know-it-alls. Maybe he should put out some job feelers just in case.

Maybe the job wasn't the problem. Maybe this bad juju he was feeling had something to do with one of his family members. His dad had mentioned his angina last night. Daniel hadn't liked hearing that. **I'll call him later and make sure Mom knows he's having chest pain. She'll make sure he sees the doctor like he promised me.**

Restless, Daniel rolled onto his side and pulled Gail over to spoon against him. She mumbled something about Soupy Lou and vegetables and managed to distract him from his dark thoughts. Daniel grinned into the darkness. He figured she was reliving last summer's garden disaster.

Gail had gone totally ballistic after their puppy had made the serious mistake of plucking green fruit off her plants and gnawing them just enough to ruin them. In her angry outburst upon discovering the crime, she'd threatened to give the dog away, which sent their four-year-old son into a panic.

Daniel had known it to be an idle threat because Gail loved the six-month-old boxer as much as Justin did. Nevertheless, it had taken him half an hour and the promise to build a fence for their backyard garden to calm down both mother and son.

So the following day when Soupy made a chew toy out of his favorite pair of sneakers, he'd chosen his own idle threats more carefully.

Remembering how Gail's eyes had sparkled as she and Justin stood united in defense of Soupy had Daniel giving the clock a second glance. He'd burned almost forty minutes with all his worrying. Still left twenty minutes before the alarm. A good husband woke his wife from her nightmares, didn't he?

He shifted his arm and slipped his hand beneath the clingy knit of her pajama top. Cupping her breast, he trailed his thumb back and forth across her nipple until she stirred and sighed his name. He nipped the soft, sensitive skin of her neck, and when she shivered in response, murmured, "I love you, Gail Garrett."

"Love you, too," she sleepily replied.

Daniel made love to his wife, and the heat they created together chased the cold from his soul.

Temporarily.

Sex as a distraction worked only until the worries came rolling back as he stood beneath a pelting hot shower at quarter after seven. Dammit, maybe he should come right out and ask Captain Hill about the downsizing rumor. Not that his boss would give him a straight answer, but his body language would betray him. In the first few seconds after posing a question to the man, Daniel could read him like a book.

However, if layoffs weren't on the horizon, Daniel didn't want to give his captain any ideas.

Another solution might be to fess up to his partner that he had the heebie-jeebies. James Reichs had twenty-seven years under his belt; he would respect hunches. Wouldn't he?

Maybe. Maybe not. **He might tell me I'm an inexperienced idiot.**

"Well, kiddo," Daniel could picture Reichs saying as he rubbed his jaw in his habitual gesture. "I don't know. There's a fortune teller over by the waterfront. Maybe we should go ask her. She could read her tarot cards and tell you what you're gonna be when you grow up."

On second thought, maybe he wouldn't say anything to Reichs.

Not that Daniel didn't give card and tea-leaf readers their due. He had some Gypsy blood in him from his father's side. His mother was full-blooded Irish. His heritage made him predisposed to accepting the reality of premonitions.

That's why he added an accessory to his workday ensemble when he dressed. He pulled on his Kevlar vest before he slipped into his sport coat and did his best not to feel foolish about it.

Exiting his bedroom, he glanced down the hallway toward Justin's room. The closed door and faint sound of local news turned low on the television downstairs meant that Justin was still asleep. Soundlessly, he pushed open his son's bedroom door. Soupy Lou immediately jumped down from the bed—where she knew she didn't belong—and into the dog bed at the foot of the boy's twin-sized bed. Daniel scolded the dog with a look, then turned his attention to his son.

An active sleeper, Justin invariably kicked off his covers so they dressed him in blanket sleepers on winter nights. He had a variety of cartoon-character versions, and the blue and gold of Daniel's collegiate team. Last night he'd chosen a green and orange Teenage Mutant Ninja Turtles selection to wear, and now he lay with his knees scrunched up under him and his butt in the air.

A tsunami of love rolled through Daniel as he gazed at the softly snoring boy. Justin was a fabulous kid. Good-natured, except when he was hungry and then he turned into Godzilla-boy ravaging the pantry. The kid was curious about everything. He'd started talking a little late, but once the floodgates had opened, the questions never stopped. All boy—the rhyme about snakes and snails and puppy dog tails fit him to a tee. Give him the Nature Channel and a show about spiders, and he was one little happy man.

A happy little **fearless** man. The boy was entirely too daring for Daniel's peace of mind. Last Saturday was the perfect example. While visiting his grandfather's barbershop, Justin had taken advantage of the adults' momentary distraction when Pitt scored a last second touchdown to clinch a come-from-behind victory over Virginia Tech. He'd fastened a barber cape around his neck, climbed onto the back of a barber chair, and jumped off à la Batman. His hand knocked scissors off a shelf on his way down, and the point missed hitting his eye by a hair.

"You will be the death of your mother and me, son," Daniel whispered now as he tucked the covers back over the boy.

He leaned down, pressed a light kiss against Justin's cheek, then trailed his knuckle across the dusting of freckles on his nose. Angel kisses, Gail called them. **We'd better hope your guardian angel covers your face in them.**

Daniel took a couple steps toward the door and his right shoe wobbled as he stepped on something. Glancing down, he spied Justin's Batman action figure. His favorite. Now, sporting a broken arm. **Kid needs to learn to keep his toys picked up.** Thinking to teach the boy a lesson, he scooped the small plastic doll up with its arm and stuck them in his pocket.

Downstairs in the kitchen, Gail had breakfast ready and waiting. He savored his first sip of coffee, but despite the early-morning exercise, his normally healthy appetite had disappeared. He had to force himself to eat the bacon and eggs.

"What's the matter, Daniel?" his wife asked when he declined a third strip of bacon. "I can tell something's been bothering you."

He took another sip of coffee to buy time to frame his response. Gail knew him better than he knew himself. High school sweethearts, they'd married young and had Justin before they'd intended to start a family—a blessing, they'd discovered recently when Gail developed fertility issues. She'd always wanted to be a stay-at-home mom, and though money was tight, they'd made it work. The promotion to detective had darn sure come in handy. "I don't like that sound the heater's been making. Really hope we can make it through the winter without having to buy a new unit."

She gave him a measured look over the

top of her coffee mug. Because the statement was true enough, Daniel managed to hold her gaze.

Gail didn't need the burden of this nameless worry of his. For a cop's wife, anxiousness came with the territory, but if fretting were a sport, she'd be a pro. On the All-Star team. She'd been more relaxed the past couple of months since he made detective and moved off patrol, but he saw no sense in causing her concern. Besides, the problem could very well **be** the furnace. They didn't need the financial hit for that right now. Not as long as they were making the hefty payments to the fertility clinic.

"What plans do you have for today?" he asked in hopes of shifting the topic of conversation.

"We have a big day planned. We're going grocery shopping this morning, then meeting Jeremy Tate and his mom at the mall for a matinee. The new Disney movie. If your day goes okay, want to meet us afterward for dinner?"

"Sure. Sounds like fun. I'll do my best to make it." Maybe he'd see about taking a half day of personal time and catch the movie with them, too. Two hours of feel-good entertainment might help him shake this funk. If he could talk her into ending their day the way they'd started it, he might put this weird mood behind him for good.

Daniel wiped his mouth with his napkin and stood. He leaned down, kissed his wife good-bye, then headed for the mud-room where he pulled on his overcoat and unlocked the gun safe to retrieve his weapon. As he slipped the revolver into the holster beneath his jacket, he heard the rattle of Soupy's tags and the thud of Justin's footsteps on the stairs. He almost turned back to greet his son, but a glance at his watch convinced him otherwise. A five-minute delay now meant another twenty minutes in traffic.

He second-guessed that decision min-utes later as he accelerated on the ramp onto the interstate that would take him downtown. The chill that skittered down his spine had little to do with the crisp November weather. **You should have taken the time. Being a few minutes late to work won't hurt anything.**

Sure. Right up until the moment they started choosing warm bodies for layoffs.

Nevertheless, the urge to see and speak to Justin was so strong that he almost took the first exit and turned around. He might have done it, too, had his phone not rung.

Two minutes later, any thought of taking a personal day had evaporated. He called Gail. "I'm not going to make it this afternoon. We caught a homicide."

"Oh, no. I just told Justin you said you'd try to join us. He'll be disappointed."

"Tell him I'll take him kite flying this week-end to make up for it. The weather's supposed to be perfect for it."

"He's standing right here. Why don't you tell him?"

She handed the phone to Justin who spoke with a whine in his little voice. "Daddy, come to the movie with us!"

"I can't, buddy. Daddy's got to work."

"But I don't want you to work. I want you to come to the movies!"

"I'm sorry, kiddo. Tell you what. You be a good boy for your mother today, and Saturday, you and I will go to the park and fly a kite."

"Promise, Daddy? Cross your heart promise?"

"Cross my heart promise."

"I love kites even more than movies. Except for the popcorn."

"Hey, we'll get us some popcorn, too."

"Yippee. Bye, Daddy."

The dial tone sounded in Daniel's ear and he chuckled. Needed to work with the little guy on phone etiquette. Then Daniel tossed his phone onto the passenger seat and turned his attention toward murder.

It was a grisly, all-consuming business, though he did manage to steal a few minutes to call his father and nag him to make the doctor's appointment. Throughout the morning, his sense of foreboding continued to simmer.

They made a one o'clock appointment with the deceased's grieving sister at her home in a Boston suburb. During the drive there after a swing through a fast food drive-through at Reichs's request, Daniel brought up the possibility of layoffs. Reichs squirted a packet of ketchup onto his fries. "Forget about it. Ain't happening. You're not getting out of this job that easy.

You're gonna have to suffer along at least until you get your twenty years like the rest of us poor saps. Is that what's been gnawing at you this week?"

"Yeah. No." Daniel watched his partner lick ketchup from his thumb, and his mind returned to the bloody scene where they'd spent much of the morning. "The husband did it."

"Yeah."

"We'll prove it."

"Considering the history of domestic violence, we'll close it by the end of the week." Reichs popped another fry into his mouth and chewed thoughtfully. "What's eating you, Garrett? Have a fight with the wife?"

"No. Gail and I are good." Daniel sucked in a breath, then exhaled a heavy sigh. "I don't know. I'm being paranoid. But... something's off. I have this spider crawling up my spine."

"That's why you're wearing your vest?"

Of course his partner had noticed. Very little got past James Reichs. Daniel described the sense of foreboding hanging over him like a storm cloud. "I don't know if it's all in my imagination or if I'm picking up on something that's real."

Reichs shook a fry at Daniel. "Doesn't matter. That's a lesson I learned many moons ago. You listen to your gut. It just might save your life."

Daniel's lips twisted in a rueful frown. "I'm listening. I just wish my gut would speak more clearly. At least let me know if this whole thing is business or personal."

"Be a detective, Garrett. Figure it out."

"Easier said than done," Daniel muttered.

Reichs finished his fry, then polished off half his burger before he spoke again. "You're still green, but you're smart. You're tenacious. You have great instincts. With a little experience, you'll be a damned fine investigator. When you're in a situation like this, you have to be methodical in your approach. Nine times out of ten, there's something there, something you're seeing but don't realize you're seeing. The place to start is your files. Take a stack of them home with you tonight."

Daniel nodded, glad to have a direction. He'd lucked out getting Reichs for a partner. The guy was a legend in the department, and Daniel knew he could learn a lot from him.

When they arrived for their appointment, Reichs grabbed a vest from the trunk and slipped into it before pulling on his suit jacket. The action made Daniel feel less foolish for having mentioned his concerns. The interview provided helpful background information about their suspect, and they left with a new lead to follow that took them downtown.

Congestion in traffic ahead caused Daniel to alter the route he'd intended to take, so chance put them on the narrow streets in the industrial area of town when all hell broke loose in front of them.

Sirens screamed from police cars pursuing a gray Mercedes sedan that turned onto the street ahead of Daniel's car. As Reichs got on the radio to report their position as half a block away, the sedan screeched to a stop and a young man bailed from the driver's seat and ran toward them.

Reichs listened intently to the radio. "Carjacking. Dragged a woman from the car. Her baby's in the backseat."

Daniel slammed on his brakes and threw the car into park even as he saw the man dart into a narrow alley.

Two of the uniformed cops stopped by the Mercedes and tended to the child. Two others joined Daniel and Reichs in pursuit of the suspect. Young and fit, Daniel outran the others, and he was the only one who saw which way the suspect turned in the narrow, twisting maze of streets and alleys.

Daniel was fast, but so was the suspect, and he obviously knew this part of the city well. Just as Daniel began to believe that he'd lose his man, the suspect stopped and whirled around.

Gun. He has a gun in his gloved hand.

Time seemed to slow to a crawl. Daniel saw the muzzle flash and tried to react, but the kick at his chest knocked the breath from his lungs and propelled him off his feet. **He shot me. I'm shot.**

He clapped a hand over his chest.

The suspect turned into another alley and disappeared.

Before Daniel caught his breath, Reichs was at his side, waving the patrolmen to continue on after the suspect while he stayed with his partner. "You hit? Show me."

Daniel shook his head. "Okay. I'm okay. The Kevlar stopped it."

He moved his hand away from his chest and revealed the hole in his overcoat. Holes, he silently corrected because the bullet had pierced his shirt, too. The temptation to stick his pinky finger through them was strong, but he resisted. Barely. Looking down at the tears in the fabric, he exhaled a heavy breath.

"Holy hell, son," Reichs breathed. "Remind me to always listen to your hunches. Your guardian angel was on the job today."

"Yeah." Thinking of his family, Daniel sent up a shaky prayer of thanks.

Reichs helped Daniel to his feet just as the two patrol officers returned empty-handed, the shooter having managed to lose them in the matrix of warehouses and shipping hubs. "Did you get a good look at him?" one of the patrolmen asked Daniel.

He nodded. "I'll recognize him when I see him again."

"And that will happen," Reichs said. "We'll find him."

When they walked back to their cars, they discovered the scene filled with a whole host of newcomers—an ambulance, fire truck, a half-dozen more patrol cars, and even the SWAT van.

"How's the baby?" he asked a paramedic.

"Appears to be just fine. He never took her out of her car seat."

"The mom?"

"She's on the way."

Daniel nodded, relieved. How frightened that poor woman must have been. Someone handed him a bottle of water, and as he twisted off the plastic cap and took a long, welcome sip of cool water, the reality of the past twenty minutes sank in.

He'd dodged a bullet. More or less.

He'd dodged that bullet because he'd listened to his gut. The sound of his partner's voice echoed through his mind. **It just might save your life.**

He dragged the back of his hand across his mouth and willed the weakness out of his knees. He was fine. He was okay. He'd listened, so he'd lived. A lesson for a lifetime.

Excellent. **Guess I don't have to comb**

through files now.

His lips quirked at the thought.

Tension rolled off him in waves and exhaustion began tugging at his bones. Adrenaline drain, he thought, just as a silver-haired man wearing a brown pin-striped suit beneath his khaki trench coat approached with his hand outstretched. "Detective Garrett? I'm Todd Barnhill. I'll be lead on this boondoggle. If you're comfortable skipping the ambulance, I'll give you a ride to the hospital and take your statement there."

"I don't need to go—"

He shook his head. "Regulations, Detective. You know that."

Yes, he did. Daniel nodded his acquiescence and glanced around. "My partner..."

"Detective Reichs is giving his statement to my partner. They'll meet us at the hospital when they're done." Barnhill hooked a thumb over his shoulder. "That's my SUV over there if you want to get out of the weather. I need to finish up with Officer Maxwell, but I'll be ready to leave in five."

"Thanks." Daniel nodded and walked toward the late-model SUV. For the first time since bailing out of his own car, he took notice of the winter chill in the air. The temperature couldn't have climbed above freezing yet. He rubbed his arms, and when Barnhill used remote ignition to unlock his vehicle, Daniel waved a thanks. He climbed into the truck and settled wearily into the passenger seat as the last of the adrenaline drained away, leaving him exhausted.

He hoped he slept better tonight. He should. Surely getting shot qualified as the big bad hanging over his head. No need to worry about layoffs or the furnace now. Not until the next time he experienced...what...a hunch? A premonition? A sixth sense inherited from his Irish/Gypsy heritage?

A warning from his guardian angel?

Well, whatever. The name didn't matter. He was a believer. He would never attempt to ignore or dismiss those feelings again. At this particular moment, he felt like the luckiest man in the world.

Maybe after Barnhill finished with him, he'd stop and buy a lottery ticket. And roses for Gail. Maybe a bottle of wine. After Justin was in bed, he'd put on some big band music and coax her into dancing with him. He'd sing to her, give them both the gift of a little romance. Maybe tonight they'd hit the jackpot in the getting-pregnant department. Why not, this was his lucky day, wasn't it?

Daniel warmed to the idea even as he held his fingers up to the heated air flowing from the vents. He also realized he needed to call Gail ASAP. News trucks would probably start showing up here any minute, and if she heard about today's events from anybody other than him, he could forget about getting any luckier.

He reached into his pocket for his cell phone, but his fingers found Justin's little Batman figure first. He pulled the doll from his pocket and studied it, newly aware of an elemental truth about himself. He didn't want to die, but he didn't really fear death. However, the thought of leaving Justin without his father cut him off at the knees.

He rubbed his thumb over the head of the Caped Crusader, smiling crookedly. He suddenly quite desperately wanted to talk to his wife and his son. **What a day this has been.**

He shifted one-armed Batman from his right hand to his left and searched once more for his phone. He dialed Gail's number and was disappointed when his call went straight to voice mail. "Hey, babe. Just calling to give you a heads-up. Had a little excitement today. You might hear about it on the news. I'm fine. Wasn't hurt. The good guys are winning. I'll tell you the whole story when I get home. Love you."

He disconnected the call and returned his phone to his pocket. He still wanted to talk to his family, but leaving a message worked out okay, he decided. Gail would give him credit for having called, but he'd be spared having to break the news to her. A win-win.

Still, it wouldn't hurt to take her flowers when he went home. Something bright and cheerful. Sunflowers, maybe. Gail always went gooey over flowers.

Then they could celebrate life, and if his good luck held just a little longer, make a new one.

His fist closed around Batman, and he

subconsciously brought it to his mouth and kissed it as a patrol screeched to a halt in front of him. A wild-eyed woman vaulted from the backseat, and Daniel watched the reunion of mother and daughter with a lump in his throat. To be part of this...even though they had yet to catch Joker...all in all..."A good day."

His phone rang. He pulled it from his pocket. His eyes on a toddler's puffy pink jacket, he answered saying, "Garrett."

His wife's panicked, fear-filled, and babbling voice chilled his soul. "I can't find Justin! Oh, God, Daniel. Somebody stole our son!"

Four days later, a jogger discovered Justin Garrett's battered and abused body in a pumpkin field two hours away from the mall. Seven months after that, Daniel returned home from work to find his wife dead from an overdose of sleeping pills.

That evening, Daniel threw his Kevlar vest off the Tobin Bridge, wishing he had the courage to jump in after it.

Chapter Two

PRESENT DAY
ETERNITY SPRINGS, COLORADO

The woman known as Shannon O'Toole around town reached for the flathead screwdriver in her toolbox just as her cell phone chimed an alarm. Almost eleven o'clock already? Where had the morning gone? She had hoped to work her way a lot farther down her to-do list by now.

"So what else is new?" she murmured as she flipped her toolbox closed. She could multitask with the best of them, but the commitment to renovate this two-bedroom dollhouse of a Victorian on Pinion Street in addition to operating Murphy's Pub and teaching yoga classes had filled her plate to overflowing. Yet, staying busy was good. It kept her sane and solvent—both of which were important to a woman in her circumstances.

In her postage stamp of a kitchen, she filled two glasses with ice and peppermint tea. She placed them and a tin filled with Fresh bakery's strawberry pinwheel cookies onto a tray and carried it outside. Setting the tray atop the flat surface of a plywood-and-sawhorse workbench, she retrieved a pair of folding lawn chairs from where they leaned against the side of the house. As she dusted grass clippings from the chairs' webbing, her cell phone rang. She pulled it from the pocket of her jeans and answered without checking the number. "Hello?"

Silence.

A shiver of apprehension skidded down her spine. **No. Please, no. Not again.**

In a flash, she was back in her Denver apartment staring at the object lying atop the lavender-colored pillow sham on her bed—fuzzy and tan with tufts of white stuffing. A teddy bear's arm. Then, back to Austin and a yellow bedspread and the bear's leg. Nashville, another arm.

Her room at Stanford and the empty bed where the bear belonged.

Fear yawned in the pit of her stomach. Her pulse began to pound. **Just when I begin to hope...**

As she yanked the phone away from her ear to check the number, she heard her closest friend, Rose Cicero, the town physician, say, "Shannon? I'm sorry. That was a butt dial. I'm at work today and had my phone in the pocket of my lab coat and a toddler in my arms."

"No problem," Shannon replied, relief washing over her, clean and sweet as a summer rain.

She ended the call a little weak-kneed and annoyed with herself. She knew better than to answer her phone without checking the number first. Letting down her guard was one thing; acting carelessly, something else entirely. She felt safe here in Eternity Springs, but she had felt safe in other places, too, hadn't she?

"Be smart. Be aware. Be alive," she murmured, repeating her personal mantra. If she didn't live, she lost. If she didn't live, he won. Unacceptable. "So get back to living and pick your paint."

It was the next item on her agenda—trim paint. If she stood a shot at finishing and flipping this house by Halloween, she needed to choose a color today.

It was proving to be a difficult task. With previous renovation projects, she'd known exactly what she wanted when it came to paint. This time she struggled to choose between two shades of red and a bright, sunshine yellow to contrast the creamy white of the siding. So an hour ago, she'd phoned for the help of a color expert, her friend and renowned artist Sage Rafferty. Sage had jumped at the opportunity for a distraction and offered to visit at eleven—provided she hadn't gone into labor.

A glance down the block revealed the heavily pregnant Sage waddling toward Shannon's house. When she drew near, Shannon said, "You look miserable."

"I am miserable." Sage grimaced as she tucked a stray strand of wavy auburn hair behind her ear. "I honestly believed I'd have this baby early, but now I'm three days late. I'm having nightmares of going into labor at Gabi and Flynn's wedding."

Shannon eyed her friend's enormous belly doubtfully. "Surely you won't last that long. The wedding's still a week away."

"You wouldn't think so, but knowing my

luck..." Sage rubbed the small of her back and nodded toward the house. "Let's change the subject and talk color. Color makes me happy. I can't tell you how much your phone call this morning cheered me. You gave me something fun to focus on rather than the noneventful state of my uterus. So, how can I be of assistance?"

"Help me settle on a trim color, please." She pulled a stack of scrap wood from beneath her workbench and carried the three painted pieces toward the house. After lining them up against the cream-colored siding, she rejoined Sage. "I cannot make up my mind."

Sage pursed her lips and studied the display. "All three of those colors are lovely."

"That's precisely the problem. I know that color preference is as individual as a favorite ice cream flavor, but in this particular instance, I need to appeal to the widest range of potential buyers possible. At the same time, I need to make this place stand out."

"Are you worried about selling it?" Sage asked, nodding when Shannon silently offered her a glass of tea.

"A little. Flipping houses is not for the faint of heart, especially when you're trying to do it in a small town. I had planned to have the house finished before tourist season ended, but I fell behind schedule because I put in longer hours at the pub this summer than I expected."

Both women took seats in the lawn chairs. Sage chose a cookie to nibble at and observed, "Murphy's Pub's new patio is the bomb."

Shannon smiled. One of a handful of buildings in town that dated back to Eternity Springs' early days in the 1880s, the pub had seen both glory days where it served as a central gathering place for citizens and long stretches of time when the vast majority of visitors walked on four legs and sported tails. But Murphy's had good bones, something she'd seen on her first walk-through following her arrival in Eternity Springs. Bringing it back to life hadn't been as difficult a job as she'd first anticipated. It helped that a strong demand existed for a family-friendly watering hole in the growing town. "The patio's popularity caught me by surprise, I'll admit.

Had I known how successful the project would prove to be, I'd have planned this one differently."

"How close are you to being finished here?"

"At least a month. Maybe six weeks. The kitchen is still a mess."

"So it won't hit the market until after tourist season," Sage said, nodding in understanding. "When traffic in town drops way down."

"Exactly. That's why I'm so concerned about color." Shannon's teeth tugged her lower lip as she studied the painted boards. "Ordinarily I'd go for the gentler red because it suits the neighborhood best. But instead of selling to drive-by tourists, I expect my buyer will have found it on the Internet, so I really need it to pop out in a photo. The yellow or hotter red might work better. What do you think?"

"Hmm…" Sage idly rubbed her glorious belly as she studied the house. "Will you plant flowers this late in the season?"

"Yes. Gabe said he'd trade a planting plan and labor for yoga classes for Nic." Gabe Callahan was a local businessman who'd trained as a landscape architect; Nic, his wife, was the town's veterinarian. Their twin daughters would be second-graders this fall.

"You are the barter queen of Eternity Springs," Sage responded, her tone warm with admiration. "Do any of your yoga students actually pay cash?"

Shannon taught yoga three mornings a week, and considering her particular situation, she'd found that barter worked very well for her. "A few. I haven't managed a local source for my nursery needs, though, but I'm working on it. I'll—"

She broke off abruptly upon seeing the startled look on her friend's face. "Not your kind of nursery, Sage. Flowers. Shrubs. Grass seed."

"Oh. Of course. I have babies on the brain." She paused, then added, "That said, if you're interested in a local source for my kind of nursery..."

"I own the only pub in town," Shannon pointed out. "My cup runneth over with local sources offering to fill that particular need."

Not that she ever took them up on the

offers. Shannon wasn't one to sleep around, and she couldn't in good conscience begin a relationship with a man when reality meant she might have to pick up and leave town at a moment's notice. Walking away from things like houses or businesses was one thing; doing it to a man she cared about enough to sleep with was something else entirely.

"I know you get hit on all the time. I've watched it happen when Colt and I are at Murphy's. Besides, men are suckers for big brown soulful eyes. But Colt has a friend—"

Shannon rolled her eyes. "So back to color choice?"

"I suggest you go with the spicy red. This is such a darling house, and I think red adds an air of romance."

Romance. Hmm. Shannon eyed the cottage with the word in mind. Sage was right. With all the gingerbread painted red, and with the right shutters, it could look like a valentine. "I could add a few cutesy heart touches to drive the point home. I hadn't thought of that."

Just showed how far away any idea of

romance was from her thoughts.

"That would be darling. You could come up with a name for the house...Love-some-thing Cottage."

A name popped into Shannon's brain like an angel's whisper. **Heartsong Cottage.**

"I like it," she murmured. In her mind's eye, she saw a heart-shaped address sign hanging from an iron bracket. The theme fit perfectly with the red, white, and black color scheme she'd been considering for the kitchen. She would redesign the mosaic tile backsplash she had planned. Do something with hearts. "It's a great idea. It will give me something to market. You're a genius, Sage."

"Thank you. As a reward for my brilliance, I think I'll have another cookie. If ever a woman needs to indulge herself, it's in the last few days of pregnancy." As Sage chose another pinwheel from the plate, motion across the street caught her atten-tion. "Speaking of romance...did I hear correctly that you threw that pair out of Murphy's last night because they were indulging in an overly enthusiastic PDA?"

The pair to whom she referred was Gabi

Romano, gorgeous in a feminine green sundress, and her fiancé, Flynn Brogan, who wore faded jeans, a blue chambray shirt, and the air of a happy man.

"I don't know that I'd term that particular public display of affection as 'overly enthusiastic,'" Shannon replied with a smirk. "I'd go for 'toe-curling.' Maybe even 'combustible.' But the couple in question involved a different tall, dark Romano. Not Gabi, but Lucca. He was extremely happy when the Rockies won the game in extra innings, and he displayed said happiness by kissing his wife. And kissing her. And kissing her."

Amusement lit Sage's eyes and she clapped her hand against her breast in exaggerated drama. "You threw our kindergarten teacher out of the pub?"

"Not because of the kiss. I told him he had to leave because his mother called looking for one of her boys. She had a broken pipe at Aspenglow Place and needed help."

"Ah."

Flynn spied them and waved, then gave Gabi's hand a tug and the pair crossed the street.

Gabi was on a phone call, and as they approached, Shannon heard her say, "I know, Mom. It'll be okay. I promise. The world won't end if one of my cousins can't make it to the wedding. Now, if one of my brothers comes down with chicken pox during this next week, it'll be another story. You quit worrying and enjoy your lunch. Tell Celeste I said hi. I'll see you both at the community center at two."

She ended the call and dropped her phone into the straw purse hanging at her side. She greeted her friends, her gaze lingering on Sage's stomach. She sadly shook her head. "Sage Rafferty, you'd better get a move on or I'm going to lose the baby pool."

"You picked today, too?" Shannon asked. "I have eleven o'clock tonight."

"Yes. Six p.m., seven pounds, three ounces."

"I'm already out of the hunt." Flynn shoved his hands into the pockets of his jeans. "I picked last week."

Sage sighed dramatically. "I like the way you think, Flynn. My fear is that Colt will be the one who guessed correctly. He bet on your wedding day."

"Now, that's just mean." Gabi gave Sage's hand a sympathetic squeeze.

"Speaking of weddings," Shannon said. "How are things going? Is everything close to being ready?"

"We're getting there. We have a few last details to wrap up about the reception and one last meeting with the florist later today. Guests start arriving on Wednesday."

"Except for the cousin with chicken pox," Flynn observed.

"That's a disappointment," Gabi admitted. "Mom is freaking out about it. She's afraid the whole family will begin spotting up like kindergarteners. Although, come to think of it, the cancellation does free up a room at Angel's Rest." She reached into her purse and pulled out a leather planner and pencil. She flipped through the pages. "Hmm...maybe we could shift the Wilsons to her room, the Camerons to the Wilsons', and get Daniel Garrett off the sofa at my brother's house."

"Daniel's on the sofa at Lucca and Hope's?" Flynn asked. "I thought your mother saved a room for him at her B and B."

"She did, but he refused it. Said to give the rooms to families and couples."

"Daniel is good people," Flynn observed.

"He'd better not weenie out of coming to the wedding," Gabi said. "He'd planned to visit last spring, but couldn't get away. Hope is worried about him. She says he works all the time."

"If Daniel said he'll be here, he will be here," Flynn said. "He's a man of his word."

Shannon tried to recall what gossip she'd heard about the Romano family's friend. She knew that he was the private investigator who brought Hope's kidnapped daughter home to her, but there was something else. "What's the deal with him? Some sort of tragedy? His wife died?"

"Not just his wife," Sage explained. "It's the most awful thing imaginable. Years ago, his young son was abducted and murdered by a stranger. It destroyed Daniel's wife. She committed suicide a few months later."

Shannon covered her mouth with her hand. "Oh, that is horrible. I never heard the details."

"It's the saddest thing." Sage wrapped protective arms around the child she carried. "Just breaks your heart."

"Did they catch the person who did it?"

"It took a few years, but yes, they got him," Gabi said. "Daniel was a police detective when it happened. He went private, and now he runs his own agency and specializes in child abduction cases."

"That has to be tough work," Shannon said.

Gabi nodded. "I worked in law enforcement and I saw a lot of ugly things, but they pale in comparison to the evils that Daniel deals with on a daily basis. I don't know how he does it. My heart couldn't bear so much pain."

"He's a hero," Sage observed.

"He's certainly our family's hero. Which is why he deserves better than a bed on my brother's sofa when he comes to our wedding."

"From the sound of it, your wedding will have Eternity Springs bursting at the seams."

Flynn spoke in a glum tone. "We should

have eloped. Six months ago."

Sage gave Shannon a droll look. "If I've heard him say that once, I've heard it a thousand times."

"I've heard it a million times." Gabi gave him a playful punch on the arm. "Stop whining. It's going to be fun."

"The honeymoon is going to be fun," Flynn corrected. "It's the reward for bearing up through all these wedding plans."

The lawn chair creaked as Sage shifted her weight. "So is the honeymoon destination still a surprise or has she wheedled it out of you?"

The bride and groom shared one of those secretive lovers' glances that could have made Shannon envious if she'd allowed it. Flynn said, "Both. We decided we'd break it up into two parts because we expect Cicero to win the Albritton Fellowship next month, and we'll want to go to California for the awards. Gabriella knows we're going to Bella Vita Isle on the first segment of the trip."

"He's being stubbornly closed-lipped about part two," Gabi complained. "All he'll tell me is that I need somebody to fill in for me at Whimsies until after Thanksgiving."

"That's a long honeymoon," Shannon said.

"Not long enough," Flynn replied. "Personally, I think it's only fair that the honeymoon last as long as the wedding planning."

Gabi gave an exaggerated roll of her eyes, and when Flynn looked like he might expand on the subject, she tugged his arm. "We need to be going. Our dog is at Nic's office and we need to pick him up."

"Is Bismarck okay?" Sage asked.

"He's had a cough. We've been a little worried about him. He needs to be healthy for next Saturday."

"Nic will get him fixed up. She's a wonderful vet." Sage tipped her head and her wavy auburn hair spilled across her shoulder. "So the rumors are true? Your dog is in your wedding party?"

Gabi's smile bloomed big and bright like a sunflower. "He saved our lives. I think it's only right that he be our ring bearer. Of course, my mother thinks I'm crazy—the rest of the wedding is supertraditional—but he's our family and we want him there."

"Then you should have him there," Shannon agreed.

The couple took their leave, and Sage and Shannon finished their iced tea and cookies. Sage levered herself to her feet. "After making a pig of myself on the sweets, I better take the long route home. I need the exercise."

"If you want to take a route past the lumber yard, I'll walk with you. I need to get my paint ordered."

"The spicy red?"

"Yes."

"Nail polish companies have such clever names for their polishes. Are house paint companies the same way? What's this color called?"

"Actually, the spicy red is a color I had mixed to match the tile I'm considering for the kitchen. The tile is listed simply as red. But as of this moment, I'm declaring that shade Heartsong Red," she announced. "And this will be Heartsong Cottage."

Sage's face brightened with pleasure. "Oh, that's perfect, Shannon. Simply perfect. It sounds like a place where special memories happen."

In her mind's eye, Shannon saw Heart-song Cottage as it would appear when she finished it. "And you just gave me my marketing tagline. 'Heartsong Cottage: Where special memories happen.'"

"Bet it sells the first day it's on the—" Sage paused mid-sentence and grabbed the edge of the plywood workbench for balance. "Market. Hey, Shannon? Does your house have a functioning bathroom at the moment?"

"Yes. I'm living here during the remodel."

"Good. Because I need it. Heartsong Cottage is working its memory magic already." Sage looked down at the ground, her smile fluttering between dismay and excitement. "My water just broke."

Chapter Three

Daniel drove the winding road over Sinner's Prayer Pass like a stunt driver in a James Bond movie. A missed connection had put him behind schedule, which served as his excuse for splurging on the rental car that handled speed and the mountain roads like a dream. Mainly, he wanted to drive hard and fast and run away from the mental images haunting him in the wake of the particularly brutal case he'd just closed.

He was exhausted. Disheartened. Discouraged by the total depravity and inhumanity of soulless monsters walking this earth. He needed a break.

The job was weighing on him. In the past ten years he'd seen too many things he wished he could **un**see and discovered a whole lot of truths he wished he could unlearn. He'd stood before way too many grieving, heartbroken parents with the grim message that he had terrible news to share, or, worse in a way, no news at all.

Gabi's wedding came at an opportune

time. For a little while, he needed to get away from the darkness and the ugliness. He wanted light and bright and positive. He needed a little fun and fellowship.

He needed a dose of Eternity Springs.

Especially now with the ten-year anniversary of Justin's death looming in November like an ominous storm cloud.

He goosed the gas and the Porsche surged forward. Rounding a hairpin curve, he caught his first glimpse of his destination. As always, at this point in the journey, upon seeing the rooftops nestled in the valley below and the sapphire waters of Hummingbird Lake, he sensed an easing of tension within him. On his first visit to town a couple of years ago, he'd discovered what a gem of a hometown his friend Hope had found here. Eternity Springs truly was a little piece of heaven in the Colorado Rockies, and coming here never failed to soothe his soul.

Although today could put an end to that streak. If he was late to Gabi's wedding, the Romano women would have his guts for garters.

He made it to the church with five minutes

to spare and found a standing-room-only crowd. A tuxedo-clad usher who bore a startling resemblance to the Romano brothers motioned him forward to a spot along the wall between a pair of stained-glass windows. Four pews back from the church's altar, the space gave him an excellent view of the proceedings. He no sooner took his spot than one of Gabi's brothers escorted her mother up the aisle to take her seat in the front row. Maggie Romano beamed with happiness, and her gaze warmed with pleasure when she saw him. Then the music changed and the groom and his groomsmen took their places.

The bridesmaids all looked like a million bucks in short forest-green dresses and stiletto heels. A smattering of laughter drifted through the congregation when the flower girl, Holly Montgomery, started up the aisle with a basket of rose petals in one hand and a dog lead in the other. Bismarck, the solid black Newfoundland, sported a smart white bow tie on his collar.

When Gabi started up the aisle on her brother Zach's arm, Daniel couldn't help but smile. For a tough, no-nonsense former cop, she was such a girly-girl.

Her dress made him think of the antebellum South—or of a Disney princess—with its big skirt and crystal beads. She wore her gorgeous auburn hair piled high and crowned with a sparkling tiara and little whiff of a veil. Flynn Brogan was a lucky man, Daniel thought. Almost as lucky as Lucca Romano, who had married the woman Daniel admired most in this world.

Daniel and Hope Romano shared a very special friendship. Nothing romantic—even before she'd met Lucca, that hadn't been part of it. But from the day he'd begun working her daughter's kidnapping case, the two of them had clicked. They understood each other. They'd come to love each other in a way that only those who've been through the fires of hell can manage. Being able to reunite Holly with her mother had been his greatest success.

Not that he'd had a huge amount of them competing for the top spot, he thought bleakly. In fact, since bringing Holly to Eternity Springs, he had not reunited another child with his parents. Not one who could smile and run into her mother's arms, anyway. In the past two years, Daniel had found only bodies. He knew more than most that such finds were not insignificant. Nevertheless, he was weary of it. Heartsick from it.

Memories of his most recent case threatened to blow into the church like a devil wind, and Daniel determinedly closed his mind against them. This was a wedding, not a funeral. **Get a grip, Garrett. The ugliness in your head has no place here.**

Deliberately, he tuned in to the service just as a young man with café-au-lait skin, Rastafarian braids, and the lilt of the Caribbean in his voice began a reading from 1 Corinthians. Daniel listened as much to the music of the man's voice as to the words he read—until his gaze drifted toward a familiar face seated near the church's baptismal font. Smiling benevolently toward the bride and groom, Celeste Blessing wore a smart tailored jacket and skirt in gold brocade. Her snowy hair was cut in a classic bob and accentuated her earrings—dangling gold and diamond angel's wings. She must have sensed the weight of his gaze because she turned her head and gave him an impish wink. Daniel grinned in response, and he thought he must have made a sound of some kind because the woman dressed in a bright summer-yellow sundress seated at the end of the pew beside him turned her head and looked at him.

Daniel instinctively straightened away from the wall. **Well now, isn't she lovely?**

Dressed in yellow, she looked like a sunbeam and her big brown doe eyes packed a punch. Set against an angular face, they were framed by thick, long lashes. Her chestnut-colored hair was cut short and sassy, and with her long, graceful neck and sharp features, she had that elegant Audrey Hepburn look that had always appealed to Daniel. As their gazes met and held, a shiver of recognition climbed up his spine, though he was certain that he'd never met her before.

He didn't think he breathed again until she returned her attention to the altar where Gabi handed her bouquet of white roses to Savannah Turner and faced her groom. Flynn took his bride's hands in his and they exchanged their vows.

In the solemn aftermath of the moment, the flower girl leaned toward her brides-maid mother. Holly's whispered "When's he going to kiss her, Mom?" floated audibly through the church and the congregation laughed.

When the service ended, Flynn kissed his wife, the church erupted in applause, and the mother of the bride rested her head on her oldest son's shoulder and allowed her tears to flow.

The dog barked. The woman didn't look Daniel's way again.

He couldn't stop himself from stealing glances her way. Wonder who she was? Wonder why he had such a visceral reaction to her? Could he have met her somewhere before and just not remembered her?

No, I'd remember her.

Mr. and Mrs. Flynn Brogan led the way back up the aisle followed by the bridal party. The wedding guests exchanged greetings and discussed the service as they filed slowly from the church. Daniel's gaze surveyed the crowd that now spilled out into the street, and he realized with a bit of embarrassment that he was looking for a particular yellow dress.

Maybe that was it. Dressed in yellow, she was the very picture of a summer day. A light, bright, warm Eternity Springs afternoon. Of course that appealed to him.

The sound of his name snagged his attention and he turned to see Cam Murphy approach with his hand outstretched. "You cut this one close, Garrett. Sarah and I were glad to see you slip into the church."

Sarah Murphy gave him a hug and added, "Holly would have been brokenhearted if you hadn't been here to watch her be her aunt Gabi's flower girl."

"I wouldn't have missed it."

Cam motioned to someone behind Daniel, and he turned halfway, expecting to see the woman in the yellow dress. Instead, the twenty-something blonde who'd been seated next to Sarah in the church stepped forward, and Cam said, "Daniel, I don't believe you've met our daughter, Lori. Lori's in vet school at Colorado State. Lori, this is Daniel Garrett."

"Oh, Mr. Garrett, you're Holly's hero. I'm so glad to finally meet you. I cannot tell you how much I admire you."

Daniel forced a smile. He knew that the families he'd helped considered him a hero. He also knew how little he deserved that accolade. Daniel did what he did out of a complicated and not completely rational need for atonement. He hadn't murdered his son or driven his wife to suicide. Nevertheless, even almost ten years later, he still felt responsible. He'd let his family down. He hadn't saved them. He was nobody's hero.

"It's nice to meet you, too, Lori." He diverted attention from himself by asking her about vet school and continued to scan the crowd for a yellow sundress. She talked about her interest in joining a large-animal practice as they joined the rest of the wedding guests who'd begun drifting toward the reception venue, the community center on the grounds of Celeste Blessing's enterprise, Angel's Rest Healing Center and Spa.

The renovation of the old Victorian mansion into a resort destination had revitalized Eternity Springs, breathing new life into a town that had been close to hanging out a closed sign. It was an appealing place with a new coat of yellow paint, white shutters, and a huge front porch and upstairs verandah. Inside, first-class accommodations and a friendly, professional staff welcomed guests like family. As he crossed the footbridge over Angel Creek onto the estate grounds, Daniel experienced a brief pang of regret for having refused the opportunity for a room here this trip. This time of year he could have slept with the window open and fallen asleep listening to the rush and bubble of the mountain stream. He would do fine at Hope and Lucca's; being around Holly would be good for him. But maybe before he left town, he'd book a room here for his return trip in November.

He and Hope had spent the anniversaries of the days they'd lost their children together for years now. After Hope remarried and Holly was found, he'd tried to cancel the tradition, but his friend wouldn't hear of it. Spending November third with her last year in the wake of her remarriage and Holly's safe return had been bittersweet. Hope's happiness soothed him and rewarded him, but on that particular day, he hadn't been able to ignore a twinge of jealousy that shamed him.

He was glad of the distraction when Colt Rafferty sidled up beside him and said, "Garrett. Glad to see you made it. Last night at the rehearsal, Gabi and Hope fretted over the fact that you hadn't arrived yet."

"Work," Daniel answered with a shrug then quickly changed the subject. "I hear congratulations are in order. A girl?"

"Eight pounds three ounces of heaven." Beaming, Colt pulled a cigar from the pocket of his jacket and handed it over. "Elizabeth Celeste. I'll refrain from whipping you with photos."

"And how is your boy enjoying his little sister?"

Colt winced. "Racer wants to send her back. Immediately. Four-year-olds aren't exactly the most generous of creatures."

A memory of a temper tantrum involving a package of animal crackers flashed in Daniel's mind. He turned toward the sounds of welcome as the wedding party arrived at the reception.

Holly ran toward him, her face alight with joy. "Daniel! Daniel! Did you see me? I was the flower girl for Aunt Gabi. Did you see?"

"I did see." He opened his arms. "You were gorgeous. You did a fabulous job."

"No I didn't." She barreled into him and Daniel's arms went around her. As he picked her up and twirled her around, she said, "I wanted to die when everyone heard my whisper. Lucca said something called acoustics made it so loud, but Aunt Gabi told me not to worry, that she'd been wondering the same thing, and that I made it a special memory for her."

"You do that for everybody. That's your gift, sunshine." Daniel gave this precious little girl a hug, conscious of how much she'd grown. She filled his arms. She filled his heart.

Broken and battered though it was.

My, oh my, doesn't he have fine shoulders? Broad and wide, just the way that always caught her eye. This particular set of shoulders attracted her gaze like a magnet.

They looked strong enough to carry even the heaviest of burdens.

Seated at a large round table draped in forest green and black with the Ciceros, the

Raffertys, and the Murphys, Shannon forced herself to look away from the handsome mountain of a stranger who stood across the room talking to Maggie Romano. Why, she wondered, had she noticed him at the wedding and thought of Ted?

He didn't look anything like Ted Colby. Ted had been a compact, brown-eyed, long-haired blond computer nerd. This guy had blue eyes, dark hair cut military short, and he was tall and powerfully built. Romano family tall, but thicker than the rangy basketball athletes who were Gabi's brothers. **Must be a cousin.**

Unable to resist, Shannon's gaze stole back toward the magnet a mere two minutes later. He wore a well-cut gray suit and blue tie that complemented his eyes. Sharp cheekbones, a square jaw, and a few fine lines etched across his face. Mid-thirties, she guessed. The hand wrapped around a pint glass was large. Was it something about his mannerisms? Did he stand like Ted or smile like Ted or maybe tilt his head that certain way when he listened?

Probably not. Probably the stranger

reminded her of Ted because her fiancé had been on her mind all day. While channel surfing the previous evening, she'd stumbled across the movie she'd been watching when the call came about his "accident." For some inexplicable reason, last night she'd set down her remote and watched **Apollo 13** through to the reentry scene. That had been the point seven years ago when her phone had rung and her world changed forever.

Yanking her thoughts away from troubling memories, she deliberately shifted her chair so that she couldn't see the stranger. She wished that Lori Murphy hadn't joined a group of younger friends upon their arrival at the reception. Her presence at the table would have added the eighth to Shannon's seventh. Ordinarily, she didn't mind attending events as a single. Tonight, however, she felt particularly alone.

Tuning into the conversation, she wished she hadn't. She loved her Eternity Springs friends. She truly did. But diapers and diaper rash ointment products truly didn't interest her. Pasting on a smile, she rose. "The bar is open. Who wants something to drink?"

"Busman's holiday?" Rose Cicero asked. "I thought Gabi and Flynn made you promise not to work the reception when they hired Murphy's Pub to supply the alcohol."

"They did, and I'm not offering to mix drinks. I'm volunteering to play server."

"I'll do it." Hunt Cicero shifted his interested stare away from the buffet table and rose. "I want to breeze by the buffet table and see if I can't score one of those little egg rolls. I'm starving. So what's your poison, everyone?"

"Wine for me," Rose said.

"Irish whiskey. Flynn is serving Bushmills 21."

"Of course he is," Cam Murphy said, standing. "Only the best for our boy. I'll help you carry, Cicero."

"I'll go with you," Colt said. "I'm going to try to snag an egg roll, too."

When the men sauntered toward the bar by way of the buffet, Shannon watched Rose's love-softened gaze follow her husband. This was almost worse than hearing about butt paste. "Gee, Rose. I know you two are still newlyweds, but you really shouldn't look at him that way in public. You don't want the bride's brother to have to arrest you for public lewdity."

"Lewdity?" Her friend's eyes twinkled. "Is that a word? I don't think that's a word."

"If it isn't, it should be. It fits that gleam in your eyes to a T."

"She's right," Sage agreed. " 'Lewdity' is a perfect word for the way you look at Cicero."

"He's hot." Rose shrugged. "Anyway, I think 'public lasciviousness' is a more suitable term. I've always wanted to be lascivious. However, you're one to talk, little sister. As your physician, may I remind you that you gave birth to a beautiful baby girl only a week ago. You still have a few weeks to go before you can scratch that itch."

"You're not my physician," Sage grumbled. "And I know exactly how long it's already been and exactly how long we still have to wait. It's just so hard when those two a.m. feedings roll around, and I stumble into the nursery to find my husband has beat me there. There's nothing sexier than a man in stubble and boxer shorts cooing at his infant daughter in the middle of the night."

"I don't know, Sage," Sarah Murphy offered. "A man in stubble and flannel pajama pants changing his son's diaper at two in the morning is pretty darn sexy, too."

Shannon gave an exaggerated groan. "Hello! Can we please change the subject? All this talk about sex and sexy men is giving me a complex. I'm single, remember? I swear I should have told Cicero to bring me a double."

The sisters and Sarah shared a significant look, then Sage said, "Oh, we remember. Weddings are great places to work on finding a special someone. I think that seeing a happy ending right before your eyes puts a person in the mood for romance. There are lots of eligible men here tonight—local and imported."

Rose ticked names off on her fingers. "Brick Callahan. Logan McClure. Max Romano. Tony Romano. The cousins Romano—Sam, Nick, and Jake. Chase Timberlake."

"Chase Timberlake!" Shannon exclaimed. "Ali's son? He's five years younger than me...and he's engaged."

"More like two years," Sage said. "And he

obviously likes older women. I suspect it wouldn't hurt Ali's feelings if you busted up that relationship."

"Or my feelings, either," Sarah grumbled, her gaze stealing across the room toward Lori.

"Well, I'm no home wrecker," Shannon declared. "And while I appreciate your concern about my love life, I'm not here looking for a man—of any variety."

Colt approached and set a glass filled with two fingers of amber liquid in front of her. "Might as well give it up. I've watched these women work for years now. When they get matchmaking in their heads, there's no stopping them."

"I'll drink to that," Sage said, lifting her glass of lemonade in toast.

Shannon wrinkled her nose in mock disgust before grinning with genuine affection toward her friends. The Ciceros, Raffertys, and Murphys were good, kind people. Eternity Springs was filled with good, kind people.

She hated that everything she'd told them about herself was a lie.

Okay, maybe not everything. She'd told

the truth about loving dogs and hating tofu. She'd been honest about her passion for music and chocolate and how fortunate she considered herself for finding a home in this small mountain town.

However, honesty and trust were two different things, weren't they? She wouldn't ...she couldn't...trust these good, kind people with the whole truth.

Nor was she about to let them play match-maker, either. Not anytime soon, anyway. As long as she might have to pick up and disappear at any moment, she couldn't risk a relationship. It wouldn't be fair. Maybe in a couple of years or five, if Eternity Springs remained safe for her, maybe then she could start to think about something with the possibility of permanence.

She took an extra big sip of the whiskey and savored the smooth, smoky flavor while she listened to the conversation taking place around her. Since the men's return, talk had veered away from her barren love life—thank goodness—and toward baseball, particularly the pennant races and the Rockies' chances of making it to the World Series.

Shannon allowed her attention to drift. She shifted in her seat, turned her head, and she wasn't surprised when her gaze found the magnet.

He was talking with a group of summer residents, the Callahans from Texas. He threw back his head and laughed at something one of the wives said. **Yum yum,** Shannon thought as she studied him. He wasn't as classically handsome as Lucca or his brothers, so what was it that made him so…magnetic?

The shoulders, she decided. Broad shoulders always did it for her. The square jaw, too. He gave the appearance of being substantial. Of being someone a person could count on. Depend on.

Yeah, well. Like they say, appearances can be deceiving. Look at me.

At that moment, he turned as if he'd tangibly felt her stare and their gazes met and held. His mouth lifted in a quick grin, and for just a moment, she thought he might head her way. Then the band played a fanfare and asked the crowd to greet Mr. and Mrs. Flynn Brogan. The beaming bride and groom danced their first dance, and then Flynn welcomed their guests and announced that the buffet was open. At that point, the party really got started.

Shannon dined, she danced, she visited with friends and touted the appeal of Eternity Springs to visitors. She accepted numerous offers to refill her glass of whiskey. She wasn't much of a drinker as a rule, but the Bushmills was a treat. It helped distract her from the ghosts that attending a wedding invariably brought to life.

She never found herself in the same group as Mr. Magnetic, and she refrained from asking about him as she moved from gathering to gathering. Sometimes a girl needed a little mystery for her fantasies, something to keep her warm on the cold winter nights that stretched ahead.

Eventually, the combination of loud music, a crowded dance floor, and her old friend the Ghost of Weddings Past drove her outside to cool off and indulge in a rare moment of self-pity. The perfume of roses drifted on the nighttime air and she slowly wandered away from the community center toward the rose garden. She was a sucker for roses. This was one of her best-loved places in Eternity Springs.

A section of the garden had been named in memory of Ali Timberlake's mother. Peace roses had been her favorite, and since they were one of Shannon's favorites, too, she instinctively headed toward that section of the garden. Peace would be a darned nice thing to find tonight.

When was the last time she'd experienced real and lasting peace? She'd known bouts of it since she'd settled in Eternity Springs. The isolation helped. So, too, did the fact that when she moved here last year, she'd sworn off making any Internet searches that involved anyone in her past.

The fact that she'd gone almost a year without finding a teddy bear part on her bed or hanging from her rearview mirror gave her hope, but having hope didn't necessarily bring a person peace. In her experience, hope actually made her more anxious.

She was tired of being anxious. She was tired of living a lie. She wanted rather desperately to make the lie the reality. Only then would she find the tranquility she craved.

"Well, I'm working on it," she murmured. In the meantime, she'd sit in the memorial rose garden among Peace roses and think a little about Ted—her beloved but misguided lover.

Light from a nearly full moon bathed the grounds in a silver glow. The perfume of roses mingled with the sound of music drifting from the community center, and Shannon hummed along to James Taylor as she made her way along a graveled path remembering Ted and their life together.

How young and idealistic they'd been. How naïve. Nothing in either of their relatively innocent upbringings had prepared them for the wild side of life they'd found in northern California.

They'd been drawn into Russell Wilbarger's orbit so easily. The charismatic son of a Silicon Valley billionaire-turned-politician, Russell had a brilliant mind and an ability to proselytize with the zeal of a television preacher and the subtlety of a fine wine. It had taken her two semesters to recognize how sneaky and manipulative he could be. Three semesters to discover that the golden boy had a criminal streak.

By then, Ted was in too deep. He wouldn't listen to her. Didn't believe her. Refused to recognize that what he was doing was wrong—until it was too late.

Melancholy suffused her, and as if her mood ordered up the song, the band struck up the old Hank Williams ballad "I'm So Lonesome I Could Cry."

"Why in the world would they choose to play that at a wedding?" Shannon murmured aloud as she stepped up into the gazebo.

The male voice spoke from the shadows. "Because it is the third-best country music song of all time, a great slow-dancing song, and it's an inside joke among the Romano brothers."

The magnet. Though she couldn't see him and had never heard him speak, she knew that's who had spoken. "You are so totally wrong."

"About what?"

"No way is that the third-best country music song of all time. I'll give it top ten. Maybe even top eight. But three? No way."

"Oh, yeah?" She could make out his shadowed form now that she knew he was there.

He leaned against one of the support posts. "So what do you think is number three?"

Shannon took a seat on the bench that ringed the gazebo's five sides and rolled her tongue around her mouth. "I'd have to go with 'Honky Tonk Badonkadonk.'"

He gave an exaggerated flinch and she laughed. "Hey, it hit all the charts. Was a gold record. It can be argued that the song changed country music."

"Not for the better," he fired back.

"All right, then. My real number three is Johnny Cash's 'I Walk the Line.'"

"Arguable, I'll admit. Wrong, but at least you didn't throw out 'Achy Breaky Heart.'"

Shannon vowed solemnly, "And I never will."

His teeth flashed. He stepped away from the post and she heard the sound of ice cubes hitting a glass, then the splash of liquid. "I have to say, this is the best-equipped gazebo I've ever seen. There's a complete bar set up here. Can I get you something to drink?"

"Bushmills, please. Straight up. Flynn told the facility's owner that he wanted everything completely stocked."

A moment later, he handed her the drink then said, "To the bride and groom."

"To Gabi and Flynn." They clinked glasses.

The little buzz she felt had more to do with the delicious timbre of his voice than the alcohol, she admitted as the final notes of the Hank Williams song faded away and the tempo of the music changed. "Hip-hop," the stranger observed. "Eclectic selection of music tonight."

"I heard that the playlist took quite a bit of negotiation. Gabi wanted guests to enjoy themselves, and she's made it a personal goal to lure everyone onto the dance floor at some point. There are a lot of young people here tonight, and Gabi does go all in when she commits to something."

"It's an admirable quality, though I'll admit that I could have gone all night without hearing the 'Hokey Pokey.' That's what drove me out into the night."

"Then you missed one of the highlights of the evening. It's not every day you see a former federal judge shaking it all about."

"Hmm...who's the judge?"

"Mac Timberlake."

"I don't think I've met him. But then, I

haven't met you, either."

Shannon extended her hand. "I'm Shannon."

"Nice to meet you, Shannon." His large hand closed around hers, his handshake firm. "I'm..."

As he said his name an owl sitting unnoticed atop the gazebo let out a loud **whoo hoo whoo** and flapped his wings, flying away.

"...Samuel," Shannon heard, distracted and unnerved by the little jolt of electricity she felt at his touch. Needing something to occupy herself with, she took another sip of her drink, then said, "Nice to meet you, too."

"Are you a local?"

"Yes. How about you? You're visiting from...?"

"Back East. I'm from—" He lifted his head and turned his ear toward the community center. "Now, there's a top five country song."

"Top five? Willie Nelson? Don't be ridiculous. 'Blue Eyes Crying in the Rain' is maybe top twenty. Maybe. That's if you count 'A Man of Constant Sorrow' as bluegrass rather than country because it's definitely top five."

"It's definitely bluegrass and you are so wrong." And they were off.

Just how long they debated artists and covers and vocal styles Shannon hadn't a clue. A long time. They ended up seated beside each other with the bottle of Bushmills within reach. She lost track of the number of times he refilled her glass. She knew her music, but the depth of his knowledge put her to shame. He knew Nashville today and yesterday, but he also knew Texas country and bluegrass and Gospel. When he threw in an Andrea Bocelli reference, she feared she might have whimpered a bit.

"Enough," she eventually declared. "Next you'll be rattling off the playlist the bands played at halftime of the Florida/Auburn football game last year."

"You follow college football?" he asked, a hopeful note in his voice.

Shannon giggled. She couldn't help it. She was a little bit looped and buzzed with sexual awareness, and she'd better do something different before she did something stupid. Like lean forward and nibble at that sexy square jaw of his. "I think that the running back out of Arkansas will win the Heisman this year."

He closed his eyes and tilted his head away, holding up his hand palm out. "Built, beautiful, knows who wrote 'Me and Bobby McGee,' and the difference between a zone read and the veer option? Honey, I think...wait." Now he looked at her, his stare intent. "Hear that?"

He reached out and rested his hand on her knee. Shannon shivered at his touch. She couldn't hear anything over the sudden pounding of her heart. "Hear what?"

He leaned forward. His eyes glittered like a cat's in the moonlight. "The song. It's number one. The best country song of all time."

She heard it then. Patsy Cline. "'Crazy.'"

"Dance with me, Shannon."

She nodded, her mouth suddenly dry. He took her hand in his and slowly pulled her to her feet. His arm slid around her waist, and he led her into the dance. By the end of the first stanza, he held her tucked close like a lover. Before the first refrain had finished, she rested her head against his lapel, lost in the music, the scent of him, the heat of him, the rare pleasure of being held.

When he began to softly sing along with the second verse, her knees went weak and she melted.

She felt the rumble of his rich baritone voice against her cheek. The music...the moment...reached down into her soul and filled a place within her that had been empty for too long.

Shannon didn't want the song to end. She wished the band would play it a second time. A third. A dozen more times. But far too soon, Samuel crooned the final line, and Shannon summoned the strength to lift her head and smile up at him. Thinking to hide the intensity of her reaction to him with a light and breezy remark about his including two Willie Nelson songs in his top five, Shannon opened her mouth to speak, but the look in his eyes stopped her cold.

Only, not cold. It scorched her. An answering heat flared inside her. She went hot. Anticipation sizzled in her veins.

A glimmer of sense and sobriety fluttered to life inside her. He wasn't wearing a wedding ring—she'd already noticed that. But..."Are you with anyone?"

His voice a bit raspy, he said, "No, Shannon. I'm alone. I'm so very alone."

Deliberately, he lowered his mouth and kissed her, rattling Shannon's world.

Her whole body reacted, aching as if the hollow emptiness inside her was finally sated. Despite her sadness, despite the warmth of a whiskey glow, despite being kissed by a virtual stranger, Shannon was more aware of this man than she had ever been of anything or anyone else in her life. When he deepened the kiss, she responded to him as if she would otherwise drown.

Explosions erupted. Screaming whistles and booms. **Boom boom boom. Crackle crackle crackle.** It took her a moment to realize that the fireworks were bursting in the sky above Angel's Rest, not inside of her.

She started to laugh. She couldn't help herself. It bubbled up from within her like the champagne in the newlyweds' flutes. Samuel released her and stepped back, seemingly startled at first. Then he, too, began to grin.

Shannon melted all over again.

"Thank you for the dance, Shannon."

"Thank you. I enjoyed it."

"Me, too."

They stood staring at each other for a long minute, until she finally felt like a fool and tore her gaze away from him to stare up at the starbursts in the sky. "Wedding fireworks. How totally Gabi."

"Yes. Absolutely."

Shannon sighed wistfully when a huge gold sunburst filled the night sky. "She and Flynn will be leaving soon. We should be there."

"You're probably right."

"This was nice."

"Very nice. I'm so glad you wandered my way."

"Me, too."

He set their empty glasses on a tray beside the bar station and led her from the gazebo, taking her hand in support when she wobbled a bit descending the stairs to the ground. He didn't release it as they wound their way through the rose garden, and Shannon didn't mind. She'd had enough to drink that she appreciated the support. Besides, she was in no hurry for the evening to end. She had nothing but old ghosts and memories waiting for her at home.

The wedding guests had gathered on the

sprawling lawn of Angel's Rest to observe the show. Shannon and Samuel joined the crowd gazing up at the night sky, and judging by some of the interested looks she caught coming their way, the fact that they'd arrived together did not go unnoticed. In fact, she sensed Hope Romano's gaze for the rest of the show.

The fireworks concluded with a finale that left the crowd cheering and clapping. When the time came to pass out sparklers for the bride and groom's leave-taking, Shannon pitched in to help. She lost track of Samuel as guests lined the path leading to the limo to give Gabi and Flynn a rousing send-off.

The crowd was slow to disperse. The band continued to play and the wait staff hired for the event still circulated with flutes filled with champagne. Shannon incautiously accepted more than one glass. Finally, though, the band announced the final song. When she recognized "At Last," made famous by Etta James, a wave of emotion rolled over her and tears pooled in her eyes. That was her all-time favorite song, but tonight, she really didn't want to hear it. **Lonely days over? Not hardly.**

Was anything more lonely than leaving a wedding by yourself?

She grabbed her evening purse from the table where she'd left it and hurried toward the door. Once she escaped into the darkness, she could let her tears fall and no one would be the wiser.

She was almost to the footbridge crossing Angel Creek when she heard someone call her name. Samuel.

She almost didn't stop. By now, tears were rolling steadily down her face, and the music seemed to flow into her ears and down into her heart where it pumped emptiness throughout her body. The sooner she was away from Angel's Rest, away from the music and the happiness and the gaiety, the better.

"Shannon, wait up!"

She could go home and wallow in the misery. Or, she could delay the moment when she'd be alone, surrounded by four walls, paint cans, and regret.

I should get a dog.

Swiping the tears from her cheeks, she slowed her steps and drew in a deep, bracing breath. Then she stopped, summoned a smile, and turned.

"Are you okay?" he asked, worry in his tone. "You left in a rush."

"I'm fine. I just needed some air." Thankful for the shadows that hid evidence of her tears, she continued with a self-deprecating note in her voice. "That last glass of champagne hit me a little hard."

"Ah. Better now?"

"I am. Thanks."

He gestured toward the parking lot that remained half full of cars. "You're not driving home, are you?"

"No. I walked over. That's one of the benefits of living in a small town. It's a short walk to just about everywhere."

"You have a point. Mind if I walk along with you? I'm bunking at the Romanos'. Their couch is calling my name."

"I'm glad to have the company," she said, meaning it.

Since those who had left the reception shortly after the bride and groom's departure had had time to reach their destinations and the close-the-party-down types had yet to leave the community center,

Shannon and Samuel had the streets mostly to themselves. The air was crisp, the moon a golden coin rising over Murphy Mountain. They strolled side by side, mostly not speaking, but sharing a comfortable silence.

For almost the first time Shannon didn't look forward to going home to her little work-in-progress. There in the anonymity of the deepening shadows, her tongue loosened by too much alcohol, she observed, "On nights like this, being alone sucks."

"Yeah, it does." He shoved his hands in his pockets.

"Ordinarily, I don't mind being alone. I'm around people all the time at work, so usually I like having my house to myself."

"What sort of work do you do?"

"My primary work is tending bar. I run Murphy's Pub. That's why I know my music. The jukebox plays all the time."

"Aha. The mystery is solved."

"How about you? Why do you know so much about music?"

His lips twisted in a rueful smile. "I spend a lot of time in pubs."

"Not mine," she said. "I'd remember you."

"No, not yours."

"How come?"

"I seldom visit Eternity Springs."

She shook her head—a mistake because it offset her precarious balance and she teetered. He reached out and grabbed her elbow to steady her...and didn't let her go. Good. She didn't want him to let her go. They were almost to her house. Her lonely house. Heartsong Cottage. Heartbreak Hotel. Empty, but for the ghosts. "I mean, how come you spend a lot of time in pubs? Are you an entertainer? You have a beautiful voice. Would you sing for me again?"

He made a sound that was part laughter, part groan. "I'm not an entertainer. I can't believe I did that. I don't sing in public."

"It wasn't very public at the time."

"No, it wasn't."

"We should go somewhere private and you can sing for me. I'd like that. I'd love that. Your voice is such a gorgeous deep baritone. Like Elvis singing 'Can't Help Falling in Love.' It sort of rumbled through me and I heard it in my heart. I didn't feel so alone."

"Now I'm embarrassed."

"Don't be embarrassed." She was the one who should be embarrassed. She had a lump of emotion in her throat and the small, sober part of her heard desperation in her voice.

They stood at the base of her sidewalk. Her cottage loomed dark and empty and so lonesome she could cry. Maybe she should reconsider the staging she'd planned for when she listed it for sale. Forget the cutesy, romantic, Victorian bed-and-breakfast décor. She should go rustic with leather and wood and maybe some iron. **Go west, young woman.** Heartsong Cottage was a country-western song.

Shannon was a prideful woman. She was a hard worker and as good a friend as circumstances would allow. She didn't ask for special treatment and she never, ever begged for attention from a man.

But tonight she was lonely and vulnerable and a bit beyond a little drunk. So she touched Samuel on the sleeve and said, "This is my house. Come inside with me. Dance with me again. Sing for me again. I don't want to be alone. Do you?"

Chapter Four

No.

Daniel didn't want to be alone. He very much didn't want to be alone.

He should tell her good night and take his happy ass home to Hope's. Hadn't he decided when he saw her sitting with the Murphys and Raffertys at the reception that approaching her, pursuing her, would be a serious mistake? This was a small town. She was a friend of his friends. He valued his friendships. He didn't have all that many of them. He didn't want to complicate those he did have.

It would be stupid as hell to go inside with this beautiful, witty, fascinating woman.

If he went inside, he wouldn't have the strength to leave. Not before morning. **Hey, it's one way to get off the Romano couch.**

Yes. By being a jerk.

He cleared his throat and forced himself to say, "We've both had too much to drink."

"Then come in and I'll make coffee. We can sober up."

That sounded safer than dancing. Not nearly as appealing, but infinitely safer. "I'd like that."

Daniel was in a mood. He'd brought it with him over Sinner's Prayer Pass, and Eternity Springs had yet to work its magic on him. Seeing Holly had helped, but when they'd brought the little kids out of the babysitting rooms and the band launched into the "Hokey Pokey," a tsunami of loneliness had rolled over him and propelled him out into the night.

When he'd spied the yellow dress floating toward him, he couldn't help but reach for the lifeline.

Now, her smile lit up the night. She grabbed his hand and tugged him up the narrow walk toward the front door of a small Victorian cottage. "You'll have to excuse the mess. I'm in the middle of some serious kitchen and bath renovations. I'm having an undeclared war with my plumber. He's not getting paid until he fixes what he broke last time he was here. I'm functional enough to make coffee, though."

She hadn't locked the front door—typical behavior in Eternity Springs, he knew. He followed her into a living room sparsely furnished with a small easy chair and otto-man, a floor lamp, and a wall unit of book-shelves filled with books. A sawhorse worktable filled a corner of the room. One wall was painted in…he counted nine different colors. "Fascinating color scheme you have going on."

"I need to live with color for a time before I decide on what I want." She waved a hand toward the chair. "Make yourself at home. I'd invite you into the kitchen but I don't want to get in trouble with OSHA. You'd need a hard hat. I'll get…oh, wait."

She veered off toward the bookshelves, used her foot to shove aside a brown corru-gated box. "I bet you'll find this interesting."

Her action revealed a 1950s-era record player. "It works like new. There are 33s, 45s, and 78s in the box. Why don't you pick something out while I make coffee?"

Delighted, he hunkered down beside the box and started flipping through the collection of vinyls. It was an eclectic collection—country, big band, gospel, even a Simon and Garfunkel album.

When he saw Patsy Cline's **Showcase**

with the Jordanaires, he couldn't resist. When Shannon entered the living room from the kitchen looking sexy and soft and warm, he didn't even try.

He needed. He wanted. He was so damned lonely. As Patsy Cline fell to pieces, he extended his arm. "Dance?"

Shannon moved into his arms as if she belonged there.

Daniel led her in the dance, the faintly floral scent of woman and perfume wafting around them, the warm heat of her soft skin beckoning him close. He closed his eyes and allowed the music to sink into his soul.

Once upon a time, music had been a big part of his life. During high school he'd been part of a garage band. Bass guitar and vocals. He'd made spending money in college playing little bars and clubs three nights a week, offering a mix of rock and country tailored for the venue. He'd only quit the band when he moved home to Boston and joined the police department, but he'd continued to play the guitar. Gail had loved for him to sing to her. Not country—she didn't like country music— but she'd loved the ballads of the sixties.

He'd sung to Justin every time he rocked him to sleep. Traditional lullabies, but also contemporary love songs. When he lowered his sleeping son into his crib, he'd stand and watch him and sing a verse or two of John Lennon's "Beautiful Boy."

He hadn't picked up a guitar since Justin died. He had not sung, not even in the shower, since then, either. **So why did I sing to her tonight? Why did it feel so right?**

The question left Daniel shaken. The sound of Shannon's sigh vibrated through him.

"Torch songs," she said. "That's what these types of songs are called. I never listened to them until I ran across this box of records in the basement at the pub, but I like them. They're so...moody."

He'd read an article about Patsy Cline a while back, and something she'd said had stayed with him. He murmured, "I sing like I hurt inside."

Shannon lifted her head from his shoulder. "What?"

"They're songs of unrequited love. Of lost lovers."

A sheen of moisture dampened her warm brown eyes. "They're evocative. Sad and lonely...so why do I like listening to them?"

"Country songs are about everyday people living everyday lives. There's a lot of pain in this world. Country music expresses what we're feeling inside. 'Misery loves company' is a cliché for a reason."

"Are you miserable?"

Yes. Rather than tell the truth, he fell back on a line. "Not right this minute, no. I have a beautiful woman in my arms."

In her broken smile, Daniel thought he recognized a kindred spirit, a lonely woman to his lonesome man. His response was as natural as the moth being attracted to a flame. He lowered his mouth and kissed her again.

They kissed.

And kissed.

And kissed.

And ended up in her bedroom, in her bed.

There was a quiet desperation in the urgency they shared, their actions physical. Mindless. Both of them fleeing from pain.

Sad country-music lyrics.

Daniel hadn't been with a woman in almost a year, so he didn't last long. Her reaction in the aftermath suggested that she didn't mind. As he lay trying to summon the energy to leave her bed, she snuggled up against him, her hand resting on his chest. Sleepily, she said, "Samuel, I'd like it very much if you'd stay the night."

This was what she'd wanted, he realized. The sex was the end to her means. That actually gave him absolution to avoid Hope Romano's couch. "Okay. I'd like it very much, too." Then, because he was a little bit ashamed and annoyed that he'd had sex with someone who didn't even know his name, he corrected her. "Only, it's Daniel. Not Samuel."

"Mmm...Daniel..." she murmured. "Pretty name for a magnet."

They both dropped off to sleep.

Shannon stroked a two-inch brush dipped in bloodred paint down chalkboard siding on Heartsong Cottage. It screeched like fingernails. She was thirsty. Oh, so thirsty. Her mouth was as dry as...she glanced around...the desert sand beneath her feet. What had happened to Eternity Springs?

It was so hot. She was so hot. And she was naked. The streak of paint in front of her dried and began to blister. The blisters swelled and popped and her head exploded in pain.

Shannon's eyes flew open. Light pierced like a sword of fire. She slammed her eyelids shut. Slowly, awareness seeped through the pounding in her head. That had been a dream. She was home in bed. With a ferocious hangover.

Home, hungover, and…naked.

Lying beside a naked man.

Oh, holy cow.

Water. She needed water. He put off heat like a furnace.

The magnet. Samuel. Samuel of the piercing, beautiful blue-gray eyes and seductive, melt-your-bones voice.

She needed clothes.

She needed water.

She needed a hole to crawl into to hide.

I got drunk at Gabi's wedding and picked up a man and slept with him. What in the world? She never did stupid, slutty things! And this hadn't been just stupid and slutty. It had been the epitome of stupid and slutty! The Taj Mahal of stupid and slutty. What had she been thinking?

She hadn't been thinking. She'd been running hard and fast from her memories and regrets and the what-ifs that haunted her. But she hadn't been able to outrun her feelings. Last night she'd felt horribly, disastrously alone...and look what she'd done.

I don't even know his last name.

She thought he was a Romano cousin, but he'd never really said that, had he? Oh, sweet kitten feet. Hazy recollections of the previous evening began to seep through the pounding pain of her headache. Coffee she'd brewed but never poured. Thank goodness for automatic shutoffs. The scratch of the phonograph needle at the end of the record. Hadn't he switched it off on their way to the bedroom? The soft, silky texture of his suit jacket beneath her fingertips as she pushed it off his shoulders.

The frantic digging through her nightstand drawer to find one of the condoms she'd brought home from her stock for the men's room machine at the pub.

She exhaled a relieved breath. Not as

stupid as she could have been, then. Thank God.

Other hazy images floated through her mind. Samuel above her, his head thrown back, jaw set, the cords of his neck prominent as he came. She riding him. Snuggled up against him, asking him to stay.

"Not Samuel. Daniel."

"Pretty name for a magnet."

Daniel. His name was Daniel.

"I'm bunking at the Romanos'. Their couch is calling my name."

The Romanos', he'd said. Not his cousin's house or his aunt's house. His last name probably wasn't Romano.

Shannon then had a clear, vivid memory of Gabi standing in her front yard a week ago talking about a guest and Lucca Romano's couch. Daniel. The Daniel who had located Holly and brought her home to Hope.

Daniel Garrett.

The same Daniel Garrett who made his living as a private investigator. **He makes his living by finding people!**

And she lived in hiding, under a name that wasn't her own.

In that moment, her stomach rebelled. She threw back the covers and dashed for the bathroom and made it just in time before she became violently sick.

Stupid. Slutty. And dangerous behavior.

Daniel knocks on the front door of the Holman house in an upscale Kansas City suburb, a local police detective at his side. At the sound of the gunshot, the two men share a look. Daniel doesn't hesitate. He draws back his leg and kicks in the door and finds...carnage.

Blood. So much blood. No no no! Suicide is too easy for the perverted piece of filth. He looks around. Spies the bookshelf filled with dolls and bile rises within him.

Movement beside him jerks him awake. He opens his eyes to see a woman's naked backside running into the bathroom. He sits up, blinks hard, shakes his head, and winces—from the headache and the lingering horror of his dream.

When the memory of his actions the previous night flowed through his thoughts, he groaned aloud.

"Dumbass," he muttered as sounds of retching reached him.

He sighed and reached for his slacks. He didn't often do things that left him cringing, but his actions of the previous night darn sure did. No wonder he'd dreamed of a scumbag. He'd acted like one himself last night. He'd taken advantage of Shannon...damn. He didn't even know her last name.

The sound of the shower running reached him as he buckled his belt. He slipped into his shirt and walked into the kitchen as he buttoned it. She hadn't been kidding about the renovations. Her refrigerator was a dorm-sized one. The lone remaining cabinet held the kitchen sink. He focused on the coffeemaker that sat on a shelf made of cinder blocks and lumber. He dumped out the untouched coffee from last night, washed the carafe, then looked around for the coffee and filters, finally finding them inside a bread box on the cinder-block shelf.

The fresh pot of coffee had almost finished brewing when Shannon joined him in the kitchen. She'd dressed in jeans and a Colorado Rockies T-shirt. With her hair wet and wearing no makeup, she looked fresh and lovely and about seventeen years old—which made Daniel feel about seventy.

"Well..." she said, not quite meeting his gaze. "This is awkward. I hope you'll believe me when I tell you I don't have much experience with this morning-after-with-a-stranger sort of thing."

One corner of his mouth lifted in a rueful smile. "I hope you'll believe me when I say I don't, either."

"I'm sorry that—"

"I need to apologize about—"

They'd spoken simultaneously. They both stopped mid-sentence. She blushed and turned away and pulled one coffee mug from the breadbox. She opened a cardboard box in the mudroom and removed a second mug. "I don't have cream. I have milk if you'd like that."

"Black is fine."

He stood awkwardly in the middle of her tiny, torn-up kitchen while she filled a mug and handed it to him, careful not to brush his fingers with hers. Daniel took a grateful sip and debated what to say. He could attempt another apology. He could make excuses. He could make a stab at small talk.

Had he ever felt this uncomfortable in his life?

Daniel hadn't been celibate in the years since Gail's death. He'd dated a number of women, and he'd had two relatively long-term relationships. He'd never in his life had a one-night stand. He had no experience with this sort of thing.

In the end, he went with the one thing he needed to say most of all. "Shannon, thank you for a very nice evening."

She stared down at her coffee cup and appeared to brace herself. In a soft, small voice, she said, "Thank you, Daniel. I was glad to have company last night."

Then in a stronger tone, she said, "I set out a new toothbrush and razor and clean towels if you'd like to shower."

"Yes. Thanks." He made the escape gratefully, and took his time cleaning up. When he returned he found her standing at the kitchen window staring into the backyard. She glanced over her shoulder and gave him a smile that didn't reach her eyes.

"Feel better?"

"I do, thanks."

"More coffee?"

"Please."

As she filled his mug, she asked, "Would you like a piece of toast? I'm sorry I can't offer you a real breakfast, but I don't eat my meals here. My cupboard isn't only bare, it's nonexistent."

"Thanks, but coffee is all I need. Unless... can I take you out to breakfast?"

"Oh, no. That's not necessary. No, thank you."

Daniel got the impression that she'd have liked to put his coffee in a to-go cup. The needy woman from last night had completely disappeared in the light of day.

"So, how long will you be in Eternity Springs?"

He could tell she'd strived for a tone of general interest, but he didn't miss the dread in her voice. He'd left his return open-ended, thinking he'd spend some time in town, visit with the Romanos, do some fishing. Soak up the peace this town had to offer. But now, after last night, something told him he wouldn't find Eternity Springs peaceful in the least. **You really screwed up a good thing, Garrett.** "I need to leave this morning."

Her obvious relief bordered on insulting. "Well, it's supposed to be beautiful weather. A nice day for a drive."

"That's good." He took another sip of his coffee, and then set the mug down. "I guess I'd better get going."

She followed him into her living room where he picked up his suit jacket from where it lay draped over the back of a chair. She opened the front door. Daniel searched his mind awkwardly for the right words to say. **I'll call you?** No. He had no intention of calling her, and he'd never been one of those men who left women hanging that way. Besides, judging by the look on her face, she'd change her number if he dared say it. So, what? Another thank you? That didn't feel right.

Nothing about this morning felt right.

He'd never been good at this sort of thing.

He'd never done this sort of thing.

Damn. He leaned down and pressed a

kiss against her cheek, and said the one thing that mattered most, apparently to them both. "Good-bye, Shannon."

Relief glimmered in those big brown eyes. "Good-bye, Daniel. Drive safely."

She shut the door behind him. Daniel hooked his jacket over his shoulder and stood without moving for a long moment as he tried to remember where he'd left his car. It seemed like a month ago since he'd locked the door and hotfooted it for the church.

As he started up the walk, music began to drift from Shannon's open window— Patsy Cline singing "Have You Ever Been Lonely."

FIVE WEEKS LATER

Her eyes scrunched shut, her mouth dry with fright, Shannon tightened her arms around the motorcycle driver's waist and held on for dear life. Why had she ever agreed to this trip? What had she been thinking? Despite all of her problems then and now, she'd never had a death wish. In fact she'd been trying oh-so-hard to stay alive, had she not?

Then she'd gone and opened her mouth and admitted she'd never ridden a motorcycle before. Admitted it to Celeste Blessing, the Evil Knievel of Eternity Springs. Who would have thought that the warm, friendly, edging-toward-elderly former Southern charmer would behave like a maniac on twisting mountain roads? Not Shannon.

Finally, thirty minutes out of town—thirty minutes that felt more like thirty days—Celeste slowed down and turned off the road. **Thank you, God,** Shannon prayed.

Then Celeste gunned the engine as the Gold Wing topped a small rise and the motorcycle actually left the ground. Shannon let out a squeal and feared she'd prayed too soon. She gritted her teeth, ducked her head, and didn't breathe easy until Celeste braked to a complete stop and observed, "Why, isn't it delightful! Is this the right spot?"

Cautiously, Shannon opened her eyes.

In a small, narrow valley below, three cabins fashioned from rough-hewn logs stood nestled between a bubbling mountain creek running in front and a heavily wooded hill rising behind. "Yes, we're in the right place. That is Mr. Hamilton's truck parked in front of the big house. He told me his first thought upon seeing the property was Papa Bear, Mama Bear, and Baby Bear, so that's why he's calling it Three Bears Valley."

"It's a perfect name. Though Baby Bear is a bit of a wreck."

Shannon nodded, eyeing the broken windows and missing shingles. No telling how many four-legged creatures called it home. "From this viewpoint, Mama needs a little work, too."

"Maybe he'll hire you to do more than the kitchen and bath mosaics."

"Maybe," Shannon said, and the hope that had sparked to life inside her yesterday burned a little brighter. A job like this could solve so many of her short-term problems.

The long-term ones were another matter entirely, but then they weren't what had put her on the back of Celeste Blessing's death machine this morning. Today was all about the possibility of a well-paying job brought to her by kismet—and the influence of her own personal angel.

"Hold on, dear." Celeste guided the Gold Wing down the hill toward the lone bridge spanning the creek and toward what Shannon hoped would be her next project.

Celeste's timely offer to one of her guests of an advertising flyer about the open house at Heartsong Cottage had brought Bob Hamilton to Shannon's door. When the gentleman from Hobbs, New Mexico, asked dozens of questions about the remodel and showed particular interest in the kitchen mosaic, Shannon had thought she might have found a buyer for her home. Instead, he'd asked if she'd be interested in doing mosaics in the kitchens and baths of structures on property he'd recently purchased half an hour from town.

Celeste pulled the motorcycle to a halt next to the red truck, and cut the motor. "I can't believe I missed hearing about this property when it came on the market."

"Mr. Hamilton said it was a private sale. He's a personal acquaintance of the former owner."

The women dismounted, and Shannon turned in a slow circle, taking a moment to drink in the beauty, peace, and quiet of the spot. On the hillside behind the cabins, a band of aspen cut a glowing golden swath across the deep green of the forest of pine and fir. To the north, the granite cliffs of Murphy Mountain climbed high into the sky. A beaver dam stretched across the creek downstream of the bridge. Upstream, the bubble and rush of water hitting rocks joined the song of a meadowlark perched atop the cabin's stone chimney to provide nature's music to the moment. Turning in a slow circle, she asked, "It's a feast for the eyes, isn't it?"

"Food for the soul," Celeste observed.

Heaven knows, she needed soul nourishment these days, Shannon thought as the front door opened and the property owner walked out onto the front porch. Tall, lean, with a thick mane of silver hair, Bob Hamilton welcomed them with a hearty hello.

Then he proceeded to turn on the flirt toward Celeste. To Shannon's delight, her friend flirted right back. Shannon watched the back-and-forth with blatant interest.

She reviewed what she knew of the older woman's background. It didn't take long, because despite her prominence in town, Celeste remained a bit of a mystery. Shannon knew that she was widowed, but she rarely spoke of her husband, and Shannon wasn't certain how long ago she'd lost him. Celeste had mentioned her regret over never having had children, and she did speak of a sister upon occasion. Rose had told Shannon that Celeste had a whole bunch of cousins. Shannon was curious about the source of Celeste's obviously considerable wealth, but she wasn't rude enough to ask.

"I'll have the president of my motorcycle club send you the information, Bob. Now, I know Shannon is anxious to see what your plans are for your place."

Bob Hamilton explained how he'd pur-chased the property from a business part-ner with the hope of it becoming a meeting place for his children and grandchildren. "I have good kids, but they are spread out all over the country. My goal is to lure them to Colorado. My wife was the glue that held us together, and after she died, we drifted apart. I want my kids to be part of each other's lives again. I think that's important."

"Yes, I agree," Celeste said. "Young people often don't understand the comfort of having someone with whom you're able to reflect upon shared memories and experiences of your formative years as you grow older."

"Exactly." Bob beamed at her. "And I also want my grandkids off the Internet and out in the great outdoors fishing and hiking and riding horses. They need to learn the joys of communing with nature, but they're city kids, so I don't want to make it too difficult for them to adjust. Gotta have some creature comforts out here, though I draw the line at luxury. That's why I'm renovating instead of demolishing and rebuilding. I want the kids to visit, but not move in."

"Wise words of empty-nesters everywhere," Celeste agreed.

Bob flashed a grin. "So, are you ready for the grand tour?"

Shannon nodded. "Absolutely."

They walked through the main house first, and spent some time at his kitchen table looking at the architectural drawings. Bob explained that he'd wanted to preserve as much of the original structures as possible, and his architect had done a fabulous job incorporating those wishes into the design. "But I don't have that something special that I want for Three Bears yet. I'm not overwhelmed by the interior design. I want each of these houses to have something unique and special that will make a memory for my grandchildren. When I saw the mosaics at Heartsong Cottage, I knew I'd found what's been missing.

"Shannon, I want a series of mosaics in each of the houses—the kitchen, the baths, the fireplaces. I want you to tell Goldilocks's story in a unique and inventive way that incorporates the history of this valley and this part of Colorado."

Excitement skittered along Shannon's nerves as design ideas fired in her mind. "How long would I have to do them?"

"All winter. As soon as they get a new roof on Baby Bear, my work crew is headed home for the winter. That was our deal when I sent them up here this summer. They worked their tails off to accomplish as much as they have, and they've assured me when they return in the spring, they can finish up before my deadline, which is Memorial Day."

"Your crew came into Murphy's a few times this summer," Shannon said. "They seemed like good guys."

"They are. I've used the same men for years on a number of different projects, and they do an excellent job. They're hard workers. Gotta be that way if you work for me. Celeste assures me that you're one of the hardest workers she knows."

Shannon smiled her thanks toward Celeste, who shrugged and said, "It's true. The girl works too hard at too many jobs, in my opinion."

That's what happens when you're living by your wits.

"She's the poster child for burning the candle at both ends," Celeste continued. "It's starting to show, too. You dragged into the early-morning yoga class this week. It's not like you, Shannon."

"Careful, Celeste, you'll talk my way out of this job."

The other woman patted her arm. "Nonsense. Bob understands that he'll need to pay you a sufficient amount to allow you to cut back your hours elsewhere. Right, Bob?"

"I pay all my people good wages."

"And, you pay based on the job, not the gender of your employee, correct?"

"Are you asking me if I'll pay her less than I would if she were a man?"

"Of course not." This time, Celeste patted Bob Hamilton's arm. "If anything, I expect you'll pay her a premium because you recognize what a gem she is."

"Brought your agent with you to negotiate, did you?" he said to Shannon, though his admiring gaze remained fixed on Celeste.

Shannon didn't know how to respond to that. Before she could formulate an answer, he added, "I don't doubt you'll be very pleased with what I have to offer."

He then named a number that almost made Shannon's chin drop in shock. This job would be a lifesaver in more ways than one.

"You bring the project in on time and on budget, and you'll earn a fifteen percent bonus, too."

Fifteen percent? For a second there, Shannon thought she might have to sit down.

"The plan is to hold our first family reunion

here on Memorial Day weekend. I want my kiddos to be wowed when they walk inside for the first time. My crew returns mid-March. Think we can have everything finished by then?"

"If there's a holdup, it won't be because of me." She needed to have this project done by Easter. "If I might make one suggestion. I know the local contractors because of the work I've had done at the pub and the cottage, and due to the fact that most of them are patrons at the pub. If your foreman wants to sub anything out to get a start on the springtime work, I can give him recommendations. Getting a few things done over the winter might save your crew some grief in March if winter drags on."

"I like the way you think, young lady. So do we have an agreement?"

"I'll get started on design drawings tonight."

They shook hands and the deal was done. Celeste and Shannon's new boss visited while Shannon made notes and took measurements and reviewed the plans. Her mind spun as she mentally reworked her schedule. Yoga. Murphy's. Heartsong Cottage. Now the Three Bears. Celeste had a point. Something would have to give. Maybe the time had come to list Heartsong Cottage with a Realtor. She'd gone the for-sale-by-owner route because the commission took too big a chunk out of her profits, but she was spending too many hours answering e-mails and Internet queries. Time now better spent here at Three Bears.

Unless I keep Heartsong Cottage. Make it my home instead of a property I flip.

The notion floated through her mind like a forbidden fantasy.

Dare she do it? Dare she even dream about sinking roots in the rich, fertile soil of Eternity Springs?

She was so tired of running. So tired of always looking over her shoulder. Ever so tired of always being afraid.

As if it were yesterday, she recalled meeting Russell Wilbarger's intense, green-eyed gaze over the spray of yellow roses atop Ted's closed casket. For just a moment, she'd seen triumph in those eyes and the first of many shudders of apprehension had crawled up her spine.

The memory put today's wild ride with Celeste into perspective. There was fear... and then there was FEAR.

Shannon turned her attention away from the past and toward the near future—since "near" was as far as she could force herself to go at this particular moment. She rejoined Celeste and Bob as he waxed on about a trout he'd pulled from the creek earlier that morning.

"The fishing is good here," he said. "You should bring your rod next time you come up, Celeste. Wear your hiking boots, too. There's a small box canyon over the hill that is so isolated that it makes this valley look like Times Square. It has the prettiest little waterfall, though. There's a game trail that leads right to it. Makes for a nice hike. Nothing too strenuous. You should both give it a try sometime."

"Oh? I love waterfalls." She glanced around then asked, "Where is the trailhead?"

Bob pointed it out using a boulder and the downstairs bathroom window of Mama

Bear as landmarks. "It'll take you about half an hour to hike to the waterfall. Reaching the box canyon by car would take you more than twice as long."

Celeste pursed her lips thoughtfully. "Is it accessible by road? It might be a fun ride on the Gold Wing."

"I wouldn't recommend it," Bob said with a frown. "The road into the box canyon is rough. Much worse than the one leading here. Takes a four-wheeler to get to the one cabin that's there. I looked at it before I bought this property, but it was too remote for my purposes." He described the route to reach it, then added, "The road stops at the cabin, so you'd still have to hike to the waterfall."

"Oh, I know that road," Celeste said. "That box canyon property was on the market for quite some time, but it sold recently. An agent out of South Fork showed it to me. He didn't mention a waterfall or I would have asked to see it despite the remoteness of the spot."

Shannon steered the conversation back to the job by asking a question about winter road maintenance. Half an hour later, she shook hands with her new employer, said good-bye, and did her best to psych herself up for the return ride to town.

"I'm so excited for you, Shannon," Celeste said, her light blue eyes warm with pleasure as she fitted her motorcycle helmet onto her head. "I have a feeling that this job is just what you need to make all your dreams come true."

Assuming I survive this trip back to Eternity Springs. "The money will certainly come in handy. I'll be able to keep Honey on at the pub."

"I had hoped you would. Isn't it lovely when things work out this way?"

Shannon had hired Honey Tarantino in June during the height of the tourist season, and the fifty-something, newly separated Eternity Springs native had taken over cooking duties at Murphy's. In addition to tweaking a few of Shannon's pub-grub recipes to great success, she'd added the local-gossip touch that, as an outsider, Shannon hadn't been able to provide. Honey loved her job and her job loved her, but when the tourist season had ended, so too had the need for an extra pair of hands at Murphy's. No matter how many ways she'd run the numbers, Shannon had been unable to figure a way to keep Honey on—until now. "She's an excellent bartender and a fabulous cook. Frankly, the work suits her better than it does me. I'm happier with a hammer in my hand."

"What about the yoga classes? Will you keep those up?"

"I'll continue to teach a morning class, but I imagine I'll have to drop the one at lunch."

"In that case, the sleepyheads will simply need to get up with us early birds." Celeste linked her arm through Shannon's. "Although, speaking of birds, a little one passed along the tidbit that Lillian Jenkins instructed at a yoga studio at Lake Tahoe before she and her husband moved to town. Perhaps she'd be willing to take over the noon class."

Shannon grinned. "I don't know why the town council chose to hire a city manager when Eternity Springs has you."

"I'm no manager," Celeste said, swinging her leg over the Gold Wing's seat. "I just like to invest. In businesses. In people. I have a knack for it."

"That you do, Celeste." Shannon took her place behind Eternity Springs' investment angel and sent up a brief, silent prayer for safety. "Eternity Springs needs you."

Ten days later as she prepped a wall in the kitchen at Papa Bear, Shannon recalled the conversation. Having worked late last night and being ahead of schedule despite the whirlwind trip to California to watch Cicero win the Albritton award, she decided to take that hike her boss had suggested.

She felt relatively good today. She had more energy than she'd had for a month. She finally felt strong enough to face her worries and concerns and make some decisions. She'd exercise and exorcise her ghosts.

Filled with purpose, Shannon tossed a couple of water bottles and the sack lunch she'd brought into a backpack. She grabbed a hat, her sunglasses, lip balm, a compass, and her notebook and a pencil and started out.

She had to hunt a little bit to locate the trail since brush and fallen leaves effectively camouflaged the path. Had she not known it was there, she'd never have found it. Within minutes of entering the forest, a most welcome sense of peace enveloped her.

It was a beautiful afternoon. Sunlight dappled the forest floor and the loamy scent of autumn wafted on the gentle breeze. The woods were alive with sound— the crunch of leaves beneath her hiking boots, the distant sound of a babbling mountain stream, the music of a songbird from a hidden perch above her. Shannon felt her spirits lift.

Her life had taken some curious turns, but she truly should count her blessings. She loved Eternity Springs. She had friends. She had work she enjoyed. And in the springtime, she would have a start at something else she'd always wanted. A family.

A baby.

"My baby," she murmured, saying the words aloud for the very first time.

She'd taken the home pregnancy test a week ago. The positive result hadn't surprised her. She was attuned to her body and she'd sensed the changes weeks ago. The prospect of motherhood both scared her to death and made her heart sing. Once upon a time, she'd wanted nothing more than to be a wife and stay-at-home mom to three or four little ones. She had thought that dream had ended with Ted's death and Russell's pursuit.

Apparently, she'd been wrong.

Shannon daydreamed about sugar and spice and everything nice as she climbed the gently sloping trail over the mountain. On the downside, snakes and snails and puppy dog tails held her attention. She decided that she truly didn't care whether her baby was a boy or a girl. "As long as the baby is healthy." That's what potential parents always said, wasn't it? For the first time, she understood how true that statement was.

The trail broke from the trees in a postage stamp of a meadow and Shannon got her first glimpse of the waterfall. It wasn't very big—the drop only fifteen feet or so—but Shannon found the spot enchanting. Rainbows of color bloomed on the mist from frothing white water at the base of the falls. Leaves of autumn red, orange, and yellow circled slowly on the surface of a comparatively placid pool along the bank of the creek. Water clean and clear revealed the presence of a speckled brown trout. A cry in the blue sky above caught her notice and she looked up to see the white-tipped wings of a hawk sailing on the breeze. It was a picture-perfect moment. Nature at its most beautiful, unspoiled. Elemental.

And she was part of it. The life growing inside her was part of it. In that moment, a sensation as powerful as any she'd ever known filled her. Joy. Gratitude. All-encompassing love.

"Thank you," she said aloud. "Thank you for this unexpected gift, difficult though it certainly will be."

Suddenly, she was starving.

She made her way to a flat rock beside the eddy, and she sat cross-legged and dug in her backpack for her roast beef sandwich. She scarfed it down, along with carrot sticks and an apple and the sack of trail mix she'd brought along for her mid-afternoon snack.

"Should have packed more," she murmured. She leaned back on her elbows, lifted her face toward the sunshine, closed her eyes, and inhaled a deep breath. She gave herself five minutes to enjoy the moment and absorb the peace it offered.

Then, sufficiently strengthened, she prepared to tackle that decision-making task.

She had to decide what to do about Daniel Garrett.

Did she reach out to the man and let him know that the precautions they'd taken hadn't proved cautionary enough? Should she be honest about the baby?

Shannon scooped up a handful of pebbles from the edge of the creek and began tossing them one by one into the water. **Plop. Plop. Plop.**

If her circumstances were different, she would never consider keeping knowledge of the baby from his father. She'd always thought that to be one of the scummiest things a woman could do. The fact that Daniel had already lost one child would only compound the betrayal. Guilt would eat her alive if she kept this secret.

And yet...**Plop. Plop. Plop.** Shouldn't her child's safety be her greatest concern? Didn't her child's best interests trump those of his father's? Children needed their fathers, true. But better to forgo having a father if it meant preserving life. Nothing she'd learned about Daniel Garrett led her to believe that he'd be content to live his life in hiding from Russell Wilbarger—and she dare not do anything else.

Imagine what he might do if he found her. Found them.

No, she didn't want to imagine it. It didn't bear thinking about. He'd left cut-up stuffed-animal pieces on her pillow, for goodness' sake! She'd never prove it, just like she'd never prove that he murdered Ted, but she knew it. In her heart of hearts, she knew it.

She'd seen it in his eyes as he'd stood as pallbearer for his friend.

She couldn't tell Daniel. Nor could she remain in Eternity Springs. Not with a child. Not around Daniel Garrett's friends.

Plop. Plop. Plop. She gathered a second handful of pebbles. She'd have to grab her nest egg and flee. Maybe she could find another little mountain town in which to live. Maybe she should try a beach town this time around. Or a city. Philly or Phoenix or Farmington.

Plop plop plop. Come inside with me. Dance with me. Sing to me again.

Actions have consequences. **Plop. Plop. Plop.** Ripples upon ripples upon ripples.

I'm going to be a mother.

A tentative combination of fear and delight fluttered in her heart like hummingbird wings.

She wouldn't have chosen this path on purpose, but she couldn't regret it. She wouldn't regret it. What she needed to do was to figure out a way to live with it. How to live with him or her.

And maybe with Daniel? What if...

For a few minutes, she allowed herself to daydream. Since Flynn and Gabi's wedding, she'd asked a few discreet questions about Daniel Garrett around town. Everything she'd learned about him reinforced her first opinion of the man. He was a good person, a real hero to a number of people. He was loyal and smart and determined. He was a man of his word. If she'd set out to get pregnant on purpose, she couldn't have picked a better father for her baby. If only he made his living some other way. Why couldn't she have slept with an accountant?

No, that might actually be worse. Who knew if her false documents would hold up beneath an accountant's scrutiny?

Daniel Garrett wasn't an accountant. He was a detective.

A detective who'd kept looking for Holly Montgomery for years. Who wouldn't give up. Who never gave up.

Maybe you could ask for his help.

The idea drifted through her mind like an angel's sigh. What if she told him? What if he tried to help? What if...

She remembered the look in Russell's eyes at the funeral.

No. She wouldn't be responsible for another man's death.

She tossed the last three rocks into the creek, her mood going bleak. Could she even keep her baby safe? Maybe the most loving thing to do would be to tell Daniel and offer him custody, but everything inside her rebelled at the thought.

Well, this was a problem she wasn't going to solve today. She didn't **need** to solve it today. She had plenty of time to figure out the best thing for all three of them.

In the meantime, she'd better get back to work.

Rising, Shannon dusted off her hands and bent to scoop up her backpack just as a sound reached her ears. The hair on the nape of her neck rose. What sort of animal made a noise like a crying child? There had been a discussion about it at Murphy's one night. Maybe a wildcat? No... something less threatening. What was it?

"A fox," she recalled just as movement on the other side of the creek caught her attention. Her mouth gaped in surprise. Not a wild animal, but a wild child. The boy was seven or maybe eight years old, and he was sobbing his heart out.

He was running straight for the creek.

Shannon frowned. Why was a child alone in the forest? He was darting straight toward the waterfall. Did he see where he was going? This might not be Niagara Falls, but a headlong tumble off the creek bank could cause a serious injury. Concern rolled through Shannon. Her gaze swept the little meadow. There...maybe fifteen yards away, the stream was narrow enough for her to cross. She began moving that way even as she called, "Hello? Hello! Little boy! Are you okay?"

Shannon took a running start to leap across the creek and angled her pursuit to intercept the child. "Stop!" she shouted. "Please stop!"

This time, the boy heard her. He slowed, allowing Shannon time to place herself between the water and the boy. "Whoa... whoa...whoa," she said, grabbing him by the shoulders. "There's a big drop-off. You need to be careful. Honey, who are you? Why are you out here by yourself?"

"I'm running away! I don't like it here. I don't want to be here anymore." He lifted tear-filled big brown eyes to Shannon. "She's fighting with him and it's because of me. I didn't mean to do something stupid. I just wanted to talk to my friend Jeremy. I'm so lonely here. There's no TV!"

Shannon placed a comforting hand on the boy's shoulder. "What's your name, honey?"

"I'm not supposed to tell!"

Oh. Shannon didn't like the sound of that. She hoped this was simple stranger-danger protocol, but her own circumstances made her suspicious. But before she said any more, another figure burst from the trees. An attractive blonde wearing expensive jeans and a tight red sweater exclaimed, "Benjamin Robert, you are in so much trouble. You scared me to death!"

"Mommy."

Upon seeing Shannon near her child, the woman's face flushed with alarm. Shannon removed her hand from the boy's shoulder, lifted both hands palms up, and took a step backward in her effort to be nonthreatening. "I was worried he was going to run over the edge."

"I'm sorry, Mommy," the boy said. "I shouldn't have used his satellite phone to call Jeremy. I was bad."

"You made a poor decision."

"He yelled at me."

"Yes, and he shouldn't have done that."

"You yelled back at him."

"Yes."

"It's just like at home. It scared me."

"Oh, honey." The blonde wrapped her arms around the boy. "I'm sorry. We shouldn't have yelled." She met Shannon's gaze and her lips lifted with an embarrassed smile.

"I'm afraid our family disagreement spilled beyond our boundaries."

Shannon's gaze skimmed over both the woman and child, searching for bruising or other signs of abuse. Nothing was obvious, but clothing could hide a lot. Quietly, she asked, "Do you need help? I have a car. It's not far from here. Half an hour along that path and it will be mostly downhill."

"Help? Oh, no. Thank you. We're fine."

"We're not fine!" the boy said. "There's nothing to do here! Do you have TV, lady? Or Wi-Fi?"

The blonde released a frustrated sigh and gave her son a stern look. "Enough." To Shannon, she explained, "My husband wanted a back-to-nature holiday, but I'm afraid the isolation here takes some getting used to for city folk like my son and me. We'll adjust. We just need to give it some time. Honey, we need to get back to the house. Daddy will be wondering if we got lost."

"He is not my daddy!"

"Stepfather, then." The blonde's voice held an unmistakable note of warning. She extended her hand toward Shannon, her manner flustered. "Thank you so very much for watching out for my boy. It frightens me to think of what might have happened to him. He had no business being on that mountain trail all alone."

"The Rockies do require respect," Shannon said. Casting a smile toward the boy, she added, "I came here from the city, too. It took me a little while to adjust to life in the mountains. But the outdoor life does have much to offer if you give it a chance."

"Fishing is stupid," the boy said with a shrug. Sullenly, he added, "It's really stupid not to have Wi-Fi."

Shannon experienced a wave of sympathy for his back-to-nature stepdad. She'd bet ten dollars that this boy was one of those children who'd been given his own smartphone or tablet before he could walk.

His mother gave Shannon an apologetic smile. "Colorado has been a bit of a culture shock for us. I didn't think this was the best place for our vacation, but my husband insisted."

"Well, if you decide you simply can't do

without creature comforts, you should ask your husband to bring you over to Eternity Springs. Angel's Rest Healing Center and Spa has Internet and offers half-price spa services on Wednesdays through the end of October."

"Really? Well, we might need to look into that. Thanks. You know, a little pampering sounds wonderful. I'll see if I can't talk my husband into taking us to...Eternity Springs, you said?"

"Yes." Shannon figured she might as well play ambassador. "In addition to Angel's Rest resort, we have fabulous shopping. You'll want to visit Vistas art gallery and our wonderful art glass shop, Whimsies. Heavenscents is our handmade-soap store. I highly recommend the lavender bath melt. Whatever you do, don't miss the strawberry pinwheel cookies at our bakery, Fresh."

"Cookies?" the boy repeated. "Do they have chocolate chip?"

Shannon nodded. "With big hunks of chocolate. And..." She paused dramatically, then added, "We do have Wi-Fi readily available."

"Mom, can we go?"

The woman's smile was a little strained. "We'll see. It truly does sound lovely. I'll see if I can talk my husband into a trip. Although he's not going to want to reward your bad behavior, son."

"I'm not going fishing! I'm not going to touch worms and those eggs are slimy. Tell him, Mom." He pointed and announced the demand. "There he is now. You tell him!"

The blonde winced and glanced nervously over her shoulder. Shannon followed the path of the little brat's finger toward the man who emerged from the trees. When he spied them, he came to an abrupt halt. Time seemed to stand still as his gaze locked on Shannon's.

Her stomach dropped. The nausea that accompanied her mornings of late stirred and her sandwich threatened to come up.

"He doesn't look happy," the blonde observed.

No, he doesn't.

In fact, Daniel Garrett looked furious.

Chapter Five

Married.

Daniel Garrett was married.

He had a wife. A stepson.

Why, the lying, cheating, sorry son of a swamp rat.

You slept with a married man.

Shannon sucked in a quick breath at the realization. Her gaze flicked to the boy and then to his mother. To Daniel's wife.

OMG. I'm the other woman!

It went against everything she believed in. It violated her core beliefs.

She was going to have a married man's baby.

Dazed and shaken, Shannon only vaguely noticed when Daniel's wife took hold of her son's hand and said, "We'd better go. Thanks again."

The blonde tugged the boy toward the edge of the forest where Daniel stood beside a boulder almost exactly the same height as he was. Shannon watched them go and wanted to dash off in the other direction. Pride kept her rooted her to her spot and provided fuel for her actions as she lifted her chin and shot Daniel a contemptuous look.

He said something to the boy, then he and his wife exchanged a few words. The blonde wrapped her arms around Daniel's waist and gave him a hug. Mother and son then disappeared into the trees.

Once his family departed, Daniel faced Shannon. She tilted her chin even higher. He glanced back into the trees, then again at her.

His mouth set, his expression grim, Daniel Garrett headed her way.

What a cluster. What a train wreck. What a colossal screwup his decision to bring Linda and Benny to Colorado had been. The kid was unhappy. Mom was unhappy. Daniel was downright miserable.

What the hell had he been thinking? Just because the idea of spending a few weeks in a remote no-frills mountain cabin sounded like heaven to him didn't mean an eight-year-old boy raised on iEverything would see the appeal. He should have realized that just because a boy had never been fishing didn't mean he'd fall in love with the activity when he had the chance.

Face it, Garrett. You don't know eight-year-old boys from hedgehogs.

No, his experience ended at age four, didn't it?

Daniel gritted his teeth. He'd had a list of worries involving Benny a mile long, but having the kid run off into the woods hadn't been on it. It almost required an act of God to get the boy to put down his electronics and leave the cabin. When Daniel discovered Benny chatting away on the sat phone, he'd lost it.

Guilt rolled through him like a wave. He seldom raised his voice. He never raised it with children or women. Why today?

At least when the boy decided to take off, he'd had the sense to follow a trail. If he'd dashed into the trees in a different direction, he could have easily gotten lost. Daniel's expertise lay in tracking children through the maze of adult depravity, not through a forest of pine and fir and aspen. All he needed was to have to call in the authorities to find a missing kid—one who was already in the news for being missing.

Not that what had just happened was a whole helluva lot better. Benny had managed to lead him to the one person in Colorado whom Daniel least wanted to see.

Wasn't it just his luck?

Not that he hadn't imagined running across her dozens of times in the past six weeks. He'd imagined seeing her out hiking in the woods—in tight little short shorts and a midriff-baring top. And sunning herself beside a mountain stream—topless. And lying beside him in bed—naked.

Instead, he found her standing in a meadow with a chip the size of a boulder on her shoulder.

Dammit, Garrett. Could you be a bigger dumbass?

He should have taken Linda and Benny to New York City or San Antonio or San Francisco. Hell, he never should have accepted this job to begin with. He was a detective, not a bodyguard. The skill sets were different.

So what if ten years of close association with evil had left him heartsick and soul weary and ready for a change? If he wanted innocence, he should have gone to work at a scrapbooking store or taking baby portraits.

No, not baby portraits. He wanted nothing to do with kids.

Taking this job had been a big mistake. After his behavior at Gabi and Flynn's wedding, he'd decided he needed to deal with this kid phobia of his. Had he not let the "Hokey Pokey" screw with his brain, he wouldn't have gone outside and he wouldn't have downed half a bottle of Bushmills and he wouldn't have ended up in Shannon O'Toole's bed. A night of good sex—okay, great sex—wasn't worth the possible repercussions to his life. She was a friend of his friends. Eternity Springs was his refuge, his pool of tranquility, and he'd gone and pissed in it. So when Linda reached out to him, he'd said yes.

What a disaster.

Living with Benny was like walking barefoot on broken glass. He looked so much like Daniel's image of Justin as an eight-year-old that every day with the boy sliced open a new wound. So he'd been on edge when he discovered Benny chatting up a friend on the satellite phone. He'd barked at the boy, frightened him, and sent him running.

Now he had to do damage control. And do it with none other than Shannon O'Toole —the very woman who had haunted his thoughts and dreams for weeks.

Great. Just effing great. So now what did he do? Slink back into the forest without speaking to Shannon and hope she wouldn't mention having seen him to the Romanos or anybody else? Or should he cross the meadow and confront her?

He didn't really have a choice. The last thing he needed was for her to spread word of his whereabouts around Eternity Springs or, even worse, connect the mother and child she'd just met to a certain man in the news in New England.

He had to do something—anything—to prevent that.

His mood grim, Daniel headed across the meadow toward Shannon. He tried not to notice how beautiful she looked, standing beside the frothing mountain creek, her arms folded, sunlight glinting off the strands of red in her hair. He tried not to recall how gorgeous she'd been naked and sitting astride him, riding him, her head thrown back as she found her release.

Daniel noticed. He recalled. He couldn't help but notice and recall. His indulgence with Shannon the night of Gabi's wedding had been the lone bright spot in his life for longer than he wanted to admit. The evening with her had been the only time he'd been warm. Now, just seeing her again, the need to experience it again...to experience **her** again...pulled at him.

The futility of that emotion poked a temper already on edge. As a result, maybe he did clench his teeth and harden his jaw, but his reaction still didn't give her leave to ball up her fist and pop him on the chin. "What the—"

"You jerk!"

"What was that for?"

"Seriously?" Her eyes widened. "You seriously ask me that?"

He rubbed his aching jaw. "Yeah."

"Gee...I dunno. Maybe your **wife** can explain it to you."

His wife? What the...oh. Linda must have stuck to their cover story. Daniel hesitated.

This presented him with a bit of a dilemma. How should he respond to Shannon? What was best for her to believe? Could he trust her with the truth?

His instincts told him he could, but the stakes here were huge. Lives were on the line.

In an effort to buy time, he said, "I didn't expect to run across anyone out here in the middle of nowhere. Eternity Springs is two hours away."

She folded her arms. "Actually, it's only a bit of a hike through the forest and a twenty-two-minute drive."

He mentally pictured a map of the area. The lone road out of the canyon where his cabin was located led in the opposite direction of Eternity Springs. There were not any public hiking trails marked. "But this is private property."

"Oh, really?" Her smile was all teeth. "Does your wife own it?"

Knowing he had that one coming, he swallowed a sigh. "Now, Shannon. It's not what you think."

"I'll say it's not. You sure had me fooled. You have everyone fooled, don't you,

Daniel? Everyone sings your praises. They don't know that you are a lying, cheating hound dog."

Okay, fine. She had her mind made up. Why should he try to convince her otherwise? She was making this easy for him. "Are you going to tell them?"

"I should." She folded her arms.

"Please don't."

"Don't what? Tell our friends that you're married? That you're visiting Colorado with your wife and stepson? Or that I made the exceedingly poor decision to sleep with you?"

"All of the above."

She narrowed her eyes. If this were a cartoon rather than real life, she'd have steam shooting out of her ears. At the thought, Daniel had the most ridiculous urge to grin. **I am losing my ever-loving mind.**

"You have more nerve than an abscessed tooth."

He stifled the urge to touch her and decided he'd tell her a portion of the truth. "Again, it's not what you think."

"Oh, spare me," she drawled, her tone

ripe with derision. "It's exactly what I think. I wouldn't believe a word out of your mouth if you tried to tell me that the sky is blue and water is wet. This is pretty much the middle of nowhere, and you obviously thought you were safe bringing your family here."

"Obviously I made a mistake."

"You don't know the half of it. Dammit, Daniel, you made me the other woman!" She bunched up her fist again, and he stepped back just in time when she threw it a second time. "My father had a lover and I saw what that did to my mother. I know what it did to my family. I won't be party to it. So don't worry. I won't rat out the rat. Your secret is safe with me."

Daniel abruptly shut his mouth. That made everything easier. He didn't like lying to her, even if technically, he hadn't come right out and stated a falsehood. **No, Linda is the one who did that.** He just hadn't corrected it.

He cleared his throat and said, "Thank you."

Her mouth set in a bitter line, Shannon backed away from him, her big brown eyes gone wet. She blinked repeatedly, fighting back the tears. "You sure had me fooled, Daniel Garrett. You have everyone in town fooled. Everyone thinks you're a hero."

Hero. He didn't try to stop the bitter laugh. Two graves on the hillside of a Boston suburb proved her wrong. "That's their mistake. I'm nobody's hero. Don't forget that."

He turned to go and silently added, **I sure as hell can't.**

Shannon's temper added energy to her step and cut her hike back to Bob's cabins by almost five full minutes. The nausea in her stomach had nothing to do with morning sickness and everything to do with the reality of her current situation.

Pregnant by a married man.

She was embarrassed, humiliated, and ashamed. She would never forget the moment as a fifteen-year-old when she learned that her father had been unfaithful to her mother. The sense of betrayal had been devastating, and watching her mother fall apart had broken her heart. To think that she'd been party to a similar hurt...Shannon blinked back angry tears. It didn't bear thinking about.

At Gabi and Flynn's wedding, Daniel had denied being in a relationship. Unless he'd met and married that woman in six short weeks, he'd lied to Shannon.

So, the precedent was set. Made her decision easy as pie, didn't it? She could darn sure lie right back at him and not feel one twinge of guilt. Maybe she could even stay in Eternity Springs!

She pictured herself behind the bar at Murphy's, the strings of her apron tied high over her baby belly. When somebody asked, she'd repeat the question. My baby's father? Why, he's a professional soccer player from Brazil.

Although considering that she'd be poor as a church mouse, perhaps she'd better rethink that claim. Maybe say the father was a golf cart mechanic. Who worked for a ski resort. That was only open in February.

"I'm losing it. Completely. Totally. Losing it."

She wished she could talk to somebody. She'd like nothing better than to cry on her best friend's shoulder. But she couldn't talk to Rose. Even if she was ready to confess all about Russell and her situation—which she wasn't—she couldn't talk about the baby because she couldn't ask Rose not to tell her husband. Cicero worked with Gabi Brogan who was the sister-in-law of Hope Romano who was Daniel's close friend.

Pregnant by a married slimeball of a man.

Maybe she'd drop by Angel's Rest and talk to Celeste. Or actually, not talk at all. Just cry on her shoulder. Ask for a hug. Ask for some words of wisdom. More often than not, Celeste had words of wisdom to share. Heaven knows, Shannon needed wisdom right now.

That evening she attempted to do just that, but upon arriving at the resort, she learned that Celeste was out of town and wouldn't return until the end of the following week. Shannon wanted to sit down on the front porch steps and bawl.

She'd never felt so alone in her life.

Not even when she'd realized Russell had killed Ted, and absolutely nobody would believe her.

But as she strolled across the grounds of

the Angel's Rest estate toward the footbridge headed back to Heartsong Cottage, it occurred to her that she wasn't actually alone now, was she? She had a little person living inside her. Someone who depended on her.

Someone who deserved better than to be born to a mother in hiding for her life and a father who was married to someone else.

"What am I going to do?" she murmured.

"About what?" came a voice from out of the darkness.

Zach Turner. **Sheriff** Zach Turner. Nope, definitely not someone she could confide in. As always when she found herself in the sheriff's company, her mouth went a little dry and her heart began to pound. She reached deep inside herself and summoned a friendly smile. "Internet marketing. I've been advised to jump into social media to drum up business for the pub during the winter. I don't want to do it. It's not my milieu."

"Mine, either," Zach said as he crossed the footbridge and joined her. "I'm afraid I have no advice for you on that subject. Are you coming or going from Angel's Rest?"

"Going. I'm on my way to the pub now."

"Did you by any chance see my wife? She said she had soaps to deliver here, but she's not answering her phone. One of my deputies called in sick, so Savannah and I need to coordinate child care for this evening."

"I did see her up at the main house unloading a box from the trunk of her car probably five minutes ago."

"Good. I'll track her down. Thanks, Shannon."

"You're welcome, Zach."

She breathed a little easier when he walked on toward Angel's Rest and she hurried off in the opposite direction. As she started up Spruce Street, a bone-deep weariness unlike any she'd known before overcame her. The trek ahead of her to Murphy's felt more like a three-mile hike than a short six-block stroll.

She arrived to find the pub relatively quiet. Grateful that Honey had the situation well in hand, Shannon spent twenty productive minutes in her office approving orders and writing checks before eating a bowl of soup and calling it a night. At home, she crawled into bed and fell swiftly asleep.

She slept soundly and awoke refreshed and surprisingly energetic. Just as important, she awoke with a more positive outlook toward the future. This baby wouldn't be due until May. She had time yet to make her decisions. All she needed to do was to take care of herself and her baby—eat properly, rest when she needed to rest, and make a doctor's appointment. With someone other than Rose.

If Shannon knew how to do one thing, that was how to survive. She would survive this challenge, and she and her baby would thrive.

With that positive thought in mind, she buried her concerns, turned her music up loud, and spent a productive day at work at Bob's—until nausea and exhaustion hit her again at three p.m. The pattern continued, and she took to playing Goldilocks at Mama Bear and napping on a cot she'd set up for that purpose.

So she was asleep when someone came knocking at the door. "Hello? Shannon? Are you here? Hello? I need help!"

Groggy, she sat up and shook her head,

thinking she'd been dreaming.

"Mom, I'm bleeding!"

Mom? Shannon's hand immediately went protectively toward her belly. **Knock. Knock. Knock.** "Hello? Help us, please!"

Shannon rolled up off the cot and had taken two steps toward the door when it opened. Her stomach sank when she realized that Daniel's wife stood on the threshold. "You **are** here," the woman said. "I saw the truck outside so I thought somebody was here but..."

The boy held up his arms to reveal a torn shirtsleeve and an angry scratch on his forearm. "Do you have any of that spray stuff, lady, so I don't get an infection and my hands fall off because of these stupid mountains?"

"Honey, please." Daniel's wife offered Shannon a tired smile. "He fell. Skinned his hands."

"And knees, too. I tore my jeans."

"I have a first-aid kit, but it's up in the main house. Come with me, and we'll get you fixed up, young man."

"Oh, good. Thank you," the woman said, following Shannon back onto the porch.

"First aid is what brought me here to begin with. Do you have any aspirin or acetaminophen? My husband has a bad fever, and I'm afraid we had an accident with our bottle of pills."

"I knocked it over into the bathtub and ruined 'em," the boy piped up.

The harried blonde explained, "You don't have to worry that he's contagious or anything. I'm not bringing a horrible disease to you while we're out in the middle of nowhere. It's a genetic condition."

Shannon's head whipped around. "A genetic condition?"

"Yes. It's something he's had since he was a child. Part of it is that he gets these bad fevers that last a few days."

"What's the name of it?"

She pursed her full lips. "Hyper something something. Three words run together."

"Can you remember the exact name? I'm very interested."

"That's a strange thing to be interested in."

"I'm writing a novel. Having a recurring fever could come in very handy for my plot."

"Oh. That's cool. Let me think a moment.

I recall the three words...hyper...and hmm...something that made me think of vaccines." She snapped her fingers. "I remember. Let me see if I can get this right. Hyperimmunoglobulin and there's a letter at the end. A, D, or C or E, I believe. Sounds like something a weight-loss doctor would give you, doesn't it?"

It took all of Shannon's discipline not to whip out her phone and Google it right then. "It sounds serious."

"Daniel says there is nothing to do but take aspirin and wait it out. I feel terrible because he feels so horrible, and my son had his little accident with the pain reliever."

"The bottle of acetaminophen is with the first-aid kit. I'm happy to send it home with you for Daniel."

"Thank goodness. Maybe if he's resting easier, my son and I will be able to get some sleep."

That comment struck Shannon as something less than what a loving wife would make, but then, she had reason to know that the marriage had cracks in it, didn't she? She wondered if this woman knew her husband had cheated? She wondered if she was a cheater, herself.

Don't go there, Shannon. You'll do yourself no favors wondering about the state of affairs—literal and otherwise—where that marriage is concerned.

It's not like she would want Daniel if he were free. She had enough trouble in her life as it was, thank you very much.

She stole a sidelong look at the woman walking beside her. She was fashion-model gorgeous with sharp cheekbones, a squarish jaw, and big green eyes. Something about her looked vaguely familiar. Could she be a model? "I'm sorry. Did you mention your name the other day?"

"Oh. Maybe not. I'm Linda."

Yes, but what's your last name? Something-hyphen-Garrett? Or maybe she didn't use his name at all. **It doesn't matter. It's not your concern.**

"Oh, that's right." She couldn't stop herself from adding, "You remind me of someone, but I can't put my finger on just who."

Linda's smile momentarily froze before she airily said, "You must be a catalogue shopper. Maybe you saw me wearing flannel shirts from L.L. Bean?"

I knew it! "That could be it." Except, she didn't shop catalogues.

Linda pressed on. "I'm so glad you were here. I didn't know where else to go for help. Daniel won't be happy that we hiked over the mountain to beg drugs for him, but he'd be furious if I left our place on my own in search of a store. I'd surely get lost—he doesn't have a GPS in his truck—but he's just so pitiful."

"I'm pitiful, too, Mom," the boy declared. "My knee hurts. My elbow hurts."

"I'm sorry. Yes, yes, you are pitiful, too, poor baby."

It was the first of a litany of complaints the child made over the next few minutes while Shannon retrieved the first-aid kit and handed it to his mother so she could tend to his injuries. When Linda sprayed the cut with antiseptic lotion, the boy began to cry. "Shush, now, honey."

Instead of shushing, the boy wound up to a wail. "Son, please."

"It hurts!"

"I know. Crying won't make it feel better."

"It makes me feel better."

Linda frowned at her son, then turned her own teary eyes toward Shannon. "He's not ordinarily so cranky, but it's been a long few days. I've been short-tempered and he's tired. We're both just so tired." An unhappy smile flitted across her lips before she added, "I'm pregnant."

Shannon's inadvertent gasp was drowned out by the boy's whine. "I **am** tired, Mommy. I need to go to the bathroom. I don't want to climb the mountain to go back. Can we stay here?"

"No!" Shannon burst out, the reaction as basic as any she'd ever experienced. She needed Daniel's wife and stepson out of Papa Bear, away from her little valley, gone from her side of the mountain—as fast as possible.

Pregnant. She's pregnant. Daniel's wife is pregnant, too!

"I can't walk another step!" the boy insisted.

Shannon could tell that he meant it. Wonderful. Simply wonderful.

"We'll sit down and rest for a little bit before we start back," Linda said.

"No!" Shannon blurted. Linda drew back,

obviously surprised by Shannon's rudeness. "I'll drive you."

Gratitude gleamed in Daniel's pregnant wife's smile and beautiful green eyes. "Oh, that would be wonderful, but I hate to put you out. I think it's a long way by road. Honestly, I don't even know how to get there."

"I do." Shannon had looked up the route to the box canyon after the encounter with Daniel beside the waterfall. Shannon grabbed up the bottle of acetaminophen and pointed toward a door. "The bathroom is through there. I'll go pull the truck up."

Shannon fled, her mind spinning. **Oh, jeeze. Oh, jeeze. Oh, jeeze. Could this situation get any more bizarre?**

She's pregnant. I'm pregnant. Daniel's going to be a double-dip father.

My baby has a sibling. I wonder which child will be older? A semihysterical laugh bubbled from her lips. What if the babies were born on the same day? They'd be like twins! What's that saying…a brother from another mother?

She shoved her hands into the pockets of her jeans as she made her way to the garage at Mama Bear where she'd left the truck. She wanted nothing more than to speed away from the work site—alone— and head for home where she would climb into her bed and pull the covers over her head and pretend this was all a bad dream.

Daniel Garrett, you sorry sack of slime.

She cleared the stack of samples and supplies off her backseat so that the kid had a place to sit, then climbed behind the wheel and started the truck. In an effort to discourage small talk, she turned on the radio before she pulled up in front of Papa Bear. The front door opened and Linda and her son walked out onto the front porch. For just a moment, the angle of the sun bathed Daniel's little family in a sunbeam, lighting them up.

Why did the men in her life invariably let her down?

Please, let my baby be a girl.

Linda buckled her son into the backseat before joining Shannon in the front seat of the passenger cab. Her eyes shone with gratitude as she smiled and said, "Thank you so much for doing this. I admit I wasn't looking forward to the trek back over the mountain, either. It's not far, but the trail from the waterfall to here has some steep sections I wasn't anxious to make again."

"Why don't you close your eyes and rest," Shannon suggested. "You can get in a nice nap in the time it will take us to get to the canyon."

"I don't want to be rude."

"Nonsense. Please, sleep." **Please!**

Linda glanced back over her shoulder where Benny already showed signs of drifting off and smiled gratefully. "I'll do that."

Thank goodness.

Her passengers both drifted off almost immediately and Shannon switched the satellite radio station to a country channel because it suited her mood, but when a Patsy Cline song came on, she muttered a curse and changed to news radio.

The winding, twisting, and narrow state of the mountain road leading to the canyon proved to be a blessing since it required her attention and gave her something to think about instead of the turmoil churning inside her over this latest emotional bomb-shell. If she thought about her personal situation right now, she didn't think she'd be able to hold back the tears. Blubbering in front of Linda and her son would be the cherry on top of today's humiliation.

Determined to delay her tears and concerns for the future until at least the return drive to Three Bears, Shannon kept her focus on the road immediately and literally before her. Mostly, anyway. She couldn't help but be aware of her passengers to some extent. She tried not to hear the little boyish snuffles coming from the backseat or notice the subtle floral fragrance drifting from the seat beside her. What sort of woman put on perfume to go hiking through the woods, anyway?

A beautiful, pregnant, catalogue-model, sophisticated city woman. That's who.

Thirty minutes after leaving Shannon's work site, Linda stirred. Her eyes fluttered open and she sat up.

"Feel better?" Shannon asked, keeping her voice soft. She didn't want to wake the boy.

"A little, yes. I don't remember being this exhausted when I carried Benny. It must be the stress of...the trip."

"Why don't you try to sleep a little more? We still have a ways to go."

Linda glanced over her shoulder at her sleeping son, then settled back against her seat and closed her eyes. "I think I will."

Shannon drummed her fingers on the steering wheel and tried to think about her grocery list. She needed eggs and milk, and she kept forgetting to buy paper towels. She was totally out of paper towels.

And, she should buy tissues. Boxes and boxes of tissues—to wipe her eyes and blow her nose during the pity party she intended to throw for herself at the soonest opportunity.

Fifty minutes after leaving the Three Bears, she reached the entrance to the box canyon just as rain began to fall in sheets. The truck bounced over the rough dirt road and twice hit potholes big enough to rattle her teeth. To Shannon's total surprise, the jarring motion failed to awaken either of her passengers. Neither did they stir when she pulled up in front of the two-story cabin and switched off the motor. Finally, she said, "Linda?"

The woman didn't stir.

Shannon sighed and spoke louder. "Linda? We're here."

Slowly, she sat up. "Where...oh. Yes." She groaned softly, then said, "I can't thank you enough for your kindness. I don't know that Benny and I would have made it if we'd had to hike back. We both were more tired than I realized when we started out. And we'd have been miserable in the rain."

Benny was a cute name for a boy. Wonder what they plan to name the baby?

"Glad to help," Shannon replied. **Now, please get out of my truck so that I can fall apart.**

Linda unbuckled her seat belt, opened the passenger door, then slid out. After opening the back passenger door, she shook her son awake and attempted to assist him from the truck. He let out a wail. "My knees hurt! Carry me, Mommy!"

"Okay. Okay."

"And it's raining. I don't want to get wet. It's cold."

"I'll go as fast as I can."

As Linda started to slip her arms beneath her son, Shannon spied the medicine bottle on the seat where the other woman had been sitting. She handed it back over the seat. "Wait. Don't forget the acetaminophen."

"I'm such a ditz." Linda slipped the bottle into the side pocket of the windbreaker she wore, then picked up her son, and carried him toward the house. As she stepped up onto the porch, the bottle of medicine slipped out of her pocket and landed on the rain-soaked ground.

Shannon waited for her to notice, but Linda never looked back. "Not my problem," Shannon murmured.

Raindrops pounded the white plastic bottle.

Upstairs, a light switched on. Shannon put her truck in gear and moved her foot off the brake pedal. Daniel's wife would realize she'd dropped the bottle at some point. The pills wouldn't be ruined. They'd be fine.

Shannon gave the truck a little gas and it began to roll. "Not my problem," she repeated.

Just before she slammed her foot on the brake and muttered a curse.

Sighing, she put her truck in park, switched off the motor, then dashed out into the rain. She scooped up the bottle and bounded up the front porch steps. Linda had left the door slightly ajar, so Shannon pushed it open and stepped inside. "Hello?"

She heard Benny wailing upstairs.

But it was the sound emanating from the room off to her right that sent a chill running down her back. It was a cry of anguish. A wounded howl of pain. A name.

"Justin!"

Daniel's hoarse, tortured voice cried, "Please, God, no. No. No. No. My boy. My little boy."

Drawn by a force she had no will to resist, Shannon walked toward the room where Daniel lay.

Fever dreams.

Pumpkins.

God, he hated pumpkins.

And blueberries. Baskets of freshly picked blueberries. "Your teeth are blue, Justin."

The smile as big and bright as the sun. "I'm blue like Cookie Monster. I'm

Blueberry Monster."

"Eat too many more and you'll be Bellyache Monster."

Two little hands raised, blue-stained fingers bent into claws. "Grrr."

Fever dreams.

The pumpkin patch after harvest. Brown and barren and dotted with rotting gourds.

Two little hands raised, fingers bent into claws.

A stranger's voice on the phone. "...child predator arrested in Pennsylvania...hit on DNA evidence from fingernail scrapings. Detective Garrett, we have a name."

Little hands. Little claws.

Pulling on a baseball mitt. "It's perfect! Thanks, Dad!"

The crack of a wooden bat hitting a baseball. "It's coming our way. Help me catch it, Dad. Help me catch it!"

Screaming. Screaming. Screaming. Daddy, help me! Daddy, help me! He's hurting me. Daddy! Daddy! Daddy!

Fever dreams.

Find him. I have to find him.

"We'll find him, Gail. It's okay. It's not your fault."

It's her fault. Her fault. Why didn't she watch him?

It's not her fault. Forgive me. "Forgive me."

"Detective Garrett, we've found a body."

Peter, Peter pumpkin eater. Had a boy and couldn't keep him.

"Daddy, Daddy. Look at that one. It's as big as Cinderella's carriage. I love the pumpkin patch."

Tonight on News at Five. The body of a four-year-old Natick boy who went missing from the Framingham mall last week has been found in a pumpkin patch.

Peter, Peter pumpkin eater.

Reichs's big hairy hand grabs the report. "Don't read it, Daniel. Don't do that to yourself. You can't put that genie back in the bottle."

"Aladdin, Daddy. Aladdin!" Blood beads from the paper cut. Pain, slicing deep. It hurts. God, it hurts so much.

Fever dreams.

Hellfire. The fires of hell. Consuming me.

"Lift your head up. C'mon, now. Swallow."

Water. Blessedly cold.

Cold as the grave. Gail's grave. Justin's grave. "I saved a stranger and lost our son."

"Shush, Daniel. Shush." **A cool cloth against his brow. Big brown eyes. Sad eyes.**

"I know you. You're Patsy Cline." He crooned, "I'm crazy."

Peter, Peter pumpkin eater. Sexual assault. Broken tibia. Broken teeth. Broken baby teeth.

"Look, Daniel. It's a little cloth tooth bag. It's for visits from the Tooth Fairy."

"Already? He's too young to be losing his teeth."

Broken baby. My broken baby.

Fever dreams.

"One more." Feminine hands lifted his head. "Swallow this, Daniel."

"One? Damn her." He swallowed the pill. "She swallowed them all. A whole bottle. She didn't leave me any. She left me. She left me to deal with it alone. Alone. So alone."

"I'm so sorry, Daniel. Here, sip the water."
Cool. Wet. She's so hot. So alive.
Fever dreams.

He blinked. "Not Patsy. Shannon. Pretty, pretty Shannon. She's alive, and I'm dead. I'm sick of dealing with dead kids, Shannon. Done with gaping throats and lacerated livers and glassy blank eyes that accuse me. Always accusing. Why are you always too late?"

"You're not always too late. You found Holly."

He waved his arm expansively. "One in a million. They break my heart, pretty Shannon."

"Drink some more water, Daniel."

Cool. Refreshing. Wet. She'd been wet. He remembered her naked breasts. Plump and pretty. He'd had sex. The first in forever.

"I'm no bodyguard," he said, his voice solemn.

"You're a detective."

"I'm no damned bodyguard. The cops can't find him. He's not going to find them. Justin didn't whine that way."

Peter, Peter pumpkin eater. Left in the field to rot.

Detective Garrett? We found a body.
Halloween is over. There shouldn't be
skeletons.

Hot, so hot. Beads of sweat trickling across his skin. Overflowing his eyes. He sang, "I'm falling. I'm in pieces."

"Where's your wife?"

"Dead. Gail is dead. Took all the pills and cut her wrists." **Gail? Gail! Moses has been in the master bathroom. With my staff I will strike the water of the Nile and it will be changed into blood.**

"Detective Garrett. Coroner is here. I need you to step away."

Fever dreams.

Shannon glanced over her shoulder wondering where the heck Daniel's wife had gotten off to. Precious little Benny was still upstairs crying, and apparently his mother couldn't drag herself away from her little snowflake long enough to offer Daniel the pain reliever she'd hiked over the mountain to get. Shannon understood the brain fog that pregnancy could cause —of late she'd been plagued by it herself. But seriously, what kind of wife went to such effort then totally dropped the ball five yards from the goal line?

Shannon flattened her lips into a grim line. She wanted nothing more than to walk out the door and climb into her truck and kick up dust as she floored it getting away from this man. Only, with the way it was raining, she'd kick up mud instead of dust and probably get stuck.

She felt stuck. She couldn't leave without speaking to Linda. She needed to tell her that she'd gotten two pills down the raving man so that his wife didn't accidentally overdose him.

"Gail took all the pills and then cut her wrists."

Wow. Wonder if he'd been talking out of his mind that way the whole time he'd been feverish. If so, she should cut Linda a little slack. It would be difficult for a wife to listen to her husband's emotional pain and anguish. It wasn't pleasant for one-night-stand Shannon to hear it.

It made her feel sympathetic toward him —just when she had every reason to fire a great big ball of anger his way.

Shannon scowled at Daniel. He'd kicked

all the covers off his bed, and at the moment, he lay still as death, wearing flannel pajama bottoms and nothing else. He looked like he'd lost ten pounds since she'd last seen him without his shirt. What if this wasn't some weird genetic thing? Daniel was burning up. Maybe he was seriously ill. "If you throw up, I'm out of here."

Maybe that's why Linda had disappeared upstairs. **She's pregnant. She doesn't want to expose her baby to anything dire.**

I'm pregnant. I don't want to expose my baby to anything dire.

"Well, too late now," she muttered. **What's done is done.** And when it came right down to it, she believed Linda about this being a genetic thing. Hyperimmunoglobulin C, D, or E wasn't a term a person pulled out of thin air.

"Where is your wife?" she muttered as she pulled the sheet up over his shoulders. Linda should be here wiping his skin with a damp washcloth.

She glanced around the room looking for a paper and pen, thinking she'd leave a note about giving him the pills before she beat a retreat. That's when she realized just how…male…the room appeared to be. A man's wallet, watch, and what looked like a college ring sat atop the dresser. A man's robe lay draped over the back of the overstuffed chair in front of the fireplace. A paperback thriller served as a coaster for a brown stoneware coffee mug on one bedside nightstand. The other nightstand was bare but for a lamp.

Linda must be the neatest woman of Shannon's acquaintance. The master bedroom showed no sign of her presence at all.

Daniel wrenched his head from side to side and began mumbling once again. This time Shannon picked up two words: "Justin" and "soup."

Soup? "Are you hungry, Daniel?"

He sat up abruptly and the white sheet slid to his lap. He turned feverish eyes her way and asked, "Has Soupy been out?"

"What?"

"Soupy!

"Gotta find her," Daniel said. "She gave her away." He shifted his feet off the bed and stood—and swayed. Teetered.

"Oh, no you don't," Shannon said, rushing toward him. No way could she pick him up herself if he fell. The man was two-hundred-plus pounds of solid muscle. She put her hands around his waist and tried to guide him back onto the mattress. Daniel's arms wrapped around her and his knees began to buckle. Shannon had no choice but to shove him backward. Tangled together, they fell onto the bed.

"You smell good," Daniel said, nuzzling her neck. "I remember how you smell."

"You need a shower."

"Let's shower together."

"Oh, for goodness' sake." He was dead weight atop her and she pushed against his chest. She couldn't budge him.

"You're in my head. Pretty and bright. Bright. Shannon. Earthy angel." He cupped her breast with his big hand and flicked his thumb across her nipple. "So pretty."

"Daniel!" Shannon was horrified.

"I'm so tired of darkness. Have sex with me again."

Shocked and embarrassed and panicked by his words and actions considering that his wife was in the house, Shannon shoved and squirmed and wriggled and finally freed herself.

"Don't go."

"Would you be quiet!" she demanded as she found her feet. "You can't say those things."

He rose up on his elbows and gazed at her with troubled, feverish eyes. "I'm lonely."

"Oh, Daniel." Shannon sighed as pity found a foothold among the anger and contempt she felt toward this man.

Behind her, a feminine voice drawled. "Well, this has certainly been interesting."

Shannon's stomach dropped to her knees and she closed her eyes. Linda.

She wanted to melt like the wicked witch in a rainstorm. She heard the lyrics of a song from the musical **Wicked** blasting repeatedly through her mind. "**No One Mourns the Wicked**" **could have been written about you!**

Wait a minute. I'm not the only one he duped. Remember who the real villain is here.

And honestly, a part of Shannon was glad to have light shined on the situation. She had enough lies and secrets in her life as it was. She didn't need more.

Bracing herself, she turned around. Shannon was shocked to see an amused smile on Linda's face. Where was the betrayed wife?

"I think under the circumstances, it's time we get this out of the way," Linda said. "I knew there was more to his decision to bring us to Colorado than he let on. He won't like it that I spilled the beans, but you've been kind to me. I'm going to trust that you won't give us away. Shannon, we're not married."

"Excuse me?"

"Daniel and I. We're not married. He's not my husband. Daniel is our bodyguard. Benny and I are in hiding. You won't tell anyone we are here, will you?"

Chapter Six

Three days after recovering from his fever, Daniel skulked in the shadows of a moon-less autumn night, spying on Shannon as she removed a stack of envelopes and circulars from her mailbox beside the front door of her dollhouse of a home. The warm glow of her porch light spilled over her, highlighting the fiery strands of red shot through the burnished strands of her hair. She wore tight jeans tucked into riding boots, a short wool coat the same brown as her eyes, and fluffy muffs on her ears.

Despite his good sense and best inten-tions, Daniel watched her and yearned. Need for this woman pulsed through him like a song.

He'd followed her home from the pub to-night. Home to Heartsong Cottage.

The for sale sign that had hung from the white picket fence in August was gone, and he knew a real sense of regret. The house must have sold. He'd snooped the real estate listings on the Internet after his return to Boston and found it listed for sale at what he judged to be a fair price. The desire to make an offer on the place had been strong, stupid, and had caught him by surprise. He'd come close to making that call, but better sense had prevailed. Never mind that he found the cottage as appealing as the woman. He had enough trouble sleeping as it was. No way would he rest easy surrounded by memories of Shannon O'Toole.

He watched her disappear inside the house and wondered where she planned to move after she left Heartsong Cottage. Did she have another project lined up to begin after she finished the tile work he'd learned she was doing out at the cabins near his rental?

And what business is it of yours if she does? Enough with this skulking and speculation, Garrett. You're procrastinating. Grow a pair. Go knock on her front door and get this conversation behind you.

He'd come to apologize and to beg her cooperation. Chances were slim, but the possibility did exist that Mason Tate would use some of his gobs of money not just to hide, but to hire a competent investigator to find Linda and Benny. Daniel had been extraordinarily careful since agreeing to help them, and he felt confident they wouldn't be found stashed out in the valley. Shannon O'Toole was a vulnerable spot in his wall of defenses.

In more ways than one.

He muttered a curse and stepped away from the gnarled tree trunk against which he'd leaned and crossed the street to Heartsong Cottage. Pushing open the front gate, he strode decisively up the walkway and onto the front porch.

Music floated on the air from inside. Big band. Glenn Miller. Tommy Dorsey. He made a fist and rapped on the painted red door.

"Just a minute," he heard her call.

Daniel shoved his hands into his pants pockets and rocked back on his heels. Softly, nervously, he hummed along to the tune.

Shannon started talking before the door swung fully open. "Celeste, I'm running late. I need three minutes to—oh. You."

"Hello, Shannon."

"What are you doing here?"

"I need to talk to you."

"About what?"

"May I come inside?"

"No, thank you." She slammed the door shut in his face.

Despite her less-than-welcoming reception, Daniel's spirits lifted. This house, this woman, had a way of doing that for him. His nervousness had disappeared and he realized he felt almost...light.

Weird.

He hadn't heard the lock click, so he opened the door and walked in.

She folded her arms and scowled at him. "Go away. I have plans tonight."

"I just need five minutes of your time." The more agitated she appeared, the more relaxed he felt.

"I don't have five minutes. I'm already late. Celeste will be here any minute. You don't need to worry. I haven't told anyone that you're here."

"Five minutes. Celeste isn't here yet. If you're headed to the chamber of commerce meeting, it's been rescheduled to next Wednesday."

"How do you know about the chamber meeting?"

She stepped back inadvertently when he walked inside as if he owned the place. **I wish. I really like this little house.** The energy of the place seeped into his soul like a hug. "There's a notice posted on the announcement board in front of city hall. Please, Shannon. Let me have my say, ask my questions, and I'll be out of your hair. I promise."

"If only," she muttered.

Daniel crossed the small parlor to the record player. He turned down the volume on "Stardust." He liked Glenn Miller, but he needed to be sure that she heard this conversation loud and clear. "Linda told me what happened the other day."

Shannon glanced toward the cell phone lying on the mantel when a ping announced a text message. She picked it up, read it, then asked, "Which part?"

"The part about her telling you that she and I aren't married, and that I'm helping her hide from her husband after he tried to hire me to find her."

She studied him for a long minute, then

she returned her phone to the mantel and took a seat in an antique wooden rocker. She gestured for him to sit across from her on the love seat. "That's not exactly what she said. Okay. You've hooked me. I'm listening."

"Benny's father is a prominent physician. He called me not long after Gabi and Flynn's wedding and said his wife was unstable, that she'd taken his son and disappeared. He wanted to hire me to find them. I told him to call the cops, but he threw out a handful of reasons why he didn't want to notify the authorities and offered me three times my normal daily rate plus a significant bonus when I found them. I still turned him down, but the whole thing bugged me. Something about the situation, about him, felt off. I decided to look into it on my own."

"You found them."

"It wasn't difficult. Linda tried, but going off the grid is harder than you'd think."

A strange look flashed across Shannon's face that intrigued him. He filed it away to consider at another time.

"When I found her, she told me her story."

Propping his elbows on his knees, Daniel clasped his hands and leaned forward, gazing at her intently. "Her husband had been making secret trips to a colleague's private island in the Caribbean. It's been in the news lately, too. You might have heard about it. They call it Sex Island."

Shannon sat up straight. "The place with politicians and orgies and underage girls?"

"And boys. Linda found compromising pictures on her husband's computer."

"Oh, that's terrible. So why isn't the piece of filth in jail?"

"Because she confronted him without securing the computer. He destroyed the computer in front of her and said that if she repeated the story, he'd divorce her and make sure she lost custody of Benny. Linda took the kid and, at the first opportunity, ran. She doesn't have the means to fight him. She signed a prenup. She has no money. She has no power."

"Well, that's not exactly true, is it? She has your belief in her story."

"Like I said. Something about him was off."

"Does he know she's pregnant?"

Daniel shook his head. "No, thank

goodness. He's crazed enough as it is over just Benny."

"So what's the plan?" Her caramel-colored eyes met his, her gaze direct as she asked, "You're going after him?"

"Not me personally, but yes, I called in a few markers and a friend in the bureau is building a case against him. We're hoping for an arrest soon. They'll get him for child porn, I expect. In the meantime, I'll do whatever it takes to keep Benny away from the bastard. That's why I'm asking for your discretion, Shannon. It's best that no one knows I'm in Colorado. My friends would ask questions, and if Zach got curious, well…it's just better for everyone that our local sheriff doesn't know I'm harboring runaways. Can I count on you?"

"Your secret is safe with me."

"Thank you. So, will you come to dinner tomorrow night?"

Daniel didn't know who he'd surprised the most, Shannon or himself. He'd knocked on her front door with the sole purpose of damage control in the wake of the other night's revelations. He hadn't planned the invitation. He hadn't thought it through before the words popped from his mouth. The fever must have addled his mind.

Nevertheless, he didn't backtrack. He wanted her to come to dinner. He wanted it rather desperately. "Linda and the kid are going stir crazy with only me to talk to. I'm thinking Italian. I make an excellent veal marsala."

A cloud of doubt rolled across Shannon's face, and he saw refusal in her eyes. Quickly, he added, "Please, Shannon. Let me thank you for your kindness and apologize for mauling you the other night."

"You didn't maul me."

"I was out of line."

"You were out of your head." She shoved to her feet and crossed to the record player. She switched Glenn Miller out for...who was that?...someone from the sixties? Turning back to him, she asked, "You're okay now? Linda said you weren't contagious."

The name of the band and the song came to him in a flash of memory. Herb Alpert and the Tijuana Brass's "A Taste of Honey." Daniel couldn't stop his gaze from shifting toward her bedroom. He cleared his throat.

"I'm fine. Don't worry. You didn't catch anything from me."

"Don't be so sure," she muttered, almost beneath her breath. "She said it's genetic?"

He dragged his attention back to where it belonged, which was anywhere other than her bedroom.

"Yes." Daniel had never been a particularly smooth operator, and now that his primary business for being here was out of the way and he wasn't fortified by either alcohol or anger, awkwardness rolled over him like morning fog in the valley. So in his attempt to reassure her that she hadn't been exposed to anything dreadful, he babbled on more than necessary. "It's called HIDS—Hyperimmunoglobulin D syndrome. It's a rare genetic syndrome, and I've had it since I was a child. Recurring fevers are part of it. The frequency of attacks has decreased since adolescence."

Jeeze, Garrett, could you be more of an idiotic bore? "Google it. Then come to dinner."

"I can't. I have to cover Honey's shift at Murphy's tomorrow night."

"All right." Despite being embarrassed by

his babbling, he pressed. "What's the next night you're free?"

She paused an eternal moment before answering. "Tuesday."

"Perfect. Come then."

"Okay. What time?

Daniel bit back a silly grin. "Seven?"

"Okay," she repeated. "Seven. I'll bring dessert."

"Great. I'm glad. Not about dessert. I'm glad you accepted the invitation. Well, and I guess I'm glad about dessert, too. I can cook, but I'm not much of a baker."

"I was thinking ice cream."

"Ice cream is good. Everybody loves ice cream."

"Chocolate? Vanilla? Strawberry?"

"I don't care for chocolate."

"You don't like chocolate! Who doesn't like chocolate?"

She looked so appalled that he found himself backtracking. "It's been years since I tried it. Maybe I'd like it now."

"So do you want chocolate ice cream?"

"Surprise me. Apparently I'm in the mood for surprises."

A knock on Shannon's front door put an

end to the ridiculous conversation. She glanced toward the sound and said, "That will be Celeste."

Too bad she hadn't knocked before he babbled on about ice cream. You'd think he was fifteen and asking a girl on a first date. Wincing, Daniel rose to his feet. "I guess I took longer than I'd intended. Care if I slip out your back door?"

"She would keep your secret."

"Yes, I imagine she would, but I'd rather not have to ask her to do it."

"I understand." Shannon waved her arm toward her kitchen. "Go, then."

A single step took Daniel to her side. He wanted to dip his head and brush her mouth with a quick kiss. Instead, as Herb Alpert's trumpet began to belt out "Love Potion No. 9," Daniel simply touched her arm. "Tuesday at seven. It's a date."

"With chaperones."

He almost blew his exit by giving away his presence when he strode into her kitchen and caught sight of the tile mosaic on the wall. Distracted, he bumped into a chair, and when it rattled, he quickly moved to silence it. He never took his gaze off the tiles.

A treble clef and five parallel lines on the backsplash running across three of the kitchen's walls fashioned a music staff. Note heads were shaped like hearts; the flags, angel's wings. Beneath it on a banner he read a quote: "If music be the food of love, play on—William Shakespeare." Under other circumstances, he'd hum the melody the notes constructed, but right now he needed to leave.

If he could yank his gaze from the scene above the cooktop, that is. She'd depicted this cottage in springtime with pots of red geraniums in bloom and yellow daffodils trumpeting the end of winter. But what brought the art to life were the details she'd put in that made the house a home: the tricycle on the front walk, the ball gloves and bat on the porch, the dog sunning himself in the flower bed.

His heart gave a vicious twist of longing.

From the front room, he heard Shannon say, "Hi, Celeste. Let me grab my pages off the printer and I'll be ready to go."

Daniel shook off his reverie and slipped quietly out the back door. He was halfway to the spot where he'd left his truck when his phone began to ring.

Ten minutes later, everything had changed.

"You go on to the conference room, dear," Celeste told Shannon as they arrived at the Eternity Springs public library for the weekly meeting of their writers' group. "I'll be along in a couple of minutes. I need to drop off some brochures for Margaret Rhodes for the librarians' retreat she's planning at Angel's Rest in March."

"All right," Shannon replied, a bit absent-mindedly. Her mind was spinning. What the heck was wrong with her? Had she really just agreed to a date with Daniel? Daniel Garrett, Private Eye? What in the world had gotten into her?

She'd been surprised to see him standing on her front porch looking hale and hearty and determined when she'd opened her door. His dinner invitation had shocked her.

Maybe it was nothing more than needing a distraction for Linda and Benny, but the look in his eyes had made it seem…more.

And she'd agreed to go. Why?

Because his marriage-that-wasn't had changed the status quo, that's why. Now the question of telling him about the baby was back on the table—with new information.

The man was protecting the vulnerable. He'd listened to Linda's story. He'd believed in her.

Maybe...just maybe...he would listen to her, believe in **her.**

And what if he did? What would it change? She had no evidence against Russell. He'd always been too careful, too sneaky. Too smart. His money and his intelligence made him a powerful foe.

Was she willing to tell Daniel the truth and put her life in his hands? Put their baby's life in his hands?

No. You can't tell him. He's an investigator. He would investigate, and his investigation would undoubtedly trip some of Russell's alerts and lead him right back to me. To us.

But if she could trust him to listen to her like he'd listened to Linda, maybe—

"Earth to Shannon," Rose Cicero said from directly behind her. "Hello."

Shannon realized she stood blocking the door. She'd walked to the conference room without even realizing it. "Oh. Hi. I didn't see you."

"The last time I saw such a faraway look on your face you were plotting murder. Thinking about your story?"

"Sort of." Shannon smiled weakly. She flipped the light switch on. **If you only knew.** "I've been stuck on where to go next with the plot."

"Well, we will figure it out."

Rose set her tote on top of the conference table and pulled two thick stacks of pages from the bag. Shannon inwardly winced at the thought of her own meager word production the previous week. At this rate, she'd never finish her book. Heaven knows, it needed an ending.

Shannon had begun writing her novel as a way of coping with her nightmares. After all, nobody could tell a stalker story like someone who knew what it was like to be a mouse with a cat on her tail. Not long after moving to Eternity Springs, she'd discovered that Rose shared her interest in writing and the two women began meeting and trading pages for critique. Celeste had joined their group three weeks ago after she'd decided to accept her friends' challenge to put together a collection of inspirational sayings. She'd been a great addition to the effort.

"Looks like you had a good work week," she said.

"That's because I quit trying to write at home."

Shannon looked from the piles of paper to Rose, then back to the pages again. "So, what happened? The writing fairies sneaked in and worked on your book?"

"Slow shifts at the clinic and a new office manager who has taken some more of the scut work off my shoulders. I had some time to myself this past week. Blessed, wonderful alone time."

"Don't tell me that the bloom is off the marriage-and-motherhood rose, Dr. Cicero."

In July, Rose had married the glass artist and heartthrob Hunt Cicero, and in the process became the new mother of four young orphans. "No. I'm happy as a clam. But I was single for a very long time, and I've figured out that as much as I love my oh-so-full life, I need a little down time, too. A little 'me' time."

"I think I have the opposite problem," Shannon said as she tugged her week's work from her own bag. "Too much alone time. Too much time to think. Next thing I know, I'm second-guessing myself about everything. Then when I sit down to write, I can't find the zone. My mind flits from one subject to another. My concentration is shot, Rose. I'm a mess and I hate it because I really want to finish this story."

It was true. While the story had begun as therapy to deal with her nightmares, over time it had grown to represent something bigger. For Shannon, the idea of The End had become intertwined with the end of a life spent looking over her shoulder. In her mind, it was as if bringing her fictional character to justice would somehow settle things with Russell.

Nonsensical, she could admit, but there it was.

Celeste had glided into the room as Shannon was speaking. "Now, dear. Don't be so hard on yourself. Keep in mind that as life pushes and pulls and sometimes shoves at us, a positive attitude can be the lift beneath your wings that helps you maintain your balance."

"That sounds like excellent aspiring angel advice, Celeste," Shannon replied, basking in the warmth of her friend's encouraging smile.

"Why, you're right. Let me make a note of that."

While Celeste pulled a spiral-bound book out of her purse and jotted a few notes, Rose studied Shannon with a look. "You know what I think? You've just finished your first summer in Eternity Springs where you worked your tail off doing the jobs of three women. It's no wonder you are distracted. The pace of life slows down now and you won't have as many distractions. I'll bet you have it done by Easter."

"I hope so." She might be living somewhere else, but that'd be okay. Safety for her and her child was her most cherished wish.

Why Daniel's image flashed through her mind at that particular moment didn't bear dwelling upon.

The women got down to work. Shannon quickly lost herself in the dramatic tension Rose had created for her protagonist, a medical lab worker who had stumbled on a bioterrorism plot. The story was fast paced and vivid, and as usual, the plotting tight. Shannon found little to critique in this week's read from Rose. The new working routine was obviously working for her friend.

Upon finishing Rose's pages, Shannon turned to Celeste's offering. Written in her beautiful, easily legible longhand, Celeste Blessing's **Guidelines for Aspiring Angels** was a work of art itself. For every guideline, she added a few paragraphs of exposition followed by some concrete examples of implementation. She'd added three new guidelines this week, and as always, each of them resonated in Shannon's heart.

Number Fourteen: Acts of kindness are feathers for an aspiring angel's wings.

Number Fifteen: Friendship is the glitter that makes an angel's wings shimmer.

Number Sixteen: Clear the cotton balls of fear from your ears and

**listen to your inner angel's voice.
It always speaks the truth.**

"'Cotton balls of fear'?" she asked when the discussion turned to Celeste's work. "Maybe a different descriptive term?"

"Shannon has a point," Rose agreed. "'Cotton balls' seems too soft and gentle for fear. Fear is...I dunno—"

The words tumbled from Shannon's lips. "Fear is a ragged shard of glass or rusty teeth on a saw blade that slices to your soul. Other times it's a chilling mist that covers you, sinking into your bones and seeping into your lungs and making it impossible to breathe. Always, it's a monster. Cold. Heavy. Harsh. Metallic."

A million-pound monster draped around her shoulders.

She briefly closed her eyes, a bit embarrassed by her outburst. Celeste and Rose shared a glance, then gazed at her with expectant expressions. When she kept her mouth shut, Celeste nodded. "Thank you. You are right. I'll rethink the use of 'cotton balls.' I have such a difficult time coming up with darker analogies."

"It's because you are a creature of light, Celeste," Rose said. "You warm and illuminate those around you."

"Thank you, dear. That's such a nice thing to say."

"There's another guideline for you," Shannon said. "'Aspiring angels light the way.'"

"Oh, that's nice." Celeste made notes in her spiral-bound journal. "This is so much fun. I'm so glad you girls invited me to join your group. Although, I will admit, your pages this week are especially disturbing, Shannon."

Rose nodded in agreement. "I'll say. The stalker's viewpoint is as creepy as anything I've read in a long time. You put us right there with poor Isabelle."

Like they say, write what you know.

"Where are you going next, Shannon?"

To dinner at Daniel's. But of course, Rose spoke of her plot. "I don't know. I'm stuck. I guess that's why I produced so few pages this week."

"You know what I think?" Celeste suggested. "I think you should give Isabelle a love interest."

Rose nodded. "Ooh, I like that."

"She had a love interest. The villain killed him."

"Give her another one. She's grown strong over the course of the story. Give her a man who complements that strength. One who will help her defeat her foe."

Shannon stiffened. "Isabelle isn't a damsel in distress. She can defeat her foe on her own."

"Yes, but why should she have to? She's been alone long enough. She deserves happiness."

"She doesn't need a man to be happy. She might have believed she did at the beginning of her character arc, but she's grown."

"True, very true. I just think it would be a nice way to circle back around to the beginning of the story."

"She has a point, Shannon," Rose said.

"I'm writing a thriller."

"So?" Rose shrugged. "Add a little romance and appeal to a broader readership."

No one is ever going to read my book. Even if this was the best thriller manuscript ever penned she couldn't publish it. She couldn't risk Russell recognizing himself in the pages.

Celeste reached over and patted Shannon's hand. "Think about it, dear. Satisfying endings are nice. Happy endings are better."

Once she worked past her initial resistance, Shannon conceded that the idea did have appeal. "I will think about it, Celeste. Thank you. It's a direction I hadn't considered before, but I see how a love interest for Isabelle adds an opportunity for suspense."

"Will she or won't she?" Rose drew a heart in the margin of Shannon's story.

"More likely will **he** or won't **he**."

"Fall in love?"

"Fall to a serial killer's knife."

Celeste reached across the table and patted Shannon's hand. "You must be willing to risk the fall in order to learn to fly."

"Better write that one down, too, Celeste," Rose said.

Shannon considered the idea of giving her protagonist a love interest as she walked home from the library. It was a clear, crisp night with the scent of wood smoke rising from hearths all across town drifting in the air. As she lifted her gaze to the heavens, she spied a shooting star, thought of Celeste's angels, and smiled. Maybe her friends were right. Maybe she **should** give her heroine a happy ending and begin a new story.

She placed her hand atop her womb. After all, the first chapter was already being written, was it not?

What if she told Daniel about Russell, and he agreed not to do anything about it? What if she told Daniel about the baby and he offered to marry her? What if they fell in love?

As she reached the intersection of Third and Pinion, an engine's backfire distracted her from her fantasy and she lifted her hand and waved as the mayor's old Ford pickup chugged past her. He tapped hello with his horn. She watched the red tail-lights disappear up the street and scolded herself for being such an idiot.

It was time she separated her plot from her life.

She repeated the admonition often during

the days that followed. On Tuesday, she awoke wishing she'd gotten his phone number so she could call and cancel. Maybe she'd simply stand him up. There was a first time for everything, right?

Knowing her luck, he would decide she'd had a flat tire or wrecked her car or something on the drive out to the remote locale. The hero in him wouldn't rest until he'd tracked her to her home where, by that time, she would probably be in bed.

That's all she needed.

Toward the end of her yoga class she decided she'd just suck it up and go. It's not as if they'd be there alone together. This time she wouldn't be caught by surprise and agree to something she'd regret.

The question settled, she spent an hour on bookkeeping at Murphy's before heading out to Three Bears to prep walls. Her work there went well and she reached a good stopping point at two o'clock, which gave her enough time to go home and take a much-needed nap before her date.

Unfortunately, she overslept. She was just out of the shower, wearing her bathrobe with a towel wrapped around her wet hair, when a loud knock sounded on her door. Shannon scowled at her reflection in the foggy bathroom mirror. She was tempted to ignore the knock. Nine times out of ten, an unexpected knock on her door meant the school had a new fund-raiser going. What were the kids selling this week? "I don't need any more Christmas wrapping paper."

Knock knock knock.

"Maybe it's the caramel corn," she said to her reflection. She really liked the caramel corn.

She adjusted her bathrobe to make sure everything was covered and retied her sash, then grabbed up her wallet as she hurried to the front door. Expecting to find a four-foot-tall visitor, she aimed her gaze that way as she opened the door saying, "What are you selling today?"

Standing on her front porch, Daniel Garrett replied, "What would you like?"

Chapter Seven

Daniel watched color bloom on Shannon's cheeks as she jerked her gaze up from his crotch. What a gorgeous picture she made, all clean and fresh and damp.

"Daniel. I thought you were a school kid."

"Not for many years." He shifted the bag of groceries in his arms. "Superior detective that I am, I deduce that you didn't see my note."

"What note?"

"In your mailbox? A folded sheet of yellow paper?"

He followed the path of her gaze toward the small table beside her door where a stack of envelopes and circulars sat. "I'd have called, but I don't have your phone number."

"I know the feeling," she muttered.

She looked so disgusted that he had to smother a smile. "May I come in?"

Wordlessly, she stepped aside and he strode into Heartsong Cottage. Immediately, a sense of homecoming, an air of belonging, enveloped him.

"I didn't look at my mail when I got home." She picked up his note and read through it. "You want to fix dinner here?"

"Either here or at one of the cabins at Angel's Rest. I can't cook at the cabin. It's uninhabitable. I had a wildlife issue. Dead raccoon in the attic. It's gonna take a few days for the place to air out."

"Oh, yuck."

"The cabin I've rented has a kitchenette so I can cook there. You tell me what you'd prefer."

Her gaze flicked down to the sack of groceries then up to him again. "Here would be fine, except my table is tiny. I don't have room for four."

"Do you have room for two?"

"Yes."

"Good. Then we're set. It's just you and me for dinner."

She went still. "What about Linda and Benny?"

Now he gave his smile full rein as satisfaction rolled through him. "My guard duty is done. They've gone home."

"Her husband's been arrested?"

"Yep. I'll tell you the whole story over supper. Now, if you don't mind me making myself at home in your kitchen, I'll get dinner started."

"Already?" she asked, a squeak in her voice. She glanced toward the clock. "You said seven."

"It's even more delicious when it simmers."

The flush on her cheeks showed that she heard the unintended innuendo. She gestured toward the doorway to the kitchen. "Make yourself at home. I'll go get dressed."

He bit back a suggestive comment that came to mind and carried his sack of groceries into the kitchen, saying, "Take your time."

A moment later he heard her bedroom door shut with a **snick**.

Not for the first time, Daniel wondered what the hell he was doing. He had no business being here. He'd gone to Murphy's this morning to call off the date, but he'd missed her. He'd driven out to Three Bears to cancel, but he'd missed her there, too. When he knocked on her door earlier today with the hope of catching her at home, he'd had every intention of begging off. But standing on her front porch, on the outside peering through her front window looking for a sign that she was home, he'd had a change of heart.

There was nowhere else on earth he'd rather be right now than standing in Shannon O'Toole's kitchen.

And what a kitchen it was. He set his grocery sack on the little kitchen table and took a moment to study the room. She'd fitted a lot of kitchen into a little space. High-end appliances, quality cabinets. Bet Gabi or Cicero had made the glass globes for that light fixture. His gaze dropped to the backsplash and he hummed the notes, recognizing the song in the first few bars. "You're a romantic, Shannon O'Toole."

And he'd better damned well be careful tonight.

Not that he thought she'd try to seduce him. Only a blind man wouldn't have seen her reluctance to let him stay. Nor had he missed her muttered remark about not having his phone number. A hundred bucks said she'd have canceled on him had she known it.

Her prickly attitude actually made it easier

for him to relax. He decided to simply enjoy the evening here at Heartsong Cottage and not overthink the situation.

He went to work. First he opened the wine to allow it to breathe. Next he got the rosemary-roasted potatoes ready to go into the oven and the asparagus ready to sauté. He was dredging the veal marsala in flour when Shannon joined him. She'd dressed in black slacks and a crisp white blouse and black ballet flats, and she wore them like armor. "It smells delicious. I love the aroma of rosemary. What can I do to help?"

"Pour us a glass of wine?"

She removed two glasses from a cabinet and poured one glass of wine. The other she filled with sparkling water. Handing him the wine, she explained, "I think I'll stick with the soft stuff tonight. Believe it or not, I'm not ordinarily a drinker."

Daniel thought it best to let that pass without comment.

"So, tell me about Linda." She leaned back against the counter and sipped her water.

"I actually got the call about it as I left

your house the other night. He's been arrested and arraigned—and, unbelievably—failed to make bail. Admittedly, it was high because he was considered a flight risk, but apparently he's had some major financial setbacks recently."

"Oh. Wow. So they've gone home?"

"Yes. I drove her and Benny to the airport yesterday. She met with a divorce attorney this morning and they plan to file by the end of the day. Even if Mason Tate is able to make bail later on, Linda will have custody. What matters most is that Benny is safe."

"Good job, Mr. Garrett. I'm so glad for them."

"Me, too. With any luck, Tate will serve some substantial time in prison where he won't be a popular guy due to the nature of his crimes. As far as I'm concerned, he'll have earned each beating he's bound to receive."

"Bloodthirsty, much?"

"For subhumans like him? You betcha. Now, it's my turn to ask a question. Why 'Unchained Melody'?"

Shannon glanced toward the backsplash,

a faint smile hovering on her lips. Daniel resisted the sudden urge to swoop in and kiss her as, suddenly, the little kitchen felt downright tiny. He turned his attention to the veal.

"Very nice, Mr. Garrett. As far as I know, you're the first person who has come into the kitchen and actually read the music. Most people don't see past the hearts and angel wings."

"I'm trained to look past the obvious. So, why that song?"

"It's a heartsong."

"Ah. I've wondered about that ever since I read the sign on your front porch. Define 'heartsong' for me."

She sipped her sparkling water and considered the question. "A heartsong gives you Grinch heart."

"Excuse me?"

"You know…Dr. Seuss? **How the Grinch Stole Christmas**? At the end of the book his heart grows three sizes."

"Ahh."

"A heartsong is beautiful. It's timeless. It's a classic."

You are a heartsong. The words hung

on Daniel's tongue, but he swallowed them. She'd think it was a line, and it wasn't. It was the truth.

"'Unchained Melody' is a good choice," he said with a nod. "This is a kitchen, after all. All that hunger..."

"And, apparently, the man who wrote the lyrics said the song was about a woman named Cookie." Her expression turned impish as she said, "And it's the number one love song."

"Seriously?" He set down his wine glass. "Are we really going there?"

Her eyes sparkling, she shrugged.

"It's a great song, but it's no higher than number four. 'Unforgettable', 'At Last', and 'Lady in Red' top 'Unchained Melody.'"

The debate lasted until they sat down to dinner.

The food turned out excellent, the veal tender and flavorful, the potatoes crisp and seasoned just right. Daniel's culinary repertoire was limited, but what he did cook, he cooked well. Shannon certainly appeared to savor her meal. He was pleased, especially once he saw her beginning to relax.

During dinner, they discussed their mutual friends, and Shannon gave him the details on Cicero's Albritton award dinner. "It was so exciting. Cicero is such a confident man, but when they announced his name, he froze in shock. Then he looked at Rose and his eyes went all soft and sort of gooey."

"That's it. No doubt about it now. You're a romantic, Ms. O'Toole."

Just like that, tension returned to the room. They both focused on their food for a few minutes until she took a deep breath and threw him a verbal bone. "This is the best meal I've had in ages. You must enjoy cooking."

That topic kept conversation going until the end of the meal. It wasn't until they shared cleanup duties that the conversation drifted toward more personal topics. Knowing that she wasn't a native Coloradan, he asked her where she was from and how she'd come to live in Eternity Springs.

"My father was a contractor and we moved around a lot when I was growing up. I was living in Miami when I learned that I'd inherited Murphy's from a distant relative. I always liked the snow, so I thought I'd give Eternity Springs a try. I'm glad I did. I love it here."

Daniel hadn't missed the shadow that flashed across her face at his question, or the note in her voice that suggested there was more to her story than what she'd revealed. "Are your parents in Florida? Any siblings?"

"No. I was an only child. My parents are both gone. How about you?"

She'd thrown up an obvious stop sign, so he took the hint. "My Bostonian native parents retired to Florida. They live in one of those senior communities and are happy as clams. She plays bridge and tennis and belongs to a book club. He plays golf six days a week. Hit his first hole in one last month. At age eighty-five."

"Go, Dad."

He lifted his wine glass in silent toast to his father. "I have siblings. No sisters, just brothers. Three of them."

Shannon drew back. "Four boys? Your poor mother!"

"Poor me. I'm the oldest. They're all a bunch of knuckleheads."

With the last pan washed and put away, and all the dirty dishes loaded in the dishwasher, Shannon suggested he pick out some music while she dished up bowls of ice cream. "I wouldn't mind having a fire if you're up to get it started."

"I'm all over it."

In her living room, he went first to her record collection. He stuck with the theme of the evening with his choices: Sinatra, Nat King Cole, Perry Como, and appropriately, he thought, the Righteous Brothers. Shannon entered the room carrying two stoneware bowls as he slid **Just Once in My Life** from its sleeve.

"I've decided that I really like the aesthetics of vinyl records," he told her. "Putting them on to play is almost a ritual. You need to do it with care."

"That's an interesting way to look at it."

Warming to the subject, he continued, "I like the tactile quality of the cardboard sleeve and the weight of the record itself, especially the older, thicker ones. Even blowing away the dust before you thread it onto the turntable is part of it. There's something about listening to one side at a time that contributes to the moment, too. You don't have that with CDs. They're more like office supplies. Digital music is handy, but it's—" He waved a hand. "Air. Vinyl records are substantive. They're an experience."

"Why, Daniel Garrett. I do believe you are sentimental and old-fashioned."

"Can't argue that." With the records loaded, he twisted the switch that started the turntable in motion. The first record dropped. The needle arm lifted and moved. Frank Sinatra began to sing and Daniel turned his attention to building a fire. She already had kindling stacked in the hearth. He called on his Boy Scout skills and soon had a nice fire burning. Taking a seat beside Shannon on the love seat, he accepted his bowl of ice cream. "So what flavor do we have?"

"I bought a gallon of Neapolitan to cover all the bases, but since dinner was so spectacular, I decided I needed to up my game. I dug into my supersecret wintertime stash from our seasonal ice cream shop."

"This is Taste of Texas ice cream?"

"Yep. Almond toffee. You can't tell anyone

I have it. My friends will beg all winter long."

"Ah, Ms. O'Toole, you are a treasure." In a movement unplanned and natural, he leaned over and kissed her.

Careful, Daniel.

Careful, Shannon.

Like a dieter in a candy shop, she told herself she could have one piece, and Shannon fell into the kiss. Both mellow and at the same time jazzed, she couldn't remember the last time she'd enjoyed an evening quite so much. The man was witty and entertaining and so fine to look at.

He ended the kiss a little sooner than she would have liked, and she heard a husky note in his voice as he said, "I'm afraid that just melted my ice cream."

Shannon's voice was a little breathy when she replied, "We can't have that."

"You're right."

She gazed at him intently, saw the promise there, and experienced a wash of both disappointment and relief. He wasn't going to try to get her back into bed tonight.

They ate their ice cream in companionable silence, watching the fire and listening to music. When Frank gave way to Nat, Daniel put his arm around her. She didn't resist snuggling up against him. "This is nice," he said, his fingers playing idly with her hair. "I really love your place, Shannon. It has such a homey feel."

"Thank you. I love it, too."

"When I was here in August, you had it up for sale. Did you change your mind?"

She recognized it as a natural opening to tell him about the baby. If she were going to do it at all, she probably **should** tell him now. It was a golden opportunity. They had privacy. He was in an affable mood. It might be her only chance to tell him face-to-face for quite some time. She knew that he always visited Hope Romano in November on the anniversary of his son's death, but that certainly wasn't the time to share news like this.

But she wasn't ready. She hadn't made that particular decision yet.

Oh, really? Don't lie to yourself.

She wasn't lying to herself. Was she?

He's a good man. A wounded man. A trustworthy man.

Her heart began to pound. She cleared

her throat. "My situation changed."

"The job out at Three Bears? I went over there looking for you earlier and snooped through the houses. The work you've done so far is very nice. Have you had artistic training? You're very talented."

Just do it. Tell him. Now.

"Daniel...I...um..."

He arched a questioning brow toward her and she chickened out and began to babble. "Thank you. No, I've had no formal training. I have had some long discussions about color with Sage Rafferty and learned quite a bit that way. I learned carpentry and a little plumbing from my dad. A visit to a tile museum during a trip to Portugal when I was at Stanford inspired my interest in tile and mosaics."

"You went to college at Stanford?" he asked, obviously impressed.

Oh, for crying out loud. You walked right into that one.

"I never finished college. I did study tile work after the Lisbon trip. I was so intrigued by the azulejo—glazed and painted tile—I saw there. I loved how the buildings were covered in tile. The patterns are fabulous.

My work with mosaics developed from that interest. Have you ever been to Portugal?"

"No. Work has taken me to Asia and Amsterdam a number of times, but that's the extent of my foreign travel."

They discussed places they'd like to visit for a few minutes before the conversation returned to Eternity Springs. Daniel said, "And I understand you teach yoga in addition to running Murphy's and remodeling houses. So you're a Jill-of-all-trades, hmm?"

"You've been checking up on me?"

"Hope likes to share town gossip with me. She thinks I need to spend more time here." He trailed his thumb slowly up and down her neck and a note of musing entered his tone. "Maybe she's right."

"Celeste says Eternity Springs has a healing energy."

"I won't argue the point."

Shannon sensed the change in his mood even before he removed his arm from around her, stood, and crossed the room to the hearth. He picked up the iron fireplace tool and poked at the fire. Logs crackled and orange sparks fluttered up the chimney. "I like this town a lot. I've thought about moving here, but I don't know what I'd do to make a living. I don't know what I **want** to do."

"You can't run your investigative firm from here?"

"Not easily or efficiently. My work involves a lot of traveling, so access to a major airport is important." He returned the poker to the holder, then stood staring down into the fire. "It wears on a man, Shannon. I don't know if I can do it anymore."

"Travel?"

He shook his head and said flatly, "Look for missing kids."

The faint lines etched across his face had deepened, she saw. Her heart went out to him. "It must be a difficult job."

"It's a beating. The losses outnumber the wins twenty to one."

In that moment, Shannon thought she'd never seen anyone look so totally alone in her life. "But you've had some glorious wins," she pointed out. "You're responsible for Eternity Springs' own missing-child miracle. You brought Holly Montgomery home to her mother."

She saw him swallow hard. A gruff note

entered his voice when he said, "That's definitely one of the best moments of my life. But times like that are few and far between. In the eight years I've been out on my own, you know how many of those home runs I've hit? Four. A whopping four!"

"Four is not an insignificant number. Especially not to those four families."

"I know." Internal conflict etched lines across his brow. "I try to remind myself of that. I understand that the base hits are important, too."

"What is a base hit in your business, Daniel?"

"Answers. The reality is that by the time parents contact me, the vast majority of the children are already dead. Most of my job is providing information to parents about when and how their child died. It's important information. I know that from personal experience. The uncertainty is soul wrenching, an absolute killer. But what I have to do in order to gather that information—"

Daniel closed his eyes. "It's ugly and it's evil and it haunts me. I don't have the heart for it anymore. I can't search child porn sites for missing children one more time."

"Oh, Daniel." Shannon followed her instincts when she went to him and wrapped her arms around him, offering the comfort of a hug.

His arms encircled her, and he buried his face against her hair as he returned the embrace. "I'm sorry. What a mood killer. I shouldn't have brought it up."

"Don't apologize." She dropped her arms and stepped away. Speaking from the heart, she said, "I know what it's like to tote a burden around wishing you had someone with which to share it. You have heavy burdens to lift, Daniel. According to Celeste that's how you grow your angel wings. You can't grow feathers by lifting air."

He let out a strained laugh. "Leave it to Celeste."

"I'm glad you can speak to me about things that matter."

"Music matters," he insisted. "I don't know why I veered off in a different direction."

"I suspect it's because you're not struggling with a major life decision about music. Sounds to me like you're at a crossroads, Daniel."

At a crossroads, but with one important highway missing from his map. **Tell him. Do it now.**

Shannon's mind started to spin. Maybe it was just the piece of information he needed to decide that he belonged here in Eternity Springs with her and with their baby. She imagined Daniel standing in the nursery and crooning a lullaby to the infant in his arms. They could be a family.

Is that what you **want?**

Panic rolled through her. How could she possibly know what she wanted? She'd spent time with the man on only a handful of occasions. She didn't know his religion, his politics, or even his favorite college football team!

Although in the big scheme of things, those things didn't matter, did they? What mattered were his viewpoints toward discipline and education and sports. Would he argue with Shannon's opinion about the dangers of peewee football? What did he think of Montessori and preschool Spanish? Would he support her efforts to raise a bilingual child?

To be perfectly honest, those things didn't

matter, either. Character mattered. She already knew all she needed to know about Daniel Garrett's character. He would love their baby. He would protect their baby with his life. He wouldn't do anything to put their baby at risk.

That much, she could trust.

She thought about Celeste and her advice for aspiring angels. Angels fly by letting go. **Heaven help me. I'm going to do it.**

She stepped back and lifted her head, seeking his gaze, but Daniel stood staring into the fire. "I don't know that 'crossroads' is the right term," he said, even as she opened her mouth to speak. "I can't do the job anymore, but I also don't think that I can walk away from it, either. How can I? They call me every day."

Shannon waited a beat, knowing the moment was lost. "Who calls you?"

He lifted a fireplace tool and gave the fire a vicious poke. "Parents. Desperate parents who need an answer to a fundamental question: is their child still alive?"

The torment in his voice twisted her heart. "That must be so hard."

"It's the worst. Invariably, by the time

they've come to me they've exhausted all of their other resources. The FBI has no answers for them. Local law enforcement has started dodging their calls. It's a horrible thing to learn that your child has been murdered, but not knowing is a whole other plane of misery. As weird as it sounds, I know that I'm terribly lucky to have a grave that I can visit."

"That's not weird. It's totally understandable."

"It's why I can't walk away from parents who aren't as lucky as I am. That, and the possibility that the next missing child could be number five. What if there's a little guy out there just waiting to be found?"

"Daniel, you can't do that to yourself. You're not the only investigator out there looking for children."

"You're right." One corner of his mouth lifted in a bitter smile. "I sound like an egotistical jerk, don't I?"

"Not at all. You sound like a committed man."

"Sometimes I think I need to be committed." He raked his fingers through his hair, and then returned the poker to its stand. "I don't know why I went off on such a tangent. Please, let me change the subject before I totally ruin this evening."

"You are not ruining the evening." What he'd done was show her a side of himself that only made her like him more. Daniel Garrett had more heart than any man she'd ever met.

He stepped to the record player and reset the needle. As the first haunting notes of "Unchained Melody" floated from the speakers, Shannon smiled. When he turned to her, held out his hand, and asked, "Dance with me?" she went a little gooey inside.

He held her close and they did more swaying than actual dancing in the small living room. When Daniel's voice crooned in her ear about needing her love, shivers ran up her spine. The rich, emotive timbre of his voice had her blinking back tears, and when the final note of the song died away, she laced her fingers behind his neck and thanked him with a kiss.

He hummed into her mouth. "Mmm..."

She sank against him a little harder, fell into the kiss more deeply. His lips tasted of mint and music and spun a sensuous spell around her as mesmerizing as northern lights—until the record changed and a rousing rendition of "Stars and Stripes Forever" startled them back to their senses. "What the heck? I didn't choose John Philip Sousa. I swear I didn't."

He looked so appalled, so offended, that Shannon threw back her head and laughed. "You have something against the Red, White, and Blue, Garrett?"

"Not at all. The Boston Pops are my peeps. In June and July around Memorial Day and the Fourth. Not when I'm busy attempting my rusty moves on a beautiful woman."

Not rusty. Not rusty at all. "Veteran's Day will be here before we know it."

"Yeah...well..." He trailed his thumb down her cheek from temple to chin. "So will morning and I have to be up at a ridiculous hour. I'd better say good night."

Shannon's heart dipped. She told herself she was glad that he was keeping the promise she'd read in his eyes earlier tonight, that he didn't assume that a dinner date meant she would sleep with him, especially considering their history. At the same time, she regretted that he didn't test her. **Face it, O'Toole. Where Daniel Garrett is concerned, you're easy.**

She wondered why he needed to get up early, and asked the most obvious question. "Do you have a plane to catch in the morning?"

"No. I have a phone appointment with Linda's attorney." He waited a beat, and then added, "My intention is to hang around town a while. I was planning to come the first week of November anyway, so I figure I might as well stay. Celeste gave me a steal of a deal on the cabin rental."

"Oh. I thought—"

His lips twitched. "That you'd be rid of me?"

"No." Then a rare spurt of candor had her admitting, "Well, yes."

"You wanted to break our date, didn't you?"

"Yes."

"I did, too."

Now she was offended. "You did?"

"You confuse me, Shannon O'Toole. You are a friend of my friends, so a relationship with you would be complicated."

And he doesn't know the half of it.

"I don't do complicated," he continued, "but I can't seem to stay away from you."

"I don't know whether to be insulted or flattered."

"Good. It's only right that we both be confused. So, why did you want to break our date?"

The moment for telling him about the baby had passed, she decided. She went for lighthearted instead. "It's the chocolate thing."

"What chocolate thing?"

"A shared love of chocolate is vital to a relationship, I believe."

"Hey, you're the one who kept the Neapolitan in the freezer. Tell you what. You need to give me another chance. Are you busy Saturday night? Gabe Callahan's brothers will be in town, and they're clearing a hunk of land they recently purchased that adjoins their property out at Hummingbird Lake. I promised I'd help. They've promised the best barbecue ever eaten Saturday night. And something called a Texas Chocolate Sheet Cake. Want to come have dinner with me?"

"Oh, I love barbecue, but it's hard for me to get away from the pub on Saturday nights. I'd better skip."

"Okay, then. I'll be out of town next week, but back the following week. I need a partner in the three-legged race that Saturday morning."

"Planning to attend the school's Fall Festival fund-raiser, are you?"

"Holly Montgomery talked me into buying a small fortune in tickets. So, want to be my date?"

She did. Shannon realized that she well and truly did.

Pleasure sparkled in his eyes. "Great. You up to making a day of it? The festivities start at ten. How about I pick you up then?"

"I'll be ready."

They exchanged cell phone numbers then she walked him to the door. "I had a lovely evening, Daniel. Thank you."

"I did, too. Thank you, Shannon." He leaned down and gave her a long, lingering good-night kiss, ending it with obvious reluctance. "I'm glad you didn't cancel."

"Me, too."

"I'm looking forward to the three-legged

race."

"Me, too. Safe travels, Daniel."

"Maybe I'll see you around town before I leave."

"Come by the pub."

"I'll do that."

She waited a beat, then said, "Well, good night."

"Good night." He gave her a quick, hard kiss and finally turned to go.

Shannon leaned back against the door as she shut it behind him. The phonograph made a clicking sound as the record changed. Moments later, Elvis began crooning "Can't Help Falling in Love," and a little laugh escaped Shannon.

She could totally hear Celeste's cheery voice ringing through her mind, saying, "Coincidences are an angel's way of working anonymously."

Chapter Eight

Daniel walked into the back room of Cam Murphy's sporting goods store, Refresh, on Wednesday night and announced, "Gentlemen, the master has arrived. Prepare yourselves for a good old-fashioned whuppin'."

The nine faces that turned his way each wore an expression of scorn. "Well, if it isn't Mr. Big Talk," Gabe Callahan said around the unlit cigar in his mouth.

"Yeah." Cam flipped his Colorado Rockies baseball cap around backward. "I'm gonna love taking his money."

Lucca Romano shuffled a deck of cards like a pro. "As I recall, last time Daniel joined us you lost everything but your shirt."

"Actually, I won that, too. Remember? He had to go to the front of the store and take something off the rack."

"I remember," Zach Turner said as he used his college ring as a bottle opener to crack open a beer. "I was getting worried that he'd insist on trying to win it back.

Didn't want to see Cam Murphy naked."

"Nobody wants to see that."

"That's right," Cam said, plunging his hand into a bag of tortilla chips. "Because one glimpse at my package will give you all such an inferiority complex that you'll need treatment, and Eternity Springs doesn't have a psychologist."

"No, it's because Sarah is sharp, and she'll notice when we all look at her with pity in our eyes."

Cam showed lots of teeth before he chomped the chip. "Bite me."

With that, poker night was officially off and running.

Daniel had played with the group on two previous occasions when his visits to town had coincided with the twice-monthly gathering. The group had grown in both size and popularity since his visit a year ago and tonight it had two separate games going. Daniel took the fifth seat at a table with Lucca Romano, Zach Turner, Mac Timberlake, and Jack Davenport. For the first hour, conversation revolved around the cards, cars, basketball, and college football. The second hour drifted toward more personal subjects—wives, kids, and jobs.

During the third hour, players began calling it quits for the evening. Seventy-three dollars up for the night, Daniel asked to be dealt out. As he rose from the table, he felt his cell phone vibrate. He checked the number and recognized the lab. He needed to take this call.

"Hello, Steve. Hold on a minute while I step outside."

"Sure."

He grabbed his jacket and slipped it on as he exited the store's back door into the crisp autumn night. Cam had turned the area behind his shop into what he called a test area for items that he sold. His wife referred to the spot as Cam's play yard. To Daniel's left, a basketball hoop hung above a rectangle of cement. To his right, a strip of artificial turf provided a putting green. Daniel turned left and headed for one of several folding chairs set along the perimeter of the court. "What do you have for me, Steve?"

"DNA matches, Daniel. You found the little girl."

Daniel closed his eyes and released a heavy sigh. It was the news he'd expected, the devastatingly awful good news. "That's good. I'll let her parents know. Thanks for rushing this for me."

"Glad to help, buddy. You know you can call on me any time."

"Thanks. I appreciate it. I owe you."

"Hey, I'm the one who owes you and you know it."

When the lab director's fifteen-year-old niece had run off with a boyfriend, Daniel had called on his law enforcement connections to facilitate the hunt for her and the story had a happy ending. "How is Katie doing these days?"

"Great. Just great. She went to summer school and got caught up. Made the varsity cross-country squad this fall."

"Good for her."

The call ended and Daniel didn't hesitate in searching his contacts list for the call he needed to make. Experience had taught him that the best way to psych himself up for calls like this was to waste no time dithering over it. Besides, he'd promised Glenn Johnson he'd call the moment he got word, day or night.

Johnson answered on the second ring. Daniel destroyed the man's world with two little words. "It's her. I just got the call from the lab and we have a positive ID. I'm sorry, Glenn."

The conversation lasted only a couple of minutes, and as the grieving father choked out his thanks prior to disconnecting, Daniel gave a tennis ball lying near his feet a vicious kick. By the time he returned the phone to his pocket, he felt as if he'd aged five years. "Well, that sucked," he said aloud.

"You do horrible and important work, Garrett."

Daniel hadn't noticed Gabe Callahan standing in the shadows with a putter in his hand.

"It takes guts to do what you do," Callahan continued. "Sorry to have eavesdropped, but I didn't want to interrupt you. I take it you just closed another case?"

"Yeah. A four-year-old girl. A former neighbor admitted to killing her in a suicide note, but didn't say what he did with the body before he ate a gun. Despite the note, her parents held out hope. They needed answers."

Callahan muttered a curse. "I hope there is a special level of hell for people like the neighbor. Four years old, huh? They'll never get over it."

The authority with which Callahan spoke reminded Daniel that they had tragedies in common. Gabe had lost a child of about that age. A boy, if he recalled correctly. Lost him as a result of a car accident that had killed Callahan's first wife and had the boy fighting for his life in the hospital for months before finally losing the battle.

"No, they won't get over it. But having an answer will help them live with it."

"Like I said, you do important work. It's actually why I followed you out here. My brother Mark and I were talking about you just this morning."

"Oh?"

"Mark was an investigator with the army before he left the service and opened his own agency. One of the things he does is give seminars to cop shops about ways that private firms can assist the men in blue. He committed to speaking in

Portland, Oregon, the week after next, but his wife is having a seriously awful bout of morning sickness and he doesn't want to leave her. I suggested your name as a sub. Would you be interested?"

Daniel found the possibility surprisingly intriguing. "Possibly. I have commitments in Texas next week and I want to be back in Eternity Springs for the Fall Festival, but I have some free time in between. Although, it's been a long time since I've done a presentation of any sort. I'm afraid I'd be rusty."

"I'll bet you'd be great at it. Can I tell Mark to give you a call?"

"Sure."

Daniel mulled over the idea as he walked back to his cabin a short time later. When his phone rang with a call from a Texas area code as he started over the Angel Creek footbridge, he guessed that Gabe had wasted no time contacting his brother.

The conversation with Mark Callahan lasted twenty minutes, and by the time it ended, Daniel had agreed to give the seminar.

His original intention of going fishing

bright and early the next morning fizzled when he worked late into the night making notes about the presentation. The spark of enthusiasm he'd felt when Gabe Callahan rolled out the idea grew with the effort. When he finally went to bed, he did so with a lighter heart than he'd known for quite some time.

He dreamed of Shannon and awoke way too early the next morning to the ringing of his phone.

Groggy and with the woman on his mind, he growled, "Garrett."

"Mr. Daniel Garrett?"

"Yes."

"I'm Dr. Norris calling from Olivia Street Animal Clinic. We have your dog."

He lowered the phone and scowled down at the number. He didn't recognize the area code. He shouldn't have answered the phone. "You must have the wrong Daniel Garrett."

"Hmm, the database registry provided this phone number and the following address." He rattled off one that Daniel knew well.

"That's my old house." The home where

he'd lived a decade ago. The sheet fell away as Daniel sat up. His mouth was suddenly sandpaper dry. "I'm sorry. Who did you say you were with again?"

"Olivia Street Animal Clinic. The granddaughter of friends of mine found your dog wandering the neighborhood a week ago, wearing no collar or tags. They put signs up, but when nobody called, they brought her to me this morning to scan her for a chip. She's a bit beat up now, but I can tell she's been well cared for in the past. She's a sweet old girl. Slept the last week at the foot of the little girl's bed. You should update your database information with your new address, Mr. Garrett."

"Soupy?" Daniel asked, barely hoping to believe it. "You found Soupy?"

"If she's a brindle boxer around ten or twelve years old, then we found Soupy. You can pick her up at my clinic. I'm open until six today."

Oh, holy hell. Daniel massaged his brow, thinking as slow as molasses. Soupy? Justin's dog? He recalled Gail standing in their living room saying, **She's gone, Daniel. She's just gone.**

But now she'd been found? Soupy was alive. "Your clinic is where?"

"We're in Old Town. Just down the street from Hemingway Home. You can't miss us. It's a pink house. I made the unfortunate decision to let Shannon choose the paint color. There is parking for patients in the back."

Old Town. Hemingway Home. Shannon? Daniel had lived in the Boston area all his life and he'd never heard anyone use that term, and Hemingway's was a restaurant, not a house. An itch of suspicion crawled up his spine. Old Town. Hemingway.

Could he possibly be calling from Key West?

Daniel wasn't about to ask. He could track down the necessary information easily enough, and selfishly, he didn't want the vet looking for whoever had lost her last. Under the law, pets were chattel. It's finders keepers. Besides, Soupy had been wandering a neighborhood without a collar for a week. Whoever lost her hadn't responded to the notices and called. She apparently hadn't been tagged since the one he'd had placed.

Whoever lost her didn't deserve to keep her. And frankly, he was too excited to care if someone else might mourn her loss. He wanted her back.

"I'm in Colorado right now, Doctor. I don't think I'll be able to make it there in time to pick her up today, but I'll definitely be there tomorrow. If you'll keep her overnight for me, I'm happy to pay boarding. In fact, if you have an open appointment, I'd appreciate it if you'd give her a thorough exam. Will that be all right?"

"That's fine." Following a moment's pause, the man asked, "Yes. When did you lose Soupy, Mr. Garrett?"

Damned if his eyes didn't flood with moisture, and he had to clear the sudden lump from his throat before he spoke. "It's been a while. I'd given up hope of finding her. Thank you, Doctor. Losing her was hard. You don't how much it means to me to get her back."

"Little Shannon will be happy to hear that."

"The girl who found her is named Shannon?" Daniel smiled as he scrambled out of bed. "That's a beautiful name. Please tell

Shannon that she has made me very happy."

"I'll do that."

Daniel disconnected the call and went immediately to the Internet. Olivia Street Animal Clinic. Olivia Street. Dr. Norris. The search results proved his suspicions correct. "Unreal."

So, what was the fastest way to Key West from Eternity Springs? As he clicked over to a travel Web site, he thought of how his final words to the veterinarian had rolled off his tongue. Wonder if there's a message in that?

Shannon lay cozy and warm beneath her pillowy down comforter and gave herself five more minutes to snooze. She really didn't want to get up this morning. For these past few weeks she'd experienced a tiredness unlike any she'd ever known. She knew she'd feel peppier after teaching her yoga class, but right now, she'd love to call in sick. "Too bad your boss is such a slave driver," she murmured toward the ceiling.

She turned her head and gazed out the window where a steady rain fell. Weather like this only made leaving her bed all the more difficult. She wondered what the forecast was for the next few days. Sunny skies, she hoped. She'd really like to be having a good hair day if Daniel came into Murphy's.

Daniel. Stretching languidly, she indulged in a little smile. Yesterday, he'd sent her a cupcake from Sarah's bakery and a note that said he was thinking of her. It had made her go gooey like the frosting on top.

I could fall in love with him so easily.

That was the thought that finally drove her from her bed. She pulled on her bath-robe and stumbled toward the kitchen. She filled her electric teakettle and stood trying to decide between a turmeric and ginger blend of herbal tea or a chamomile one when she heard a knock on her door.

Shannon's brow furrowed. Ten minutes after seven and raining outside. Who in the world would be...?

She cinched the sash on her robe and walked to her front door, not really sur-prised when a glance through the peep-hole revealed the identity of her visitor. Who else came calling when she was in her bathrobe?

"Daniel?"

The confounded man walked right inside without waiting for an invitation. His eyes were shining. His smile, beaming. "Shannon, is it all possible for you to get away from town for a couple of days? The craziest thing has happened, and I have to go to Key West. I'd very much like you to come with me. I called in a favor and there will be a private plane waiting in Gunnison to take us to Florida."

"What? Why?"

"My dog. She found my dog." Happiness rang in his voice as he grabbed her around the waist and picked her up and twirled her around. "A little girl named Shannon found Soupy so I figure it's a sign. You should come with me. Please? I very much want you to come with me to get her."

The room spun a little. "Put me down, Daniel. I'm a little slow on the uptake this morning. Why do you have a dog in Florida?"

"Beats me. How she got from Boston to Key West will probably always be a mystery. I honestly thought Gail had her put down."

"Who's Gail?"

"My wife. Justin's mother."

Shannon took a step backward. "Wait a minute. Are you saying that somebody found your dog who disappeared almost a decade ago? In Florida?"

"Yes!" He told her about the phone call from the vet. "Tell me you'll come with me."

She couldn't miss the sparkle of joy in his eyes, an emotion she'd not witnessed in him previously. He looked like a schoolboy. "Ten years?"

"I know. It's crazy. I feel like a little kid at Christmas."

His excitement was infectious and Shannon found herself wanting to tell him yes. Better sense prevailed, however.

"I can't just pick up and leave." The irony of hearing herself say those particular words had her inwardly rolling her eyes. "I have a class to teach this morning. I have orders to place for Murphy's and tile to lay at Three Bears."

A glint of mischief joined the joy in his eyes. "Haven't you ever played hooky, sunshine?"

Sunshine? He said it like an endearment and it warmed her from the inside out.

"It's been a very long time," she confessed, hearing the yearning in her own voice.

"Let me tempt you."

"Daniel, that's all you've done since the day we met," she grumbled.

She hadn't been on an airplane since the second time Russell found her. She couldn't afford to have her real name on a flight manifest, and she hadn't trusted her new identification enough to risk a TSA check. A private plane negated that concern. She loved Eternity Springs, but it would be really nice to get away for just a little bit. On a private plane, no less! She'd never flown on a private plane, and Key West was someplace she'd always wanted to visit.

However, it **was** a public place. A very public place. Lots and lots of tourists. Tourists with cameras who posted their trip photos on Facebook. No, she couldn't go with him. It was too risky. Going would be stupid.

So wear sunglasses. Wear a hat. Eternity Springs has tourists with cameras, too. I don't wear a hat and sunglasses every time I go out in public

here. It could be argued that I'd be safer there than I am here at home.

"I can't go, Daniel. My class—"

"Get a sub," he interrupted. "When was the last time you took a vacation, Shannon?"

"I can't afford a vacation." In more ways than one.

"Then isn't it handy that the whole trip is on my dime? Look, if you're worried about sleeping arrangements, don't. I'm not expecting you to sleep with me. I know someone who owns a vacation house there, so I called in a marker. We have a four-bedroom house to ourselves."

She couldn't resist him. She didn't want to resist him. For that matter, she didn't want to sleep in separate bedrooms, either.

She wanted to tell him yes. After all, this wasn't an ordinary trip to the pound to pick up your average runaway dog. She was honored to have been asked to go with him on such a personal journey.

Dare she say yes? The chances of running into Russell in Key West were remote. Florida was a long way from Chicago, the most recent address she had for him, and he wasn't a sun-and-surf kind of guy. As far as pictures went, well, if she were careful with the sunglasses and hats, she should be as safe as she was here.

"How much time do I have to get ready?"

"You'll come with me?"

"I will."

Delight filled his expression. He leaned down and smacked her loudly on the lips. "You have an hour and a half, but an hour would be better."

"I'll be ready in an hour."

He no sooner left than she began to second-guess herself. Twice she almost called him to renege. But as a result of having to live a life of lies, she'd promised herself that unless it involved Russell, she would always keep her word. If she canceled on Daniel now, she'd be breaking a promise to them both.

Packing a suitcase took no time at all since she kept one packed at all times. Actually, she kept two packed, a summer and a winter case. She did add a few items —the yellow sundress she'd worn to Gabi's wedding, a bathing suit, and a wide-brimmed straw sun hat. It took her longer to contact Honey and Lillian and make arrangements about the pub and yoga class, respectively. Lillian didn't answer her phone and Honey wouldn't hang hers up. Nevertheless, when Daniel pulled up in front of her house, she was ready to go.

"I pray this isn't a mistake." She picked up her suitcase, switched off her lights, and stepped outside to begin her adventure.

After the two-hour drive to Gunnison, they grabbed lunch then continued on to the regional airport where they boarded a sleek six-passenger Cessna Citation that belonged to Gabe Callahan's brothers' security firm. "I'm helping them out with something next week—that out-of-town trip I mentioned—and Mark made a big deal about putting the jet at my disposal. I hesitated to call for something so personal, but it's not easy to get to Key West from Eternity Springs. I'm afraid if I delayed getting there, it'd be just my luck that whoever lost her might finally go looking for her. They've had a week. They've had their chance as far as I'm concerned. Mark is a dog lover too, so he gets it."

"The Callahan brothers are good people."

"That they are."

Fatigue caught up with Shannon during the long flight, and she slept quite a bit. She awoke when they landed to refuel, then promptly fell asleep again shortly after takeoff. She woke up to find herself tucked into a blanket, and Daniel nearing the end of a novel he'd started well into their flight. "I'm sorry. I'm poor company."

"Not at all. As hard as you work, I imagine sometimes you'd like to sleep for a week."

The tender smile he gave her made her want to snuggle up against him like a kitten. "I like to stay busy, but I admit it's caught up to me lately. Napping like this has been a lovely indulgence. So, how's your book?"

"Good. I like suspense. Speaking of which, a little angel in Eternity Springs told me you're a writer?"

Shannon didn't want to talk about her writing with him. Daniel was too perceptive. Giving a dismissive shrug, she said, "It's something to do on long winter nights."

One corner of his mouth lifted in a crooked smile. "That, Ms. O'Toole, is a hanging curveball for a man trying to keep his mind off sex."

"Oh. Sorry." She meant it, too. Not because she'd sent his mind traveling down that road, but because his comment had hers heading down that path, too.

Is that so terrible? Would it be a spectacular mistake to enjoy this unexpected gift of time away from the realities of her situation? Though he seemed determined to be a gentleman about it, Daniel obviously was open to the idea. Since she'd already decided to tell him about the baby, didn't it make sense to attempt to forge a stronger bond between them?

Not based on lies, no. Every moment she didn't tell him compounded the lie.

Not true, she argued with herself. She was still very early in her pregnancy. Her first pregnancy. Before over-the-counter pregnancy tests, she wouldn't have even known for sure that she'd conceived a child with Daniel Garrett. Women didn't always tell their husbands this early in a pregnancy, much less their one-night stands.

Lots of justification there. How did that saying go? The saddest lies were the ones you told yourself?

So, why not change reality? Why not make him something more than a one-night stand? Shannon turned her head and glanced down at her shoulder, halfway expecting to see a little red devil perched there.

"So," she said with false brightness. "How long until we land?"

Daniel glanced at his watch. "Less than half an hour now."

Shannon tore her gaze away from his wrist. She couldn't recall ever before thinking that a man's wrists were sexy. His were. They were substantial like his shoulders. Everything about Daniel Garrett was substantial.

Oh, man, she was getting in deep.

"I'm nervous," he admitted with a sheepish smile. "It's ridiculous."

Glad for the distraction, she said, "Nervous about what?"

He blew out a long breath. "Damned if I know."

Shannon knew in that moment that everything else aside, she'd made the right decision to accompany him to Key West.

He needed a friend. She could be that for him at least.

Preparing for their arrival, Shannon removed her contact lenses and donned the oversized glasses she'd taken to wearing during the tourist-crowded days of summer in Eternity Springs. As camouflage during after-dark public activities, they served their purpose. Daniel did a double take upon seeing her.

"I slept too long in my contacts," she explained.

"I love them. It's the sexy secretary look. Take 'em off and chew on the arm and give me a little thrill."

"Oh, hush," she said with a laugh.

He replied with that same boyish grin he'd shown her that morning, and in that instant, Shannon fell a little bit more in love.

Chapter Nine

Daniel led a bright-eyed Shannon through the small Key West airport. They'd arrived in between any incoming or departing flights, so the place was deserted. "Good timing," he told her. "When my brothers and I came here on a fishing trip last time, the taxi line took almost an hour to work our way through. I'll call a cab if none are waiting."

He shouldn't have been surprised to find a car waiting for them at the curb. He asked the driver, "I guess the Callahans arranged for the ride?"

"No, Detective Garrett. Mr. Winsted hired me." He reached into the car and removed a bouquet of roses, which he handed to Shannon. "He said to tell you welcome to Key West on his behalf."

"How nice!" she said, delight adding color to her face that paired perfectly with the roses. She lifted the flowers to her face and inhaled the fragrance, and Daniel felt a stirring of desire as old as time.

Gary Winsted was a very nice man. An investment banker who had retired at the ripe old age of forty-two, Gary was the older brother of a woman whom Daniel had cleared of murder back before he left the police department. Gary's gratitude knew no bounds and he'd taken Daniel's purpose on as one of his own, making countless donations of time and treasure to the cause of missing children through the years.

Daniel and his brothers had stayed at Gary's house on their fishing trip, so he knew what to expect. It freed him to enjoy Shannon's reaction to the fullest at the end of their short journey to their destination. "Wow," she said. "This is lovely."

He switched on the outside lights illuminating the backyard, and she laughed with delight. "It's Cinderella's castle!"

"Gary has boys, but his sister has two girls. He dotes."

"I love it."

From out of nowhere, an unbidden thought floated through his mind. **Me. Love me.**

The idea left him shaken. **Whoa, there, buckaroo. Where the hell did that come from?**

A long travel day. That was it. He was tired. He was anxious about picking up Soupy tomorrow. "I'm hungry. Why don't we go find something to eat?"

"Sounds great."

"Seafood?"

"Absolutely."

"Excellent. I know a place that's a little off the beaten path. About a ten-minute walk from here. Unless you have your heart set on strolling up Duvall first thing?"

"Off the beaten path suits me perfectly. What should I wear?"

"It's a white-tablecloth place."

When she joined him in the living room ten minutes later, she wore the yellow sundress she'd worn to Gabi and Flynn's wedding and looked even more beautiful than she had the day they'd met.

The restaurant was dark and intimate, the food delicious. They both chose grouper, which led him to relay fish tales about the fishing trip with his brothers. When he managed to get Shannon laughing in stitches over the silly antics of Team Garrett as one of them attempted to land a sixty-pound fish, he felt as if he'd hung the moon.

Over dessert, conversation turned toward the following day. "What would you like to do after our trip to the vet clinic? Want to take any tours? Go parasailing or ride a Jet Ski or something more active? Anyplace specific you've been dreaming of visiting? I figure we'll watch the sunset from Mallory Square tomorrow night. We have to do that."

"Yes." Shannon sipped the sparkling water she'd ordered with her meal. "Honestly, I'm happy as a clam just walking around. I wouldn't mind lazing by the pool at the house, either, while you become reacquainted with Soupy. That is why we're here, after all."

"Sounds like a plan to me."

As they left the restaurant following dinner, he was far from ready to see the evening come to an end. "Can I tempt you with a walk on the beach or would you prefer a rowdier Duvall Street?"

"The beach. Definitely the beach."

He called for the car to take them to Smathers Beach. Upon reaching it, he rolled up his cuffs, and they both took off their shoes to stroll barefoot on the sand.

Without conscious thought, he took her

hand. It was a beautiful night with a huge full moon and a gentle breeze off the receding tide. They walked without speaking, the mood between them comfortable and mellow. The sound of the gentle surf was soothing; the woman at his side, exciting.

The urge to take her in his arms and kiss her was as natural as breathing, and Daniel made no attempt to resist it.

She placed her hands on his shoulders, then slid them up, lacing her fingers behind his neck. Her mouth was wet and hot and she tasted of chocolate and raspberries from the dessert she'd ordered. Daniel decided he liked chocolate very much, after all.

Daniel released her reluctantly when the kiss ended. He gently stroked his knuckles down the softness of her cheek. "Thank you for coming with me, Shannon."

"Thank you for inviting me."

"Want to walk some more?"

Her eyes were big brown pools of emotion in the starlight. "Why don't we go back to the house? Let's go to bed."

He saw it in her expression, but for both their sakes, he clarified. "Together?"

"Yes, Daniel. Together. I want you. Take me home and make love to me. Please?"

"It will be my pleasure."

And it was. It most definitely was.

Shannon awoke warmer than she could remember—since August, anyway—and with blue bedroom eyes staring down at her. Daniel lay on his side, propped up on his elbow, his head pillowed in his large hand. When their gazes met, he slowly smiled. "Good morning."

"Good morning." She smiled back at him easily. She hadn't felt this way in a very long time. She was happy. Genuinely happy. Content. Dare she hope that he might actually be "the one" for her?

He definitely was one of the good guys. He'd be so easy to love, but then, loving wasn't the problem, was it? Trusting him was. Could she trust him with the secret of her past, especially now that she had the baby to consider? The baby's safety had to come first.

"Are you rested?" he asked.

Her grin turned rueful. "Not particularly, considering."

"Complaining?"

"Not at all. How long have you been awake and watching me?"

"Not long. Not long enough. I could do it all day."

"Well, you don't have all day. We have to get up and get ready to go get your dog."

"Yeah." Joy leaped in his eyes. "We do, don't we? We don't want to be late, either. Why don't we shower together to save time?"

Shannon rolled her eyes. "Something tells me that wouldn't save any time at all. Besides, there's more than one shower in this house. I looked."

"Spoilsport." He leaned down and kissed her once, hard. "In that case, I'll go make coffee."

He rolled from the bed and picked up his boxers from the chair where he'd tossed them last night. Shannon sat up and watched him pull them on with frank appreciation. Large all over, the man was built. "You can still change your mind about the shower," he said, noting her interest.

She made a shooing gesture with her hand. "Just enjoying the scenery."

When he was in the kitchen, Shannon climbed out of bed and pulled on the robe she'd hung in the closet when she'd unpacked. She showered and toweled dry, spying the razor burn on her skin with a touch of smugness, then took a few extra minutes with her hair and makeup. After a moment's debate, she dressed in khaki capri pants and a forest-green top. If Soupy was a jumper, she probably didn't want to be wearing shorts, and she could always change into shorts later if she got hot.

She found a steaming cup of coffee along with a tray of bread and pastries, a bowl of fruit, and a selection of yogurts waiting for her when she exited the bedroom. Suddenly starving, she wondered who had stocked the larder and when. She yearned for a cinnamon roll but, thinking of the baby's nutritional needs, chose to begin with a yogurt instead. She could always indulge in a roll for dessert.

After all, she'd burned a lot of calories last night.

She was grinning when movement in the backyard caught her notice. Dressed in shorts and a fishing shirt, Daniel paced nervously beside the backyard pool as he talked on the phone. Concern rolled over Shannon. She hoped the vet hadn't called with some sort of dire news.

Spying her in the kitchen window, he waved for her to join him, so she grabbed an apple from a basket of fruit on the counter and stepped outside. She eavesdropped and discovered that he was talking to Mark Callahan. Good. So glad the call had nothing to do with Soupy.

Shannon sat at the edge of the pool and dipped her feet into the water. Heated. Very nice. Daniel ended the call and she asked, "Everything okay?"

"Yeah. Just making arrangements for my upcoming trip. You look gorgeous."

"Thank you. You look pretty fine, yourself. I like that shirt." The color matched his eyes. Seemed like the sort of thing a girlfriend would give him.

"Thanks. My mom gave it to me for Christmas. You found breakfast?"

"I did. The poppy-seed roll was fabulous."

Daniel hooked a thumb over his shoulder. "There's a bakery right across the alley. So, are you ready to go?"

"I am."

"Let's head that way then."

He grabbed the leash he'd bought in Eternity Springs the previous morning while she donned her sunglasses and a hat. They headed out. She sensed the tension growing in him with every block they walked. When they turned a corner and the bubblegum-pink siding of the Olivia Street Animal Clinic came into view, he sucked in an audible breath. "I'm a real head case. She's a dog. Just a dog."

"No 'just' about it, Daniel. She's **your** dog."

And he didn't have many "yours," did he? Not that he knew about, anyway. Yet.

At that thought, Shannon grew as nervous as he was. To distract them both, she said, "I've never been a fan of that shade of pink, but I must say, it's a happy color. Do dogs see in color, I wonder?"

Distractedly, he said, "I think so. I believe they're more limited than humans in the colors they see."

They started up the front walk and Daniel said, "Justin liked hats. He was always putting things on his head. He had cowboy hats and baseball caps and a little football helmet one of my brothers gave him. But he also made hats out of Tupperware bowls and pots. His absolute favorites were those pointed birthday-party hats. And of course, Soupy had to wear one, too. Damned if the dog didn't let him put it on her." A gruff note entered his voice as he added, "I'll never forget the two of them running around the backyard wearing birthday hats with red, blue, and yellow balloons on them."

Shannon touched his arm in silent support and they walked into the clinic.

The receptionist seated behind a desk looked up at them and smiled. "Mr. and Mrs. Garrett?"

The "Mrs." gave Shannon a bit of a jolt. She opened her mouth to correct her, but Daniel spoke first. "Yes."

"I'm Polly. I gave your little lady a bath this morning. She's just a doll. If you want to have a seat, I'll tell Dr. Norris you're here."

"Thanks."

Shannon took a seat on one of the waiing area's chairs. She wasn't surprised that Daniel remained standing, his hands shoved into his pants pockets. Leaning against the wall, he stood staring intently at the door through which Polly had disappeared, as stiff as she'd ever seen him.

The door began to swing open. Daniel straightened away from the wall.

Shannon saw a smushed black muzzle surrounded by a salty, brindle coat, a cute underbite, and big brown eyes. But she only gave Soupy a cursory look because, once again, Daniel drew her gaze like a magnet. When he spied the dog, a spasm of emotion flashed across his face, a heart-wrenching combination of joy and grief. Soupy's nub of a tail wiggled happily, and she strained the vet's leash toward Daniel. Shannon watched with a lump in her throat as he sank to his knees and those strong arms of his wrapped around the dog's neck. A long red tongue licked at his face and Daniel laughed, a sound of pure, unadulterated joy that she'd never heard from him before. Then he buried his head against his long-lost Soupy's neck, and his broad shoulders shook with a silent shudder.

Shannon's heart melted as she tumbled the rest of the way into love.

"She looks good for a dog who's going on

eleven. Don't you think she looks good?" Daniel knew he was babbling, but he couldn't seem to stop it.

"I think she looks great." Shannon gazed at him with indulgent amusement. "I especially like the parrots on her collar."

Daniel tried to frown, but he had trouble wiping the smile from his face to do it. "That's fine for Key West, but we'll have to get her something more dignified for Eternity Springs."

"Celeste sells dog collars with angel's wings on them in the Angel's Rest gift shop."

"A plain leather collar will be just fine. Maybe something red. So, have you figured out what you want to do?"

While Daniel had been going over the results of Soupy's exam with Dr. Norris, Polly had given Shannon a list of pet-friendly tourist activities in Key West. He'd admitted to a measure of concern about parading the boxer around in public—the last thing he wanted was for a kid to coming running up and thank him for finding his lost dog, but Polly had soothed those fears, saying, "I wouldn't worry. Anyone looking for her would have called the SPCA and the vet offices on the island. That didn't happen. As much as I hate to say it, people dump older dogs all the time."

He knew that to be true, so he relaxed and decided he'd enjoy the day. After all, he was in a beautiful place with a beautiful woman and man's best friend. And, he'd gotten laid last night. What could be better?

"I wouldn't mind visiting the botanical gardens; I'm a sucker for plants and flowers. But we'll need to take a cab."

"Actually our driver from last night is on call. He said to text him with an address whenever we wanted to be picked up."

"Seriously? You know, between private planes and personal cars, I could get accustomed to hanging around with wealthy people."

Daniel sent the text. "Having money does make life easier in many ways, but in my experience, it doesn't necessarily make them any happier than the average Joe."

"True. That's very true."

The comment resonated with a note of knowledge that he found curious, and he was about to ask her about it when Soupy spied a squirrel and suddenly started barking and yanking at the leash. "Whoa there, honeybunch. You don't need to go chasing squirrels." Tossing Shannon a grin, he added, "Guess she still has some get-up-and-go in her, after all."

They spent a couple of hours exploring the gardens. Shannon expressed a love for plants and flowers, and Daniel filed away the bit of information about flowers. He'd have to send her flowers sometime. Admittedly, he was out of practice with this sort of thing, but surely women still liked getting flowers from men. He tried to recall if Eternity Springs had a flower shop, but he couldn't remember seeing one. So what do the men do for romantic gestures? He'd have to ask.

Of course, that would mean going public with his relationship with Shannon. Was he ready to do that?

Shoot, don't be ridiculous. It's a small town. They know what you eat for breakfast, where you hide your money, and when was the last time you went to church. Of course they know who you're sleeping with.

Returning to Old Town from the botanical

gardens, they killed the rest of the morning at the dog park and beach. Daniel discovered that Soupy loved playing fetch in the surf and that Shannon looked like a million bucks in a swimsuit. Neither fact surprised him.

After burgers at a restaurant that not only welcomed Soupy, but served her a burger of her own, they returned to the house for a nap. Together. Now Shannon slept soundly beside him, all pink and rosy from love-making. It was shaping up to be as nice a day as he could remember in...a decade.

A decade. Memories fluttered on the edges of his mind and chased him away from Shannon's side. In the kitchen, he downed two full glasses of water, then cracked a beer and stepped out into the backyard. Soupy followed on his heels, seeming to be as anxious to remain at his side as he was to have her there. She plopped down at his feet when he sat on a bench beside the pool.

Daniel idly scratched her above the collar and allowed the memories to come. For the first time in a very long time, he thought about Gail.

He had loved her with all the passion and innocence of youth. She'd been his first—his only—until long after her death. Starry-eyed high school sweethearts, struggling young marrieds, parents head-over-heels in love with being parents. They'd basically grown up together and she'd left a handprint on his heart that remained today, almost a decade after she had left him.

He hadn't forgiven her for that.

Beyond the heat of the moment, he'd not held losing Justin against her. He'd have done exactly the same thing had he been in the food court that day. What he hadn't forgiven her for was killing herself. Why should she be at peace when he lived with this crushing grief all the time?

He needed to let that go. He needed to find forgiveness in his heart for the weakness that grief had carved into hers.

He'd never quite been ready to do that. Until now.

Until Shannon.

He sensed that in order to move forward, he needed to let go of the resentment, the anger, and the blame he'd nursed toward his wife because she'd left him to grieve alone.

He lifted his gaze to the cerulean sky above where a snowwhite gull sailed on the salty sea breeze. Not exactly a dove with an olive branch, but close enough.

"And there's your sign," he murmured.

For a long time and in ways he'd not allowed himself to do since coming home to find her that horrible spring day, he reflected on his past with the woman whom he'd loved and honored. With the memories, the stormy seas of a decade began to calm. Finally, with Soupy snoring contentedly at his feet, he sensed that he had turned a corner. He repeated a gesture he'd seen Gail do in the weeks after they'd buried their son. Daniel kissed his fingertips and blew the kiss toward the sky. Softly, he said, "I forgive you, baby."

When Soupy nudged his leg and then licked his hand, he felt as if Gail and Justin had sent him a kiss in return.

With a newfound sense of peace in his heart, Daniel went inside and opened his laptop, intending to do a little work while waiting for Shannon to awake. Two hours later, he finally heard her stir. "That's what I call a power nap," he said when she exited the bedroom.

"I'm sorry. I'm embarrassed. I guess I still needed to catch up on my sleep."

"Hey, don't apologize. It helps my fragile masculine ego to think I wore you out."

"Fragile. Right."

She snagged a leftover cinnamon roll and scarfed it down. When she licked her fingers lustily, it was all he could do not to drag her back to bed. But it was her first time in Key West and since they were leaving tomorrow, tonight would be her only sunset. They had to go to Mallory Square.

"Are you ready to get out and play tourist some more? I thought we could wander through the shops and grab a snack on our way to watch the sunset. We'll do dinner afterward if that suits you?"

"Absolutely."

Daniel wasn't a shopper; he was a buyer. If he needed something, he went to the store and bought it. So he never had been one to wander from store to store gawking at baubles, but he knew that's what most women liked to do. He followed her inside the ones that welcomed dogs on a leash and waited patiently outside those that didn't. She bought gifts for the manager at Murphy's and Celeste, but mostly, she jotted down notes in a little leather notebook she carried in her bag.

"Okay, I fail as a detective," Daniel finally said. "What's with the notes?"

"This is a tropical Eternity Springs on a larger scale. I'm doing intel to share with our shopkeepers for items they could carry in their stores."

"You're always working, aren't you?"

"I like to keep busy."

They puttered their way up Duvall Street toward Mallory Square, and as the afternoon wore on, the street grew more crowded—and Shannon went quiet. What had he done wrong? he wondered. He was picking up a signal of some sort, but he didn't know her well enough to read exactly what. While she tarried in an art glass shop similar to Gabi's Whimsies, he reviewed their conversations. "I'm a typically clueless male," he said to Soupy.

She bought a new pair of sunglasses and a filmy scarf in one shop, a second sun hat with a big floppy brim in another. "You could be a Hollywood star going incognito," he told her. "That's a movie star look if I've ever seen one." He hesitated a beat, then added, "Though I can't think of any actress as beautiful as you."

"You're blind, but thank you."

She seemed to relax after that, so he guessed his compliment made up for whatever slight he'd given her.

They arrived at Mallory Square an hour and forty minutes before sunset and watched the street performers do tricks on a unicycle and walk a high wire. A juggler whose performance sign read mark the magnificent juggled plates and knives and flaming torches. Soupy seemed a little too interested in the performing cats, so Daniel moved them along. He bought minty mojitos from a stand—virgin for her, since she claimed her head was already spinning from people-watching—and thick, warm pretzels, which they ate while listening to a talented steel drum trio.

"This is a zoo," she said, when a couple wearing clown paint and orange wigs walked by, followed by a man walking on his hands.

"Definitely an experience." Daniel secured them a prime viewing spot as the drone of a bagpipe rose from somewhere to their right. "Looks like there are just enough clouds to make this a spectacular sunset."

"I remember reading something about ocean sunsets. The salt in the air reflects light differently and changes the intensity of the colors. It's been a very long time since I've seen an ocean sunset."

"You should take your sunglasses off so you see the colors, honey."

Shannon hesitated a moment before following his suggestion. "Wow, it is gorgeous, isn't it?"

He glanced down at her and discovered he couldn't look away. An ocean sunset had nothing on Shannon O'Toole when it came to gorgeous. "Fiery like your hair when sunlight hits it."

Just as the sky went ablaze in shades of gold, orange, and red, the American flag atop a nearby pole began to whip. The formerly gentle breeze turned suddenly gusty, and beside him, Shannon said, "Oh, no!"

Daniel saw her floppy hat go sailing over the railing. It turned a pair of slow flips before landing in water below them. Though he was smarter than to say it to her, he thought to himself, **Good riddance.** He wanted to see her face. He loved looking at her.

Now, though, she looked a little distressed. He hated to see that. Ever the helpful companion, he reassured her, "Don't worry. The shops here stay open late. We can stop by after dinner and buy you another one."

"Yes, let's do that."

The subdued note in her voice surprised him. It was just an inexpensive hat. She'd paid seven dollars for it. Why act as if it'd cost a hundred?

Something didn't click. Daniel's cop's antenna twitched. Was she afraid of something? Someone?

Before he could pursue the thought, Soupy distracted him with a tug on her leash as a bulldog waddled over to her and the two dogs sniffed each other's butts.

"What a pretty silver girl," said the man of around Daniel's father's age who held the bulldog's leash. "How old is she?"

"She'll be eleven in the spring."

"I've always loved boxers. Our dog before Sergeant, here, was a boxer."

While the two men talked dogs, Shannon kept her gaze focused on the sunset. Daniel listened to the bulldog's owner with divided attention. What was the deal with his date? When the bulldog and his owner moved on, Daniel prepared to confront her when the young blonde standing next to Shannon said, "Excuse me, miss? Would you mind taking our picture? We're on our honeymoon, and I'd love to have one picture that's not a selfie."

"Oh. Sure. Congratulations."

"Thank you," the groom said, giving his bride a tender smile as she touched the camera app on her screen and handed Shannon her phone. "We're very happy."

Shannon lifted the camera, then stepped backward a few paces. The crowd around her politely faded back and allowed the space Shannon needed to snap a picture of the honeymoon couple. "Beautiful. Let me try one more."

The camera clicked. Shannon lowered the phone. The bride stepped toward her to take it.

A male voice said, "Chelsea?"

Chapter Ten

Shannon's blood drained toward her flip-flops.

"Chelsea Abbott? Is that really you?"

She stopped breathing as an icy hand closed around her heart. **Oh, God. Oh, God, no.**

Time slowed to a crawl. She didn't need to turn to see who called her name. Her mouth went sour with fear as she recognized the voice. Not at all sinister, but one still a bit high-pitched for a man. A nerdy voice for a nerdy boy, he'd once told her. Not the one voice she feared most in this world—but a solid number two. Three, at the very least. Alden Findley. One of the Musketeers. One for all and all for one. Alden had been Athos to Ted's Porthos, and Russell's Aramis, charter members all of AnonyBytes, the hacker group organized by Russell that had grown to over fifteen members and caused her nothing but grief.

What do I do? Please, God. What on earth do I do?

She had a split second to decide between the only two choices that occurred. Run or try to brazen it out?

She flicked her gaze toward Daniel. He watched her with a mildly interested stare that suddenly flickered with interest. **Time has run out.**

Pasting on a bright smile and hoping that nobody noticed the pounding pulse at her neck, she finally looked toward Alden. He wore a navy fishing shirt and cargo shorts and had lost most of his hair since the last time she'd seen him. Since Ted's funeral. Adding a breathy note to her voice in an effort to disguise it, she said, "Are you speaking to me? You've mistaken me for someone else. My name is Shannon."

"Oh. Well. Wow." He glanced toward Daniel, and then back toward her. "They say everyone has a doppelgänger. I went to college with yours."

"You know, I've heard that before." She exaggerated a gesture toward the western sky and effectively dismissed him by saying, "Enjoy your sunset."

Then she turned her attention back toward Daniel, slipping her hand through the crook of his elbow—appreciating the support for her still weak knees—and led him beyond Alden's range of hearing. "It's good to know that Soupy is dog friendly," she babbled. "It'll make life much easier for you in Eternity Springs since you can't walk down the street there without meeting someone out walking their dog."

She was glad that twilight was falling fast. Otherwise he might see the guilt that rippled through her eyes.

"Shannon—" he began.

She interrupted as if she hadn't heard him and put her arms around his neck. Her fingers naturally found the short, crisp hair at his nape. She'd discovered the previous night how much she'd liked the feel of his thick hair against her fingers. "This has been a truly wonderful trip. I badly needed a vacation, and I don't think I even realized it. Thank you so much for inviting me."

His hands settled around her waist, and he pulled her against him as she went up on her tiptoes and kissed him. She'd intended it to be a short thank-you kiss on his firm lips, but his mouth was hot and minty and masculine and compelled her to linger.

As did the fact that his broad shoulders shielded her and his powerful arms cradled her, his solid strength a safe, protective port in her storm. If she could stay here forever, she would.

To think that not two minutes before Alden said her name, she'd seriously considered telling Daniel about the baby tonight. It would have been a risk. If he didn't take the news well, the trip home tomorrow could have been awkward. But these past couple of days had been so wonderful, and she'd felt so encouraged and hopeful and, well, guilty over keeping the news to herself. She'd almost...almost... been ready to tell him.

Being seen by Alden changed all of that.

What a fool she'd been to come here. She'd feared photographs and face recognition software. She'd not seriously worried about actually coming face-to-face with someone who knew Chelsea Abbott. Panic flooded through her once again. Her heart thudded painfully. She'd have to run now. Wouldn't she?

She didn't know. She needed to think,

and she had trouble thinking at all when he kissed her. What was the best thing to do for the baby? The baby came first.

His mouth released hers and his lips trailed across her jaw toward her ear. "Better stop that. Otherwise I'm liable to throw you over my shoulder and cart you back to the house. I need dinner first."

"Oh, yeah?" she asked lightly. "I think I'm insulted."

"Don't be. Fuel for a long night ahead."

"Ahh." She went for a smile, but she knew what she managed was shaky.

The rest of the evening didn't go much better. Walking along Duvall, she caught herself glancing over her shoulder too often and yammering on too much. She feared Daniel would pick up on her nervousness.

Of course he'll pick up on my nervousness. The man's a detective!

Sure enough, over dinner she noticed him watching her with narrowed, speculative eyes, so she knew she had a problem. Better head it off now.

You could always tell him about the baby.

Maybe that's what she should do. As

distractions went, she probably couldn't do any better.

Over the years she'd become adept at lying, but she found the thought of lying outright to Daniel even more distasteful than lying to her friends in Eternity Springs. So she told him a truth. Not **the** truth, but a truth. She shared an event that actually happened. "I'm sorry if I'm not good company tonight. That guy made me nervous."

"The man who called you Chelsea?"

Hearing her name on his lips made her stomach do a slow flip. Of course he'd remembered it. Her luck wouldn't allow anything else. "A few years ago some guy mistook me for a friend of his wife's who he blamed for his divorce. He followed me when I left work and cornered me at my car."

Daniel went momentarily still, then slowly lowered his fork. "Oh? Did he hurt you?"

"An openhanded slap, but I felt it for a week afterward."

His lips tightened. "I hope you pressed charges."

"In hindsight, I should have. But I was young, and I let his lawyer talk me out of it." The money the attorney had given her made the decision easy. She'd been broke as a church mouse at that point. "At the time I just wanted to forget the whole thing. Ever since then I'm a little weird about being approached the way that guy did. So, distract me, Mr. Garrett. You've known the Romanos longer than I have. Tell me something about one of them that I don't know."

"You want to spend our last night in Key West gossiping?"

"No..." She made a show of plucking the maraschino cherry from the top of her virgin piña colada and sucking it suggestively. "But you haven't finished refueling yet."

Daniel eyed the surf and turf on his plate and picked up his steak knife and fork. "Mind if we skip dessert?"

Daniel drove to Texas for his work there the following week, so it was no problem to bring Soupy along. When he finished in Dallas, he traveled west to the Callahans' place in Brazos Bend because they'd insisted on sending him and his dog to Portland on their private plane. "We're dog people, Daniel," Mark had said. "It's too soon after your reunion for you two to be separated, and I don't like the thought of her riding in the cargo on a commercial plane. Take the Cessna. It's only right. You're doing us a solid."

"As you did me with the Key West flight."

"Piece of advice. Don't argue with a Callahan when we're set on something. It's a waste of breath. Besides, I'm trying to lure you into the fold. Let me dangle my perks. I'll be cranky otherwise."

So he and Soupy flew in the private jet to Oregon and stayed in a pet-friendly hotel. The conference was interesting. His presentation went great, the information he shared was well received, and he fielded questions long past his allotted time. Afterward, the conference organizers asked him to sit in on a panel scheduled for the last afternoon of the conference, so it was late Friday night before he returned home.

Home. Funny how right the term felt. Except for the years away at college, he'd lived in the Boston area all his life. Why did this little valley now seem like it was where he belonged? Why did he awake humming with a positive energy that he almost didn't recognize when he opened his eyes in Eternity Springs?

Daniel thought he might be flirting with the idea of being happy.

Eternity Springs had some powerful mojo.

So did Shannon O'Toole.

They'd spoken twice on the phone while he was gone. Their date tomorrow for the school festival remained on the schedule, after which she'd offered to cook dinner. He couldn't wait.

He knocked on Shannon's front door at precisely ten o'clock. She opened the door and smiled first at Daniel, then her gaze dropped to his dog. "Seriously, Daniel?"

"Hey, don't blame me." He followed the path of her gaze to the dog, who wore a princess costume, complete with a tutu of turquoise blue net. "I'm humiliated on Soup's behalf."

"I take it she's entered in the pet beauty pageant?"

"Holly's idea. I can't say no to that girl. Apparently there's a senior division."

"Well, turquoise is a good color on her."

"I voted for red, but Soupy thought it made her look slutty. You ready to go?"

"I am. Let me grab my purse and the cake I made for the cake walk."

"Cake walk?"

"Musical chairs with cakes for prizes. You should plan to participate in the final round of the night. I'm told it's become quite a traditional battle between the men in town. And Gabi. Everyone is glad she'll miss it this year because of her honeymoon. She apparently fights dirtier than anybody. The prize is her mother's Italian cream cake."

"Is it now?" he said with interest. "It's well worth fighting for."

They dropped Shannon's cake off at the school and continued on to the scene of the day's outdoor events, Davenport Park. Daniel felt a little better once he spied the ridiculous costumes some of the other pets wore. "People really get into the spirit of this sort of thing, don't they?"

"In small towns, schools and churches tend to be at the center of residents' social lives. This is the largest fund-raiser of the fall, so people like to support it. It's also one of the few festivals in town that are primarily for locals, rather than aimed at bringing in tourists. So, locals aren't busy working the event as much as they are participating in it, which makes for a more relaxed atmosphere. Today is all about fun—fun and a new HVAC system for the school."

"I can support that. Soup is ready to do her part. Holly told me to have her at the baseball diamond at ten-thirty. Luckily for me, she volunteered to handle the leash during the competition."

"I think the pet beauty pageant is like a stock show presentation," Shannon said. "Children always present the animals."

"Ah."

They arrived at the baseball diamond to see a collection of their friends and their pets, including Cam Murphy's devil dog, a Boston terrier named Mortimer. "They are seriously entering that dog in a beauty pageant?"

"Not this year. I do believe Cam and the PTA reached an agreement that Mortimer wouldn't defend his title again this year."

"His title?"

"He's the defending champion. Two years running."

Daniel shot her a doubting look. Shannon

shrugged. "People like underdogs. What can I say? Though he didn't win any friends when he ate his trophy."

Holly Montgomery's excited voice called out. "Daniel! Soupy Lou looks wonderful! Where's her princess hat?"

He turned to see the eleven-year-old rushing toward him. As always when he spied the girl, gladness filled his heart. She was his little miracle. He slipped the backpack he carried off his shoulder and dug inside it until he found the conical hat. "I couldn't get her to leave it on. Maybe you'll have better luck."

"I'll put it on her right when we start."

Daniel watched with amusement as his friends—females first—realized that he and Shannon attended the festival as a pair. Elbow nudges and widened eyes and significant looks spread the word. The fact that to a person, approval and encouragement lit their eyes shouldn't have mattered, but it did. His Eternity Springs friends cared about him.

"That dog looks stupid in a skirt," Zach Turner said.

"Wrong." Savannah gave her husband a

hip shove. "You're just afraid of competition for Ace."

"Different divisions," he fired back.

After a skirmish between two dogs interrupted the conversation, Cam and Sarah's adopted son, Devin, made the rounds collecting entry fees for the pageant. "Fifty bucks?" Daniel said, opening his wallet. "Little steep, isn't it? Shouldn't Soup get a senior discount?"

"Have you priced HVAC units recently?" the young man asked, the sound of his native Australia still heavy in his voice.

"Here's sixty."

"Awesome. Thanks, Daniel. Here's your entry form. You need to fill it out and give it to your presenter to hand to our emcee as she begins her walk."

"Will do. It's nice to see you again, Devin. You're home for the weekend?"

"Yes. Got a hankering for Sarah's strawberry pinwheel cookies. Plus, my sister's coming home this afternoon. Bringing her new boyfriend to meet the parents. I wasn't about to miss that."

"How is school going?" Devin attended college at Western in Gunnison, two hours away from Eternity Springs.

"All right, I guess. Grades are hanging in there, but I'm still trying to decide what I want to be when I grow up."

"I can relate to that."

Shannon asked, "So what's the scoop on Lori's new guy? I haven't heard much about him."

"Nobody has. All she has said is she has someone special who she wants the folks to meet. Mom started dusting the house at dawn and don't even get me started about Dad's posturing. They're always saying that they want her to find someone, but now that she apparently has, they're both weirded out about it. Silly, really, since she changes boyfriends as often as she changes hairstyles. But Mom and Dad are nervous and I was glad to have an excuse to beat feet before Lori and her guy arrived."

Devin handed Daniel a receipt for his entry, then turned to answer a question from a woman holding a Pekinese decked out in a nurse's costume. Shannon scratched Gabe's boxer behind the ears as he and Soup sniffed and said hello.

Then Celeste Blessing stepped up to the microphone set up at home plate and announced, "Final call for spruce-ups and potty breaks. The fourth annual Eternity Springs Canine Beauty Pageant begins in five minutes."

The silliness commenced with a small dog division, followed by large dogs, seniors, and best in show. Daniel borrowed a pen from Nic Callahan to fill out his entry, answering basic information like name, breed, and age in addition to more unusual questions like favorite dog treat and special tricks she could perform.

"The dog treat question is the one that always won it for Mortimer," Shannon told him. "The judges loved that he ate anything and everything. Anything interesting you can use for that answer will likely get you points."

"Hey, I'm in it to win it. Unfortunately, since Soupy and I are short-timers, I don't have much to say."

"No puppy tales?"

"Not really." He twisted his lips as he considered the question. "She was a relatively normal puppy. Chewed up the normal things. She did get into my wife's makeup case one day. Completely destroyed a tube of mascara."

"That's a good one. Use that. Say something about caring for her looks at an early age."

He finished up the questionnaire as the small dog parade began. Acting as emcee reading from the questionnaires, Celeste performed every bit as much as the dogs and the youngsters holding the leads, and Daniel quickly saw why the event proved to be so popular. It was fun. Silly, but entertaining. "Kids and animals... you can't beat 'em," he observed.

"Throw in our resident angel and it's a recipe for success."

The school's math and science teachers populated the judging panel, replacing last year's English and social studies judges. Sage Rafferty's bichon, Snowflake, won the small dog category. Daniel predicted the large dog prize would go to Zach Turner's Ace, whose superhero costume looked downright dashing. His expectations changed when Celeste read the entry for the librarian's Great Dane, Biscuit.

" 'Biscuit is a religious dog, as evidenced by his affinity for the plaster figures of a vintage Nativity scene.' " Celeste looked up from the entry page, her eyes wide. "Oh, dear."

Titters of laughter swept over the crowd.

" 'First, the camels disappeared, then the sheep, then the shepherds, and after that—' " Celeste gasped and clapped her hand against her chest in a dramatic exaggeration. " 'The angels!' "

"Not the angels!" Gabe Callahan called.

"It's the stuff of nightmares," Celeste declared, her eyes sparkling. Returning her attention to the page, she continued to read. " 'With three children below the age of seven in the house, it wasn't unusual to find GI Joe or a Little People figure in the Nativity. I assumed I'd discover Mary in Barbie's Dream House. It didn't occur to me that Biscuit was the culprit until I discovered the head of a wise man in his mouth.' "

"The dog ate the manger scene?" a girl in the front asked.

" 'Baby Jesus was the last to go,' " Celeste read, a solemn note to her tone. " 'I still don't know how Biscuit found him on top of the refrigerator.'"

The crowd went wild. Shannon leaned over and murmured, "Biscuit's got it in the bag."

Daniel didn't argue. His attention had fixed upon Holly and his dog as they took their place in line. Crazy as it was, he wanted the old girl to win.

With his gaze turned toward home base, Daniel didn't notice the commotion headed their way until the squirrel raced right between his legs. Cam Murphy's dog, Mortimer, followed right on the animal's bushy tail and ran right into Shannon. She let out a squeal and lost her balance. Daniel caught her before she hit the ground, just as he heard Holly shout, "Soupy Lou, no!"

He watched in dismay as his boxer pulled an old trick on the young girl. Soupy backed up, threw her collar, and took off after the squirrel. "Oh, no," Daniel groaned.

Barks and yips and yaps and laughter filled the air. Holly took off running after Soupy. A second later, Daniel, Lucca Romano, and Nic Callahan all spied the danger approaching and started after her.

It was a perfect storm of terrible circumstance. At the intersection, a towering fir tree blocked the truck driver's direct line of sight. The barking combined with the sound of the band concert happening on the school grounds drowned out the shouts of warning.

The squirrel dashed across the street. Brake lights flashed as the driver slammed the pedal. Soupy followed the squirrel into the road.

Holly Montgomery stopped at the curb like she'd been taught.

The truck's front bumper hit Soupy and sent her flying.

Chapter Eleven

Shannon gasped aloud as three distinct emotions hit her: relief that Holly wasn't hurt, fear when Soupy didn't get up, and heartache for the devastation that flashed across Daniel's face when he saw his dog go down. **This can't happen,** she prayed. **He can't lose her. Not so soon after he's found her.**

Daniel reached the boxer's side as the truck driver—the teenaged delivery boy for the lumber yard—climbed out of his cab, obviously distraught. Shannon watched Nic Callahan go down on her knees beside Soupy and Daniel, and sent up a silent prayer of thanks that a veterinarian was on the spot. Efficiently, Nic took charge, and within minutes, she, Daniel, and Soupy were on the way to her vet clinic in the lumber-yard truck.

"I'm right behind you," Shannon told him as the truck pulled away.

"My car is in the parking lot at the school if you want a ride," Hope Romano said.

Keeping one arm wrapped around her sobbing daughter, she reached into her pocket and pulled out a ring of keys.

"No, thanks. It'll be faster to walk."

"Good luck. Tell Daniel we're all praying for Soupy."

"I will."

Shannon jogged across Davenport Park and headed for the vet clinic, worry adding speed to her step. She arrived to find Daniel pacing the small waiting room. "She's taking X-rays. She'll let me know as soon as she's able. Cam's daughter Lori arrived in town a little while ago. She's due to graduate from vet school next year. She's coming in to assist."

"That's good."

He sat on one of the room's wooden chairs and leaned forward, his hands clasped, his elbows resting on his knees. "I should have used a martingale collar. She slipped her collar once when she was a puppy. I should have remembered that. I acted irresponsibly."

"Oh, Daniel. That's not being fair to yourself." When he expressed his disagreement with a downward twist of his lips, she insisted, "It's true. The entire time we were in Key West she never once pulled that sort of trick. She's an old dog. Who would have thought she'd have a big burst of puppy like she did today?"

"It doesn't matter. What's done is done." After a moment's pause, he added, "I just hope **she's** not done. Holly will feel just terrible."

Not nearly as terrible as you.

"I'm a big believer in the power of positive thinking," Shannon said, taking a seat beside him. She took his hand and gave it a squeeze as Lori Murphy rushed into the office, waved a hello, and hurried right through to the exam room.

Minutes dragged by like hours. When the silence grew heavy with tension, Shannon tried to think of an appropriate distraction for them both. "Have you heard the story about the Callahans' boxer? How he brought Nic and Gabe together?"

"Hmm?" Daniel asked, obviously distracted.

"Clarence was a stray up on Murphy Mountain in winter. After Gabe found him caught in a trap, he brought him to Nic for treatment." She rattled on about the dog's persistence in claiming Gabe as his owner, and ended with the line that always touched her heart. "Gabe says they rescued each other."

"That I can relate to." Daniel nervously tapped his foot. "I felt that way after Justin died. In a real sense, Soupy saved me."

"Want to tell me about it?"

He shoved to his feet and resumed pacing the waiting room. "You'll think I'm crazy."

When the death of a child was concerned, she wouldn't classify anything as crazy. "I'm certain I won't."

Daniel dragged his hand across his jaw. "Justin had these Sesame Street slippers with Bert on the left slipper and Ernie on the right. He wore them all the time. We had to force him to change into sneakers to leave the house. Anyway, the dog used to stick her head right between his legs and walk right along with him. Perfect coordination. She never tripped him. It was Bert, the dog, then Ernie. I used to call out for him by saying, 'Where are the Three Stooges?' That's really how her name evolved. 'Stooges' became 'Soupy' in Justin-speak."

He stopped in front of the window and stood with his back to her, gazing outside, his hands shoved into the back pockets of his jeans. Shannon sensed the pain the memory evoked as she waited patiently for him to continue his story.

Daniel cleared his throat. "The day Justin disappeared, she went up to his room and curled up on his bed. For the next two and a half days, she left only to drink a little water and take care of business outside. I was in the extra bedroom we used as an office working the phones when she left his room. She came to me, jumped up in my lap, and licked my face. Then she curled up in my lap and didn't leave."

Daniel released a long breath and finished. "That fell within the coroner's window for time of death. I've always felt that my boy managed to use his dog to give me a kiss good-bye."

"Oh, Daniel." Shannon went to him and wrapped her arms around him, hugging him tight. "That's not crazy at all."

"I know she's old and she's just a dog, but I'm not ready to lose her."

Shannon searched for words to reassure him, but everything she could think to say seemed inadequate. "She's not just a dog. She's family."

"Yeah. And losing family is a kick in the junk."

Shannon wanted to do something to help, but she didn't know what. Now certainly wasn't the time to blurt out the news about the baby.

She'd planned to do that at dinner tonight. After a thorough inner debate in the days since Alden Ramer called her name in Mallory Square, she'd decided that staying put in Eternity Springs remained her safest bet. After all, assuming that Russell learned of her visit to Key West, how was he any closer to tracking her to Eternity Springs than he'd been prior to that? If anything, it might send her stalker off on a series of wild-goose chases. He'd start tracking down the names of every female who had flown in or out of Key West in probably two weeks. Add in the cruise ship passengers and car rental agencies, and he'd have lots to filter through—and he wouldn't find the name she was using now on anything.

So she'd decided the time had come to tell Daniel that she carried his child. If Soupy didn't make it, what would be best? Hold off on the news until a happier day? Tell him now to give him good news amid the bad?

You don't know that he'll consider it good news. He might consider it to be another blow on top of this one.

Well, she darn sure wasn't going to tell him right this minute no matter what, so no sense crossing that proverbial bridge.

"Nic Callahan is an excellent veterinarian," she assured. "She will do her best for Soupy."

"I know."

Shannon kept her arms around him, offering the unspoken comfort of a hug. Eventually, they returned to their seats though Daniel kept her hand clasped firmly in his. He began to talk, telling stories about Justin and his puppy, more than once bringing tears to her eyes.

They both looked up at the squeak of door hinges. They stood. Daniel's grip on Shannon's hand grew crushing. "She's alive," Nic said, stating the most important words first. "I'm cautiously optimistic."

While Daniel released a heavy sigh, Nic described a litany of injuries and repairs, finishing with, "We will keep her here for a day or two and keep a close eye on her."

"Can I see her?" he asked.

"Sure. Come on back."

While Daniel spent a few minutes with his dog, Shannon visited with Lori Murphy about her semester and plans after graduation. "Nic has offered me a partnership," Lori explained. "There's a need for a large-animal vet in the area, and we could cover for each other. I don't know if I'm ready to move home to Eternity Springs." With a sheepish smile, she added, "The guy I'm seeing likes the city, so if we're still together then..." She shrugged. "If not, well, I don't know. It's hard to find Mr. Right in a town the size of this one."

"I don't know," Shannon said, her gaze drifting toward the door through which Daniel had disappeared. "I can count quite a few happy-ever-afters around here."

"That's what my mom is always telling me. She just wants me to come home. I still have some time to figure out what I want to do."

The clinic's telephone rang and Lori excused herself to answer it. Listening to the one-sided conversation, Shannon gathered that the teen who'd hit Soupy had called to check on her condition. Daniel entered the room and gave Shannon a crooked smile. "You ready to get out of here?"

"Sure."

After waving a good-bye to Lori, they stepped out into the bright sunshine to find Lucca Romano shooting a basketball toward the hoop suspended from the Callahans' garage. Seeing them, he held the ball. "She's okay?"

"So far so good," Daniel replied.

Lucca breathed a heavy sigh of relief. "Good. Holly is a mess over this whole thing."

"No need for that. It wasn't her fault."

"I told her that and Hope told her that, but she's feeling responsible."

"Is she still at the park? I'll talk to her."

"Hope tried to take her home. She wanted to go to church instead. Taking it straight to the source."

"St. Stephens?"

"Sacred Heart." Daniel glanced at Shannon. "Do you want to come with me? Or, I could meet you somewhere later. If you want to bail on me entirely, I'd understand. I haven't exactly shown you a good time."

"I don't bail, Daniel." Well, unless her life was at stake. "Let's go see Holly."

"Thanks, guys," Lucca said.

The walk to the church took less than five minutes. Daniel opened the door and they stepped into stained-glass peace. Standing at the back of the church with her toddler in her arms, Hope Romano turned at the sound. Her anxious expression eased somewhat when she spied Daniel's and Shannon's faces.

"Soupy is okay?" she asked softly.

"So far, so good. Lucca said the Squirt could use a little reassurance."

Hope nodded toward the front pew where her daughter knelt with her head bent in prayer. Shannon stayed at the back of the church with Hope while Daniel made his way up the aisle and took a seat next to Holly. As the two spoke quietly, Hope said, "Forgive me for being nosy, but

Daniel is a special friend, a special man. I want so badly for him to be happy. The two of you looked...close...this morning. Celeste says he's rented a cabin through mid-November. He's never visited Eternity Springs for so long before. I heard that he took you with him to pick up Soupy. It makes me wonder if this thing between you two might be serious?"

Serious as prenatal vitamins. "Are you asking if we're sleeping together?"

"I'm not **that** nosy." Hope set her squirming son down to toddle around the back of the church. "But since you brought it up...?"

"We're in church."

"Want to step outside?"

Shannon wanted to sidestep the question. She watched Daniel hand a handkerchief to Holly and observed, "He loves your daughter, doesn't he?"

"Yes. She loves him, too. We all love him. Daniel is as good a man as I've ever known. He has the heart of a warrior and the dedication of a knight in shining armor. But he's also the loneliest man I've known."

"So, before you met Lucca, you and Daniel never became an item?" The possessiveness behind the question surprised even Shannon.

"No. Always friends. Good friends. We understood each other's pain." Hope took a hymnal away from her son and slotted it back into the holder on the back of a church pew. "You do know he has a significant anniversary coming up soon?"

Ten years since the murder of his son. "Yes."

Hope's gaze flickered back to the front of the church. "My hope has been that once he gets past it, he'll finally be able to fill his life with something besides work. He needs light in his life. I think you could be that for him, Shannon. You won't find a better man."

"I know that." Daniel and Holly stood, exited the pew, then started down the aisle hand in hand. Shannon saw the tracks of tears on the girl's face and her heart gave a twist. Holly smiled tremulously and said, "Daniel says Soupy will be okay, Mom."

"I heard, baby."

"I was so worried."

"We all were worried."

"Pets are family, and Daniel needs his

family."

Hope touched his arm. "Yes, he does."

He does, Shannon silently agreed. **And I have one to give him.**

Standing in the back of the church where she'd first laid eyes on this tragic but big-hearted man, Shannon knew a sudden peace. Call it fate or destiny or God's hand at work in their lives, this pregnancy had been meant to be.

She was in love with him. Head over heels, birdsong and butterflies and perfumed rose petals crazy in love.

He was her second chance.

And you are his.

As they left church, Holly asked Daniel if he intended to return to the festival. "I sure do," he told her. "I have a stack of tickets to use, and Shannon and I are going to win the three-legged race."

"Mind if we stop by my house first?" Shannon asked. "There's something I need to do."

"Sure." He gave Holly a good-bye hug and Hope a kiss on the cheek, then they went their separate directions. Daniel was honestly glad to have the reprieve. Everyone would ask about Soupy, and he'd just as soon not retell the story a dozen times. Plus, he found the idea of spending a little time at Heartsong Cottage right now soothing. His nerves were frayed. "I could use a nap."

"I could be talked into that."

"Oh, yeah?" He took her hand. "Are we talking a nap or a **nap**?"

"I could so make a joke about the three-legged race here, but I'll do my best to refrain."

He laughed and bent to give her a quick, hard kiss. "I adore you, Ms. O'Toole."

Her gaze jerked toward his and she stared at him intently. "I think you're pretty wonderful, too."

Something in her voice—a note of solemnity—made him think it hadn't been an offhand remark like his had been. She thought he was wonderful? Was this relationship becoming something more than casual for her?

It is for you.

Daniel sucked in a breath. Whoa. He needed to think about that one.

Or did he, really? No "becoming" about it; that horse had left the barn. He cared for Shannon, more than he'd cared for anyone since Gail. Maybe—just maybe—he'd made his choice at that crossroads without even knowing it.

At home at Heartsong Cottage he started kissing her before she even got the door shut, and their lovemaking had a depth he might have found disturbing had the day's events not already laid his heart open. When it was over and she lay limp and sated upon his chest, he trailed his thumb slowly up and down the ridges of her spine. "You are precious to me, Shannon."

She lifted her head, stared down at him with those whiskey eyes of hers, and said, "I feel the same way, Daniel. You have given me more than I dared hope for."

When he opened his mouth to speak, she rested her finger against it. "I need to say something. Tell you something."

The flicker of nervousness that entered her eyes gave him warning. As she rolled off him and reached for her robe from the foot of the bed, he braced himself. Something was up.

He sat up, struck by a sudden thought. "Is it Soupy? Did Nic text you or something? Is my dog dead?"

"No, Daniel. Your dog is not dead. This has nothing to do with Soupy. It's me. Us. All of us. Three of us." Her lips fluttered with a tremulous smile. "You're going to be a father."

At first, the words didn't penetrate his brain. "What?"

"I'm pregnant, Daniel. We are going to have a baby."

The news hit him like a punch to the gut, and words he never dreamed he'd say to her flew from his mouth like bullets. "You bitch."

Chapter Twelve

The words Daniel spat and the accompanying fury that leaped into his face had Shannon taking a physical step away. He threw back the covers and shot from the bed. "You miserable bitch. Damned if you didn't have me well and truly snowed. This was a setup from the start. What happened? Whoever he is dumped you? Or do you even know who the father actually is?"

As he grabbed his jeans off the floor and shoved his feet into the pant legs, Shannon gasped at the vitriol spewing from his mouth. What had just happened? She'd known he might not be happy about her news, but this rage took her breath away.

"Shame on me for being so damned gullible. Guess no man is immune to a pretty piece of ass turning on the—"

"Whoa!" she interrupted, finally finding her voice. "Stop right there. I don't know where this temper tantrum is coming from but you have no call to speak to me that way."

"No call? No call! You try to foist your bastard off on me and—"

Whap. Her slap against his cheek was an instinctive reaction. "Don't you ever use that word again when you're talking about our child."

For a long moment he stood there fuming, a muscle tic at his temple. He yanked his belt hard. "It's. Not. **Our.** Child!"

"Sorry to wreck your world, Garrett, but she darned sure is too our child. By this point she has a heart that beats and would undoubtedly be broken if she could hear you right now."

"Let it go, O'Toole." He scooped his shirt up off the floor and jammed his arms through the sleeves. "You outsmarted yourself when you picked me for your patsy."

"Why are you saying that? You are not my patsy! The condom obviously failed!"

"For somebody, but sure as hell not me. I'm not the father of your baby. I can't have any more children. I didn't want any more children after my son died and my wife died so I got myself snipped."

"What?" Everything inside her froze.

His laugh was a vicious, unamused sound.

"Gotcha, sweetcheeks. I had a vasectomy. You're gonna have to find some other sorry sap to peddle your lies to."

Shannon's mouth dropped open. A vasectomy? Daniel had had a vasectomy? So **that's** what this was about!

And his immediate response is that I'm lying? Not only the first response, but also the second and third, too. As he shoved his feet into his shoes, Shannon's own temper kindled. His next words threw gasoline on the fire. "I'll be sure to warn all my friends around town that they'd better keep their dicks in their pants around you because you are on the hunt. That is, if you're not already porking another guy as a backup."

"That's it. Leave my house, Daniel Garrett. We're not done—our baby is due in May— but I will deal with you another time."

Renewed fury shot across his expression at her dismissal. "Haven't you listened to a word I said? It can't be my kid!"

Her chin held high, her shoulders back, Shannon sailed from her bedroom to the front door. She flung it open wide and demanded, "Get out."

"As fast as I possibly can." He shot through the door, his long legs eating up the front sidewalk.

Her bitter voice chased him. "One more thing, Mr. Hotshot Detective. Google is your friend. I suggest when you crawl back into your cave you put a few minutes into investigating the instances when vasectomies grow back together."

Slam.

Shannon leaned back against the door, breathing like she'd run five miles, her heart ripped open and bleeding. That jerk. That clueless idiot. That slimy son of a swamp rat. Angry tears pooled in her eyes and she furiously blinked them away. He didn't deserve her tears.

Why do the men in my life cause me nothing but grief?

She shoved away from the door and stormed around the room spitting curses and invectives and every insult she could squeeze past the lump of anger and pain in her chest. She even gave in to the childish desire to throw something and grabbed a pillow and sent it sailing. Twice. When the first wave of fury subsided, she switched on the shower, adjusted the temperature to near scalding, and stepped beneath the steaming water to wash the musky scent of him from her skin.

There, finally, she allowed her tears to fall. Shannon sobbed out her hurt and disappointment as her hopes and dreams circled the drain and disappeared. The storm eventually ended, helped along by the emptying of her hot water heater. She stepped from the shower and grabbed for a towel feeling as if she'd aged fifty years.

She crawled into bed, hating the scent of him on her sheets, but too bone weary to do anything about it. Immediately, she fell asleep. She dreamed of Key West and sunset on a Mallory Square strewn with decapitated teddy bears everywhere she turned. She awoke with a scream on her lips.

Sitting up, her heart pounding, she gasped for breath. Then the dream faded and reality returned and she buried her face in her hands. "What am I going to do?"

She heard a voice in her head as clear as a church bell. **"Aspiring angels don't indulge in pity parties."**

Whoa, she'd been spending too much time reading Celeste's manuscript if she now started hearing the woman's voice in her mind. And yet, the fact that she had heard it calmed her and strengthened her.

So, her fantasies about happy-ever-after with Daniel Garrett weren't going to happen. It wasn't the end of the world. She'd fallen into love with him quickly; she would fall right out of it just as quickly.

Honestly, she'd dodged a bullet. The man had more baggage than she did—which was saying something. Any relationship attempting to float that much poundage had been bound to sink eventually. Better now than later, when her heart was even more invested.

Oh, she knew he'd be back eventually. At some point—maybe years in the future—curiosity would get the better of him and he'd discover that his blessed vasectomy hadn't taken. He'd come demanding a paternity test. Maybe looking for a relationship with her child. Perhaps even absolution from her. Maybe she'd even give it to him.

Her heart, however, was another matter entirely.

In the meantime, she needed a plan. She'd already decided against running. She'd planted her flag in Eternity Springs. Now to figure out how to make the best possible life here for herself and for her child.

So the question became: what made life good? Family, friends, and financial security were a darn good start. Well, she and the baby would have each other for family, and that would be just fine. She had the means to put food on the table and a roof over their heads, so financially she'd be okay for a little while. No need to cross the child-support bridge now.

Which led to friends. This was where it got complicated. She'd rolled the dice by going public with her relationship with Daniel, and unfortunately, the die had cast snake eyes.

Once her pregnancy grew obvious, her friends would conclude that Daniel was the father. When he failed to own up to it— or followed through with his threat and accused her of trying to pass someone else's baby off as his—what would she do? He said/she said never ended well for anybody.

Maybe she should read through Celeste's advice for aspiring angels to look for an answer for a situation like this.

Her anger rekindled, fueled by hurt. She didn't begrudge him a moment of doubt— well, not too much, anyway—but the fact that he immediately concluded she was a skank and never once asked a single question totally chapped her. Perhaps he was just scared. Fear didn't excuse his behavior, but fear was something she could understand. His immediate doubt in her, however, was unforgivable.

His friends might be her friends, but Eternity Springs was her home. Barring any noise out of Russell, this would be the place where her child would grow up. Her reputation was important to her. Plus, she had the righteousness of truth on her side. Eventually, a paternity test would prove her out, but she didn't want months of suspicious looks and friends choosing sides.

It was time for war.

Daniel closed his eyes and dragged his hand down his face. He was so screwed.

Google is my friend, my ass. Google was his worst fear come to life. Come to life in May or June, apparently.

He shoved away from his computer. He'd go for a run. After the day he'd had, he either needed to run himself ragged or drink himself into oblivion. Since he didn't want to miss a doctor's call—be it Nic Callahan or his surgeon back in Boston—running was the better choice. Besides, Shannon owned the only bar in town, and she was the last person he wanted to see right now.

"It's me. Us. All three of us. You're going to be a father."

Been there, done that. Got the casket.

"Oh, God," he groaned again, dropping his head back and lifting his face toward heaven. Toward Justin. "Oh, God. I can't do this again."

Pain ripped through him, all but bringing him to his knees. A part of him recognized that if he ever gave in to that urge, he might never get up. So he changed into shorts and a T-shirt, grabbed his sneakers, and tried to outrun his reality. He ran across the grounds of Angel's Rest, through town, and headed up Cemetery Road. He'd never explored this route. Didn't know where it went once it rounded the mountain or what sort of terrain lay ahead, but the name of the road suited him.

He ran hard. Sweat beaded at his temples and dribbled down his spine. Just as he reached the turnoff to the cemetery, he felt the phone in his pocket vibrate.

He checked the number. Boston. "Hello, Jeff."

"Hey, cuz. How they hanging?"

The two men weren't cousins, but the nickname had stuck since the night they'd first met twenty years ago now when Daniel's cousin introduced them. "Do you ask all of your urology patients that?"

"Not in so many words, but yeah. I do. So, my office manager told me you said it's important. What can I do for you?"

"I have a question. I think I already know the answer, but I have to ask it anyway."

The conversation didn't take long. Daniel wasn't interested in being scolded. Yeah, he obviously should have gone in for his follow-up, but that ship had sailed. He confirmed what he'd suspected—hell, what he'd known—from almost the moment he'd left Heartsong Cottage. He'd made a really terrible assumption, and he'd reacted badly. Really badly. Beyond bad.

Dumbass.

He'd have to deal with the consequences of that. Deal with her. He'd hurt Shannon and that made him feel like pond scum, but before he did anything else, he had to process this gut-wrenching bit of news.

Because of his job, he was acquainted with more parents who'd lost their children than most, and in his experience, grieving parents ordinarily fell into two camps: those who desperately wanted another child, and those who absolutely didn't. Daniel had known from the moment the funeral director had led him and Gail into the casket room that he was finished with fatherhood. Gail's infertility had been a blessing. The pain was beyond bearing.

And the fear was overwhelming. Ten years later, time had dulled the pain but the fear—oh, the fear—it remained all-consuming.

Evil hadn't changed in the last ten years. If anything, he believed it had grown in scope and number. His experience had proved that evil souls found their way to evil deeds sooner, at younger ages than they had in the past—the influence of the Internet, he suspected.

The thought of needing to protect another child chilled him to his soul. Words pounded through his mind in rhythm with his sneakers pounding the road. **I can't do it. I can't do it. I can't do it.**

"Well, guess what, boyo. It's happening whether you like it or not. You don't get a choice."

The sound of a motorcycle approaching from in front of him had him shifting onto the shoulder of the road. When it rounded a curve and came into view, he recognized the rider. Celeste on her Gold Wing. As she drew closer, he saw she wore a white leather motorcycle jacket with gold fringe on the sleeve. She lifted a hand and waved to him, then pulled off the road and stopped. Lifting her helmet off her head, she gazed at him with compassion. "Daniel. How is your poor puppy doing?"

"So far, so good."

"I'm so glad." She tilted her head and studied him for a long moment. "You're troubled about more than Soupy."

"You remind me of my aunt Sally, Celeste. My mom always said she was a psychic."

"I admit to being intuitive, but honey, anxiety is rolling off you in waves. May I give you a quick bit of advice?"

"Of course." Daniel wasn't a fool. He knew that his Eternity Springs friends considered Celeste's advice to be golden.

"When you are lost in life, listen to your friends. Their caring will light the path so you can look inside your heart to where your angel waits—a bright, warm joy ready to light your path and show you the way home."

Daniel smiled. "Words of wisdom, there."

"You remember them."

"I will, Celeste. I promise."

"Excellent. Now, I'll let you finish your run. I need to get back to Angel's Rest, myself, since we have a busload of knitters arriving this evening for a workshop."

She gunned her engine as she departed. Daniel watched her go, her words of advice echoing through his mind. The woman had a way about her that he found soothing to his spirits.

He no sooner resumed his run than his phone vibrated once again. He pulled it from his pocket hoping that Nic was calling with an update. A positive news update, that was. A bad report might just have him throwing himself off the mountain. But instead of Eternity Springs' veterinarian, the person on the other end of the line was a former coworker on the Boston force who was calling in a marker. Within minutes, Daniel headed back down the hill.

At Angel's Rest, he took a quick shower, threw clothes in his suitcase, and headed for the vet clinic in order to check on Soupy in person and arrange boarding.

"She's doing fine," Nic told him. "Resting comfortably."

"Outstanding."

"Barring the unforeseen, you can pick her up tomorrow afternoon."

"About that..." He explained about the unanticipated trip. "Will it be a problem to board her?"

"Oh, those poor parents." Nic grimaced sympathetically. "I will keep them—and you —in my prayers. Of course Soupy can stay with us. Don't worry about her one little bit.

Feel free to check on her whenever you'd like."

"Thanks, Nic. You're a lifesaver, literally."

He was headed back toward his car when the Callahan twins blew past him, their mouths running as fast as their feet. They bounded up the steps, calling, "Mom! Mom! Guess what."

"Girls!" Gabe Callahan called as he sauntered along in his daughters' wake. "Say excuse me to Mr. Garrett."

"Excuse me, Mr. Garrett," a pair of voices shouted in unison. "Mom! You'll never believe what Dad did."

From inside the vet clinic, he heard Nic say, "Oh, I suspect I will too believe it."

Daniel tore his gaze away from the door through which the twins had disappeared, and when he met Callahan's gaze, the question just popped out. "How did you do it?"

"Do what?"

"Move on." Before Gabe had a chance to reply, Daniel closed his eyes and gave his head a shake. This was Celeste's fault. "I'm sorry. That's a personal question. I shouldn't—"

"I think I know what this is about." Gabe studied Daniel with a knowing look. "I hear you have a thing going with Shannon."

A thing? **I guess that's as good a name for this as anything.** "It's something. It's complicated."

"Women always are."

His tone wry, Daniel observed, "Now there's an observation for Celeste's book."

"I heard about that project, too. I bet it'll be a best seller."

"Look, never mind about the question. I don't know why I asked." Then, honesty compelled him to say, "Actually, I do know. I did something stupid."

"Ah, that I can understand. I do stupid all the time."

"Most men do. But you and I have a bit of a different perspective."

"We do have a terrible thing in common—the loss of our boys. We've walked in each other's shoes."

"Exactly," Daniel said.

"You can talk to me and I'll understand."

"Except guys don't talk, which I guess is part of the problem." Daniel's mouth twisted ruefully. "Celeste told me to listen to my friends."

"She is one smart cookie. So is Hope. After Gabi's wedding she asked me to talk to you if I had a chance. She's been worried about you. Want to go around to my sports shack and let me beat you at a game of billiards? I'll tell you what a dumbass I was when I met Nic."

"What's a sports shack?" Daniel asked, more to give himself time to consider the question than due to curiosity.

"I think 'man cave' is a stupid term. I had toy room envy after Cam built his, so I built one of my own."

Daniel glanced toward his car. Did he really want to do this? Today? When he was so uncertain and confused?

Yeah, he did. Shannon was having his baby. The sooner he came to terms with that, the better for all three of them. "Sports shack. I like it. Yes, I have time to whip your ass on a pool table. Just one game, though. I'm on my way out of town. I'm on the first plane out of Gunnison in the morning."

Gabe called to Nic to tell her where he'd be, and then led the way around to the stand-alone building in his backyard. Inside, he flipped a power switch and four different pinball games flashed to life. A stained-glass fixture that Daniel pegged as Cicero's work hung above the billiard table. "Sweet," Daniel said.

"An indulgence." Gabe grabbed two beers from the refrigerator, handed one to Daniel. "I work on improving my skills whenever I can steal a few moments away. When my brothers visit we have pinball wars. Matt is our family's pinball wizard, but I'm determined to unseat him. Choose your stick, Garrett."

They lagged for the break and Daniel ended up playing solids. He sank two before turning the table over to Gabe.

"The yellow stripe ball is an appropriate way for me to consider the question you asked me earlier," Gabe observed as he lined up a shot on the nine ball.

"I don't follow you."

"You asked me how I moved on. I had to quit being a damned coward to do it."

Daniel wanted to laugh at that. Gabe Callahan a coward? Right. Matt Callahan had told him that Gabe had spent six months in a Balkan prison. Whether the rumors he'd heard about Gabe having worked for the CIA were true or not didn't matter. The guy was obviously a hoss. "How were you a coward?"

"If I started outlining all of the ways, it would take the entire night and you'd miss your plane in the morning. Bottom line is that I was a fatalistic, pessimistic son of a bitch. Losing my wife and son sucked so badly that I was afraid to let myself go down that road again. My brain told me the chances of that particular lightning striking twice weren't high, but my heart wouldn't hear it. The thought of going through that kind of pain again—I knew I wouldn't survive it. So when Nic told me she was pregnant, I was an ass."

Been there, done that.

"Add in survivor's guilt, and I couldn't admit to being in love."

Daniel sipped his beer. "That's not my problem. I'm in love with Shannon and I know it."

Gabe lifted his gaze from the felt and gave Daniel a long, considering look. "Well, now, I always knew you were a brainy guy.

So you **have** moved on. In that case, what's eating you?"

Daniel bent over his cue and lined up his shot. He sank three balls before he spoke again. "I don't have a yellow stripe, Gabe. I'm yellow through to the bone. I'm afraid of so many things I could star as the Cowardly Lion on Broadway."

"If you can admit that, you're a big step ahead of where I was when I fell for Nic."

"Recognizing fears and overcoming them are two different things. That's what I need to know. How did you defeat yours?"

"I don't know that you ever defeat them, Dan. Instead, you learn to live with them. 'Live' being the key word."

"That feels like an insurmountable task. After ten years I feel as if mine are part of my DNA."

"It helped me that living was forced upon me. I might have held out longer if it was only Nic lobbing grenades at my walls, but the babies made my surrender inevitable. I had to start living again. I was responsible for two innocent little souls."

"Doesn't it tear you up to know how vulnerable they are? How much evil is out there in world waiting to eat them alive? Don't you lie awake at night worrying about how the hell you are going to protect them?"

"That sounds like we might be getting to the heart of the problem."

Daniel rubbed the back of his neck. "Maybe I could get past the fear of that lightning strike, but I don't know that I'll ever work my way beyond the reality of just how vulnerable they are. I failed one family. I failed my son. I didn't protect him. How do I risk history repeating itself?"

Gabe gave a silent whistle. "Wow, you're as big a head case as I was, aren't you?"

"I'm pretty bad."

"I don't know that I'm going to be much help to you, Daniel, because I've got nothing for you where protective instincts are concerned. My own work overtime. I guess it's simply something we face as fathers."

"At the risk of being a whiner, I don't want to face it."

"That, I can advise about. Don't make the same mistake I made. I tried to run away from my fears, and in doing it, I did something borderline unforgivable. I hurt Nic badly. I'm damned lucky that she has such a forgiving heart."

Daniel winced. "I'm afraid I might be following a bit too closely in your footsteps. What I did today was beyond stupid. I don't know if Shannon can forgive it."

"Like Nic so often tells me, sometimes it's difficult for a man to overcome the stupidity of his gender. I've got one word for you. Grovel. You can follow up with flowers and romance and fantastic sex—but lead with your best shot. Swallow your pride and grovel. It'll save you a lot of time. When you love a strong woman and you screw up, it's the price you have to pay. Take that bit of advice to the bank."

"I don't know, Callahan. I don't grovel."

"If it was as bad a screwup as it sounds, I suggest you learn."

Hope Romano and fate gave Shannon a reprieve from battle planning that evening when Hope, her husband, and their children arrived at Murphy's wanting fish-and-chips for supper. As Daniel's closest friends in town, their warm greeting assured Shannon that Daniel had yet to launch his first attack. Then Hope dropped a bombshell. "I feel so bad for Daniel, having to leave town on such short notice with Soupy still in distress. I know he hated leaving her behind."

He left? The son of a bitch ran away?

Reeling from the news, Shannon faked her way through the moment. Obviously, the Romanos expected her to already know the news.

"He's due for some good luck. Maybe this time he'll find the little boy."

A case? He's gone on a case? "I hope so," Shannon replied, meaning it.

Once she turned the Romanos' order in to the kitchen, she stole a moment for herself and ducked outside. Knees a little shaky, she sank onto a picnic table bench. "Okay, this is good," she murmured. It gave her time. Time was a good thing.

He'd be back. He'd left his dog.

She could take her time rolling out her news. She'd had a reprieve.

Exhaling a heavy breath and what felt like a year's worth of tension, she returned to work with a lighter heart.

The following week sped by. The overwhelming fatigue that had plagued her for weeks seemed to have abated, and she felt amazingly better. Her work at Three Bears was going well, the final design for all three houses finished and approved, and the first mosaic eighty percent done. It was fabulous, if she said so herself. And to think she'd been disappointed when the itinerary for her study-abroad class took her to Lisbon instead of Madrid. Her time in Portugal had sparked an interest that eventually led here to this little valley and was going to fund her obstetrician's bill and hospital expenses and allow her to buy the nursery decorations that she'd always dreamed of having.

"Heaven knows, I can't count on the baby's father to do it," she grumbled to her reflection as she donned her headband, a furry confection complete with pointy ears —part of her costume for this Halloween night at the pub. She hadn't gone all out in dressing up, but she did keep in the spirit of things with her headband and foxtail belt, though she'd forgone the matching sky-high heels. She liked her stilettos as much as the next girl, but with Halloween falling on a Saturday this year, the pub would be crazy. She'd be on her feet all night—or at least until the music started.

She had a fabulous guitarist playing tonight, beginning late. Since she'd established the pub as a family-friendly venue, Murphy's welcomed trick-or-treaters tonight until eight p.m. She'd stocked up on mini candy bars—no lame hard candy for her Halloween visitors—and when she arrived to help Honey with the early crowd, she found the Callahans' twins, Cari and Meg, already there, packing away chicken nuggets and fries and chattering away like magpies.

"Dad says Halloween is a nutrition-free zone, Miss Shannon," Cari explained when Gabe ordered stuffed potato skins to go with it.

"Gabe!" Nic protested.

Gabe grinned and shrugged. "It's Halloween. And they'll let me steal some of their Three Musketeers bars if I play the good guy now."

"And when do you ever not play the good guy?" Nic observed in a long-suffering tone.

"Hey, they're my baby girls."

"We're not babies, Daddy," Meg said.

Shannon left the Callahans to their meal and got to work. A festive mood filled the air, with plenty of excitement and laughter by children and parents alike. Shannon passed out candy to princesses and cowgirls, Elsa, Darth Vadar, and Superman. But it was Sage Rafferty's new, beautiful little girl, Ella, who reached in and grabbed hold of her heart.

Next Halloween, I'll have a baby dressed like a little pumpkin.

The crowd thinned after eight when the children and their parents all departed, but swelled again toward nine when the music was slated to begin. That's when she overheard the news that Daniel was back in town.

She knocked over a full pint of ale.

Okay, don't be ridiculous, she scolded herself as she wiped up the spill. **You knew he'd be back**.

She told herself that the little spurt of something she felt was simply indigestion. Not excitement. Not happiness. Definitely not relief. No. Absolutely not.

You're at war, remember? Don't forget how he made you feel when you told him.

Her stomach rolled and she hoped she hadn't picked up that virus going around the kindergarten class.

She rinsed out her cleanup rag, tossed it in with the other dirty towels, and grabbed a clean one. She needed to keep her mind on the goal. In the past week her heated temper had cooled—all the way to ice. Hard and frigid and solid, it was in no danger of melting.

So, her reprieve from dealing with this problem had come to an end. The time to fire the first shot in her war with Daniel Garrett was upon her. She should do it now, tonight, on her own turf. If she could just work up the nerve to do it.

Her gaze drifted toward the end of the bar. The Ciceros had taken seats there so Rose could visit with Shannon. Since Rose's new family and part-time job at the medical clinic kept her running from dawn until long past dusk most days, outside of their weekly critique group, the two women didn't see much of one another anymore.

They both regretted it.

Rose was Shannon's best friend, and while Cicero's loyalty might lie with the Romanos and, as a result, Daniel, Shannon knew that Rose would side with her. But it would help if she got out in front of the story, put Daniel on the defensive from the git-go.

The time had come to go public with her pregnancy.

Okay, then. Do it. Speak the truth and nothing but the truth. Announce the pregnancy with her head held high and name Daniel as the father whenever asked. Whenever anyone asked what their plans were—and invariably, they would—she'd say that Daniel didn't believe the baby was his. She would keep her tone neutral and nonaccusatory, hiding her anger and her pain. Let him look the fool when he blabbed his personal health history. Let him explain his reaction. Let people draw their own conclusions. Starting tonight.

As the musician began his second set with a fabulous guitar riff and the crowd settled in to listen, she delivered a pint to the patron seated next to Rose, then said,

"I'm going to fill one more round of orders and then take a break. Would you steal upstairs with me for a few minutes? I have something I need to tell you."

Rose's eyes lit with interest. "Sure."

Shannon delivered a tray of pints to Mac and Ali Timberlake and their son Chase and his fiancée, who were in town to discuss plans for their upcoming wedding. Shannon couldn't help but notice that Ali's expression appeared strained, despite her avowed determination to grow to love her son's choice. I'm not the only one with relationship challenges, Shannon thought as she motioned for Rose to join her. The newlywed leaned over and whispered something to her husband, kissed him on the cheek, and followed Shannon up the stairs to her office.

She started chatting before Shannon had the door shut behind them. "Life has been entirely too busy for both of us. I've been dying to talk to you. I picked up the phone to call yesterday and then Daisy fell and skinned her knee, which meant the world stopped turning on its axis. Tell me about Key West. I want to hear everything, beginning with how long this thing with Daniel has been going on. I can't believe you kept the news to yourself. I knew something was up—you had that air about you. But I thought maybe you'd been seeing Logan McClure or that maybe one of the Romano relatives was sneaking into town. I never guessed it was Daniel."

"I'm pregnant!" Shannon blurted out, not at all what she'd intended. As Rose's eyebrows arched with surprise, Shannon totally blew her plan by bursting into tears.

"Oh, honey." Rose wrapped her arms around Shannon and held her while she sobbed out the story.

"It happened at Gabi's wedding. I had too much to drink and I was so lonely and he was so handsome and it was dark and romantic and I love roses. We argued about music and it was fun. So much **fun!** I hadn't had fun with a man in a very long time. He walked me home and I invited him in and we're going to have a baby. I'm keeping it, but he doesn't believe me!"

"He doesn't believe you? That you're keeping it?"

"That the baby is his! He had a vasectomy!"

Shannon watched her physician friend swiftly follow the thought process. Rose said, "Oh."

"Yes. Oh. He accused me of trying to hoist somebody else's baby off on him! But she's his baby, Rose. I swear it. I haven't been with another man in over two years!"

Disgust rolled through Rose's voice. "Why, that half-wit."

The words were balm to Shannon's wounded soul.

"Seriously," Rose continued, stepping back and bracing her hands on her hips as her temper gathered steam. "I thought Daniel Garrett was smarter than that. I get that there are women out there who no one should trust, but the man's a detective. How could he spend any time at all with you—much less sleep with you—and think you could tell such a monumental lie?"

Rose wasn't trying to wound her, Shannon knew. She had no way of knowing that her words scored a direct hit on the dam holding back Shannon's reservoir of guilt.

Rose's indignation grew. "You have every right to be hurt and furious, Shannon. There's just no excuse for behavior like that from him. Why, next time I see him I just might have to kick his ass from here to Gunnison. With my steel-toed boots."

That startled a disheartened laugh from Shannon. Gentle and loving Rose Cicero devoted her life to healing, not bruising. "If you decide to do that, let me know so I can watch, would you?"

"Absolutely."

Nevertheless, by bringing up the issues of trust and truth, her friend had managed to worsen Shannon's despair rather than soothe her. The tears began to flow once more.

"Oh, honey." Rose clucked her tongue and reached for a tissue. "You just let it all out."

"I can't. I'd be here crying until closing, and Honey would kill me."

"Cry fast."

This time her laugh held real amusement. "Oh, Rose. I didn't expect him to be happy about it. I hoped, but I didn't expect it. He's got baby baggage."

"Yes, he does."

"I'm afraid I've fallen in love with him."

Rose grabbed a tissue and in a maternal manner dabbed at Shannon's tears. "I'm not surprised. Daniel is a lovable man when he's not being an idiot."

"What am I going to do?"

"Well, the truth becomes undeniable eventually, which means he'll come around."

"Maybe not without a paternity test shoved beneath his nose."

"If he continues to be an idiot, yes."

Shannon told her about his threat to spill all to their friends.

"A gold-plated idiot," Rose observed.

"I decided to try to get out ahead of it by telling everyone first."

"Good plan."

"I started with you."

"As well you should. We're best friends. I have your back, Shannon. So, how are you feeling? Fatigue? Nausea? Have you chosen an obstetrician yet?"

Basking in the glow of friendship warmed Shannon's heart and her spirit calmed. At the end of her break she returned downstairs with a bandage over the wound on her heart. The sight of the newcomer entering the pub ripped it right off again.

Well, this blows. Daniel hung a jacket and a backpack on one of the coatracks beside the door and sauntered to the bar as if nothing had happened. Just seeing his face again rekindled her fury. Of all the nerve. **Who the heck does he think he is?**

He found an open spot at the bar—not an easy feat tonight, especially for a man of his size. He met her gaze with aplomb. "I'd like the Oktoberfest on tap, please."

Shannon wasn't one to make crude gestures, but at that moment, her middle finger wanted badly to flip. She settled for hooking her thumb over her shoulder toward the sign hanging on the wall behind her that read: we reserve the right to refuse service to anyone.

The slightest of nods and uptick at one corner of his mouth acknowledged a hit. However, he didn't leave. Instead, the confounded man waited until she'd carried a tray to a table, then walked around behind the bar and poured himself a brew. Shannon stuttered when she returned. "I want you to leave."

"This is a public house. I'm the public."

"Do I have to call the sheriff?"

"I don't care if you're the owner. Zach Turner isn't going to throw me out of this bar. Will you take a break and talk with me, Shannon?"

He was right about Zach. He wouldn't throw Daniel out, and she wouldn't bother him with a call. Icicles hung from her response to his request. "No."

He nodded, as if that's exactly what he'd expected. "Okay. In that case, I'll stand here and drink my beer and enjoy the show. Your performer is a very nice guy. He and I fished the same stretch of Angel Creek earlier. He has some wild stories to tell about his days in a rock band."

Shannon fumed. How could he simply stand there and talk as if nothing had happened?

As she struggled to find the perfect putdown, a table signaled for another round, giving her an excuse for retreat. What did he want? She couldn't read that look in his eyes. The fury that had lasered from them last time they'd been together wasn't there, but neither was any other emotion she could identify.

She had to be careful here, she decided as she pulled the tap and golden ale flowed into a pint glass. She couldn't afford to show an ounce of vulnerability. Strategically, that would be a serious misstep. Righteous indignation was the order of the day.

Wasn't it a good thing that looking at him produced an abundance of that particular emotion?

For the next half hour, she did her best to ignore him and counted herself lucky that the combination of Halloween and live entertainment had brought in the crowd that kept her busy enough to do so.

She was so busy, in fact, that she didn't notice that Daniel had abandoned his place at the bar. Her back was to the stage when the singer made an announcement.

"We are going to switch gears here for a moment. I want to welcome a guest to the stage who has a special message for our wonderful barkeeper."

She almost dropped her tray as Daniel's soulful voice rang out across the tavern, launching into the classic Brenda Lee song, "I'm Sorry."

His mesmerizing gaze never looked away from her as he called himself a fool and asked her to accept his apology. By the time he sang about love being blind, she stood there with a hand covering her mouth, fighting back tears. As the last note faded away, Murphy's erupted in applause and cheers. From the table directly behind her, she heard Chase Timberlake say, "Well, I'm totally screwed. I'll never manage an apology as good as that one when I do something stupid."

Daniel had certainly managed to suck the wind out of the sails of Shannon's anger, that's for sure.

His gaze remained steady and locked on hers as he waited for her reaction. She didn't give him one. Her mind was spinning, and she could barely think. Vaguely, she heard shouts for an encore. His lips twisted wryly, then he finally looked away and nodded toward the musician. A moment later, he followed up Brenda Lee with Frank Sinatra's "What Can I Say After I Say I'm Sorry."

By the time he repeated the line lamenting making her cry, Shannon recognized the emotion fluttering to life in the pit of her stomach. Hope, spiced with a little joy. When the final note of the song faded, Daniel—along with everyone else in the pub —looked toward her.

The man had been a jerk, no doubt about it, but no one was perfect. She had to put herself in his position. Would she have reacted differently had their situations been reversed? Following a long moment of hesitation, she lifted her hands, fluttered a smile, and slowly applauded.

An answering smile bloomed across his face.

"Very prettily done, Mr. Garrett. Sit down and have a beer and we'll talk after closing time."

The crowd clapped and cheered and Daniel called, "A round for the house on me."

Chapter Thirteen

Daniel tried not to watch the clock, but it proved to be a struggle. He wanted all these people to leave so he and Shannon could hash the situation out.

At least the grovel had gone well.

During the week he'd been away, he'd had plenty of windshield time to analyze both his feelings and his missteps. He'd taken Gabe's advice to heart and directed his thoughts toward planning the apology he needed to make. Nothing he'd come up with had risen to the necessary level of grovel until the guy whom he'd ended up fishing the same stretch of creek with this morning mentioned he'd be playing tonight at Murphy's. The idea had occurred to Daniel just as a twelve-inch rainbow took his fly.

He'd taken it as a sign.

Finally, Shannon announced last call, and fifteen minutes later, shut and locked the door behind the last straggler. She flipped off the red neon open sign, then turned to face him. "Was your trip successful?"

"Yes, it was. I chased down a runaway in Minneapolis. Got her home to her parents before too much harm was done."

"That's wonderful news."

"How are you feeling?"

"Okay. Well, I actually feel pretty good. I have more energy than I've had for quite some time."

"That's good. I'm glad. So, can we talk about the baby? I'd like to attempt to explain why I went off on you the way I did."

"That's rather obvious. You thought I was lying."

"No, actually, I didn't think at all. That was all emotion talking, one emotion in particular—fear. I failed to protect my child. I failed to save my wife from her monsters. The weight of those two crosses has had me crawling on my knees for a decade. But lately, I've found my feet again. My balance isn't worth a damn—I wobble more than a college kid on a spring-break binge—but I've managed to stay upright. Your news knocked my feet right out from under me again." He paused, then shook his head. "Actually, I don't know that the metaphor sufficiently expresses my terror. When you told me I was going to be a father again, my testicles drew all the way up to my liver."

Her lips flirted with a smile, which he found encouraging, so he pressed on.

"Apparently, the vasectomy didn't take. That happens more than most men probably realize. The reason I got one is because I never wanted to experience the pain of losing another child, so when you told me about the baby, I panicked. I was an ass."

"I won't argue the point."

He nodded his acceptance of her comment. "I managed to work my way past that initial reaction, and I thought about it—about us—a lot while I was away." He grabbed the backpack he'd hung beside his jacket, and removed the gift he'd bought at an airport gift shop—a fluffy brown teddy bear.

Shannon started and her cheeks went pale. Her reaction caught Daniel by surprise. Did she think this was a good-bye gift?

Quickly, he handed her the bear and declared, "It's the first gift of many I intend to give our child. Shannon, I won't run away.

I won't abandon you and the baby. I may never **not** be afraid, but I won't let it rule me again. You've given me a second chance, one I've never expected would come my way again. I want you to know this chance, this baby is precious to me, and I'm going to treasure him or her."

She dragged her stare away from the stuffed animal and met his gaze, an expression on her face he couldn't quite read as she said, "I'm glad to hear that, Daniel. It relieves a significant worry of mine."

"Good. But I'm not finished. Let me say all of it while I'm on a roll. I'm warning you that I'm an old-fashioned man. I think it's best for a child when his mom and dad are married. I'm going to want to marry you."

Her eyes widened, and she opened her mouth to speak, but he forestalled it with a finger against her lips. "Something else I realized while I did all of my self-analysis. I'd want to marry you even if you weren't carrying my child. I'm in love with you."

"Daniel," she said, taking a step away.

"No. Don't say anything. That wasn't a proposal. A woman like you deserves a better proposal than that. It's a piece of this five-thousand-piece jigsaw puzzle that is a relationship. We build it one piece at a time. It takes some trial and error and time to fit new pieces onto the board, and you can't try to force them where they don't belong. If you do, you'll just have to go back and fix it. But if you work at it diligently and with care and consideration, you create a beautiful picture.

"So, Ms. O'Toole. In my estimation, we have the corner pieces in place and the straight edges, too. I'm ready to start working on filling the picture in. Are you?"

The look in her whiskey-brown eyes warmed him like a shot of the Jameson on the shelf behind the bar. A husky note of emotion sang through her voice when she said, "The puzzle piece that has my heart—I know where it goes. Right here. I love you, too, Daniel."

She stepped into his arms—where she belonged.

Daniel awoke the morning of November third more at peace than he'd been in a decade, and certainly happier than he'd ever dreamed of being on this day of all days. His gaze lit on the teddy bear sitting propped on the top of Shannon's dresser and he actually smiled. He was ready to face the day, ready to put this significant anniversary behind him. Ready to seal the scar on his heart with a kiss and look forward rather than behind him. All because he awoke with Shannon snuggled against him.

"Good morning," she said sleepily.

"You know what? It actually is."

Her gaze softened. "What time are you meeting Hope?"

"Nine o'clock." Daniel's tradition of spending the anniversary of his son's abduction and murder with Hope Romano had begun when her daughter was missing. Hope's flat rejection of his offer to end the practice following Holly's return had proven to be an extra blessing because it had led him to being here, today, with Shannon. "Honey, I know you have a lot on your plate, but if you can carve out the time, I'd love for you to spend the day with us, too."

"Of course I will."

On a previous anniversary in Eternity Springs, Daniel had discovered that he found mountaintops with a view to be the perfect place to spend the day. This year, since the weather appeared to be cooperating, the plan was to take a Jeep up to a high meadow on land Cam owned up on Murphy Mountain. There was an easy hike up to a rock promontory that gave a spectacular view of the valley below.

Hope was ready to go when they arrived at her house promptly at nine. "I'm so glad you're coming with us," she said to Shannon.

"I am, too," Shannon replied.

"Do we need to stop somewhere and pick up a little more for lunch?" Daniel asked, reaching for the picnic basket Hope carried.

"No. I packed enough for a dozen people. I suspected Shannon might accompany us."

"Good."

Hope gave directions, and soon they were climbing out of the valley on a little rutted road that Daniel never would have found on his own. As they ascended, the two women chatted quietly about town events during the upcoming holiday season. Daniel's thoughts drifted back in time, and his mood grew subdued.

The meadow proved to be as pretty a spot as Hope had promised. A little mountain stream burbled at the base of an evergreen hill that rose gently upward. He parked where she indicated and spied the game path at a break in the trees. Hope said, "If it's all right with you, Daniel, I'm going to let Shannon take my place on the hike."

Surprised, he glanced at her. She said, "It's time."

Following a moment's pause, he nodded once. "I guess you're right."

"Look for the little bench Cam built up there. It's a great place to sit. And take your time, Daniel. I brought a paperback to read. Actually, I brought two paperbacks to read."

"You are the best of friends, Hope Romano."

Smiling up at him, her eyes misty, she touched his cheek. "I love you, Daniel."

"I love you, too. Good thing Lucca isn't here or he'd whip my ass."

"Nah. He's a very secure husband. Now, don't forget to take water."

"Yes, Mother." As he grabbed his pack from the Jeep, he saw Hope touch Shannon's arm and heard her say, "Get him to talk to you. Don't let him lose himself entirely. There have been times I worried he was going to walk himself right off the mountain."

Shannon nodded to Hope, then arched a brow toward him. "Lead on, Magellan."

Daniel took Shannon's hand and led her into the forest. They didn't speak as they hiked, but Daniel didn't lose himself quite as thoroughly in the past as he had in previous years. He remained quietly conscious of the fact that Shannon climbed this trail with him even as his thoughts returned to that fateful day a decade ago.

The moment he'd heard Gail's panicked voice was etched into his soul. **"I can't find Justin! Oh, God, Daniel. Somebody stole our baby!"** He'd never been so afraid —before or since. He—**whoa!** Shannon slammed into him from behind, and he pitched forward, his hands flying up out of his pockets to save his balance.

The item he'd been fingering in his pocket went sailing.

"I'm so sorry," Shannon said. "I was looking up into the trees and totally missed seeing that root across the trail. I fail as an outdoorswoman."

"No harm done." He thought he'd managed to keep the panic out of his tone. Her sharp look told him he was wrong.

"What's wrong, Daniel?"

"I dropped something."

"Something important?"

His gaze scoured the ground. "Just a little piece of plastic."

An arm. With the black paint all but worn off from being carried in Daniel's pocket for a decade. **I'll never find it among the dead autumn leaves and moss littering the forest floor.** His throat tight, he added, "Batman's arm."

Shannon's tender assurance encircled him like an angel's hug. "We'll find it."

They tried. After ten fruitless minutes of search, he got scientific about it and began searching in a grid. Following another twenty minutes he said, "Enough. This is ridiculous. It's gone."

"It was Justin's?"

"Yeah."

Worry creased her brow. "Oh, Daniel, I feel terrible."

"No, don't. It's silly of me to have toted it around with me all of these years. Maybe this was meant to be. It's time I stopped that silly practice. Past time."

"It should have been your choice to make, not something I forced on you with my clumsiness."

"Stop it. I'm okay with this. Seriously. Let's finish our climb, shall we? I'm anxious to see this view Cam has bragged about, not to mention discover the contents of that picnic basket Hope brought."

Her gaze lifted to study his, then she nodded. "All right."

He leaned down and kissed her briefly, then led the way up the trail, leaving a little part of his heart behind lost in the detritus of the autumn forest floor.

Shannon sat beside a silent Daniel on the log bench Cam Murphy had placed at the scenic viewpoint and tried to recall a time she'd felt so helpless. The only event that came close was when she'd left the police department after reporting Russell as a stalker. Not only had they all but called her a liar, they'd ushered her out the door and told her not to return.

Still, that had been a different kind of helpless. This kind was probably reserved for the physical or emotional pain of her own children or the man she loved.

Daniel broke her heart.

She rested her hand on his denim-clad thigh, offering her quiet support. He took hold of her hand and squeezed it.

"I don't let myself think about that day, ordinarily. Sometimes, a thought or two will sneak in, and I'll have spells where the nightmares come in waves. Thinking about it today seems like a duty to me. Like I owe it to him. To them."

"Do you want to talk about the day, Daniel? I'm happy to listen."

"I don't talk about it. I've never talked about it. Maybe because talking about it makes it all the more real. Silly, I know. It was real. I lived it."

"I can understand not wanting to relive it, though. Why don't you tell me about Justin?"

"I wouldn't know where to start."

"You said once that he loved to fly kites?"

"Yeah. I bought him his first kite the spring before he died. A Batman kite because the kid loved superheroes—Batman, especially."

"Was Justin Robin to your Batman?"

Daniel's lips twitched with a hint of a smile. "No. We were commissioners. Commissioner Dad and Commissioner Justin. We'd send notes flying up the kite string to Commissioner Gordon. Justin loved to do that. I think it's the main reason he loved to fly kites so much. Kite flying totally rocked his world. I had to help him hold it, but he didn't care. Flying a kite was just about the only thing he didn't insist on doing himself, in fact. He was glad to have me hold it because that gave him more time to write notes to Commissioner Gordon, so that good could triumph over evil. Stupid me, I fostered that. I let him believe that the good guy always"—Daniel choked up a little as he finished—"won. It's a lie that haunts me still today."

"Oh, Daniel."

"I let him down. I know it sounds stupid, but I knew something was going to happen. I had this god-awful feeling for weeks. When

Gail called me that day that...when I figured out what she was saying...I knew...I knew." He closed his eyes and dropped his head back, his face lifted toward the sky. "Four days. They called me four days later. I went out there. They told me not to do it, but I couldn't not go. He was my boy. A jogger found him lying in a pumpkin patch. Wearing one little red tennis shoe and a Spiderman sock. That was..." His voice broke. "All."

His hand was a vise grip on hers. Shannon lifted it to her mouth and pressed kisses across his hard knuckles. She wanted to scream at the cruelty committed on an innocent little soul and to his loving parents. However, she sensed that she shouldn't interrupt Daniel. He'd opened the wound and now the poison needed to flow.

"Way too often, evil wins. It's the nightmare that won't go away. Ten years later, and it still haunts me. The vision of it all. The pumpkins. The yellow tape. The cold flash of the coroner's camera. What that monster did to him and knowing he undoubtedly called for me...begged and screamed for me...waited for me to come and save him. How frightened he must have been. And the pain…I can't remember the sound of his voice anymore, except in my nightmares. Then, ! hear him screaming, 'Daddy, Daddy, help me! Daddy, save me!' He died waiting."

Shannon's own tears flowed freely now, but she kept them silent. Daniel had lanced the wound. The poison needed to flow without interruption.

"At the crime scene, I couldn't touch him. They held me back. I knew it had to be that way. Evidence. Everything was evidence. They needed to do their thing. But, oh, how I wanted to grab him up in my arms. His broken little body. All I wanted to do was fix it, and I couldn't. I couldn't be Batman. I remember it being so quiet, just the click of the camera, and all I could do was stand there and watch until they finally put him in a black body bag and zipped it up."

A lone tear seeped from beneath his eyelid and trailed slowly down his chiseled cheek. "I didn't save him, Shannon. I didn't save him."

Shannon had known it was bad, but hearing the story through his eyes…oh. She didn't know what to say to him. The platitudes that rolled through her mind were simply that—platitudes—and so totally inadequate. So she didn't say anything, but gave him the only comfort she knew to offer—a hug.

A bit desperately, he pulled her onto his lap and held her tight, his head buried against her. A minute passed, then two. A long shudder quaked through him, then he spoke again. "I made a mistake with Gail. She wanted to see him."

Oh, Daniel. No.

"I refused to take her to the field, thank God, but I couldn't keep her away from the morgue. Terrible, terrible mistake. Maybe she would have fallen apart anyway, but I know it broke her to see him...afterward. She shut down. I took her to a grief counselor. Thought it was helping, but in hindsight, she was faking it. Everyone told me time would heal, but it turned out we didn't have time. She gave up.

"After she died, I was so angry at her. I spent a lot of years being angry, and when I wasn't angry, I was filled with despair. The work helped me. Taking action helped me because I was doing something."

"You fought back."

"Yeah. Yeah, I did. I felt good about what I was doing until lately. Now, I'm weary of it. I'm so over living in the dark every day. I've reached my limit of horror and filth."

She lifted her face and stared deeply into his eyes in order to emphasize her point. "What you went through is more than any heart should have to bear, Daniel. You've carried this cross for a decade. It's okay for you to set it down."

"I think I'm ready to do that. I need light, Shannon. I need you. You're my beacon."

It was, she thought, the nicest thing anyone had ever said to her. She gently cupped his cheek in her hand. He turned his head and pressed a kiss to her palm.

"The evil in this world scares me. I'm probably never going to wake up and not be afraid, but being with you has brought light into those dark corners of my life. I can see now that I was a good father to Justin. My son was a happy, healthy, and well-loved child. What happened wasn't my fault."

"No, it wasn't."

"I'm a man of faith so I believe he's in a far

better place, in arms even more loving than my own."

"That has to be a comfort."

"Yes, it is." He looked at her then, his blue eyes glittering and intense. "I never thought this day would come, but I'm ready to be a father again, Shannon. I'm ready to be a husband again. You and our baby are my second chance. You, Shannon, are my heartsong."

That started her crying all over again. "Oh, Daniel, I love you."

"I love you, too, Shannon O'Toole."

But that's not my name!

She couldn't tell him now. Not today. Not like this.

She'd have to tell him. She couldn't bear to lie to him any longer.

The coward in her protested. **But are you really lying?** Maybe she wasn't born Shannon O'Toole, but she'd become her since moving to Eternity Springs. Honestly, if it were safe for her to start going by Chelsea right now, she didn't know if she'd make the change.

However, that was a question for another day. She had a reprieve. Today was all about Daniel—and his lips had taken hers in a kiss as sweet as Sarah's cinnamon rolls.

The mood lightened a bit after that. He talked a little more about Justin, sharing sweet stories and happy memories this time. He even laughed once or twice, and the sound did Shannon's heart good. Following a long moment of quiet reflection, he turned to her with a smile. "This experience has been cathartic for me, but now Hope's picnic basket is calling me. How about we head down and see what is in it?"

"Sounds like a spectacular idea."

They were perhaps a quarter of the way down the trail when they first heard the voices. Daniel glanced over his shoulder. "Sounds like we have company."

Shannon smothered a smile. It appeared that the text she'd sent Hope had worked.

As a result, she wasn't surprised to see searchers combing the forest floor in the spot where her clumsiness had caused the loss of Daniel's treasured Batman's arm. However, the number of searchers astounded her. In addition to Hope's husband, Lucca, the Turners, the Murphys, the Davenports, the Callahans, Colt Rafferty,

Cicero, and Celeste were there. Zach directed what was obviously a systematic search. They must have all dropped what they were doing immediately this morning when Shannon's plea went out.

At first sight of his friends, Daniel abruptly halted. "What the—"

Hope's gaze zeroed in on him and she studied him intently. Relief flooded her eyes and she offered him a brilliant smile. "Those new cell towers that have gone in on Murphy Mountain are fabulous, and smartphones are the bomb. Don't worry, Daniel. We'll find it."

He turned to Shannon. "What did you do?"

"I sent up the bat signal, of course. I knew our friends would help. This is Eternity Springs, after all."

Because it **was** Eternity Springs, nobody was surprised when a few moments later a voice rang out. "I found it!"

Celeste Blessing stood framed by two tall aspen trees, her hand raised, her fingers holding Daniel's treasured keepsake.

Daniel's voice cracked. "God, I love this town."

Chapter Fourteen

Because the women of Eternity Springs knew their men, they'd all brought along picnic baskets of their own. The impromptu picnic led to a pickup football game in the meadow that filled the afternoon with laughter—including Daniel's. It was a first for him in a decade of November thirds and when the party finally broke up, he thanked his friends for their friendship from the bottom of his heart.

As people climbed into their vehicles and began to leave, Daniel leaned against his Jeep with his arms crossed and a smile on his face waiting for Shannon, who stood over by the Murphys' car looking at kiddo pictures on Sarah's phone. Celeste approached Daniel and said, "I'm heading out, too, but first I have something for you. A gift."

He patted the Batman arm in his pocket. "I don't need any gifts, Celeste. You've already given me the world."

"Actually, 'gift' probably isn't the right

word. This is something you've earned."

She pulled something from the pocket of her white leather motorcycle jacket—a pendant on a long silver chain. Daniel recognized it. What seemed like half the guys in town wore it.

"This is the official Angel's Rest Healing Center blazon that I award to those who have embraced love's healing grace. You have traveled a long, arduous road littered with potholes of heartbreak, Daniel, but in loving Shannon, you have reached your destination. Love heals. Wear your pendant close to your heart and carry the symbol of love's healing grace with you as you begin a new journey of joy with Shannon at your side."

He leaned over and kissed Celeste's cheek. "Thank you, Celeste. I'm honored. And I'm so grateful to have found friends and my second chance here in Eternity Springs. I know you are a big part of the rejuvenation of this town that made it all possible. You are truly the town's treasure."

"Why, that's a lovely thing to say." She beamed up at him, sunshine in her smile. "Now, I do have one word of caution before

I go. About Shannon."

"Shannon?"

"The dear girl still has a little work to do." Celeste patted him on the arm. "Remember that, Daniel. Don't let hurt block you from the truth."

What hurt? What truth? But before he could ask, she turned away and headed for her Gold Wing. Then Shannon walked up beside him with a gleam in her eyes and invited him home to Heartsong Cottage, and he forgot about everything else. He traveled back to town with lightness in his heart beyond all imagining when he'd arrived in Eternity Springs.

"This has been a bearable day," he told her, taking her hand in his as they approached her back door, having parked the Jeep in the detached garage. "Justin loved the outdoors. He loved being with friends. He loved life, and today, I remembered to remember that. Having you beside me, supporting me, helped tremendously. Thank you, sweetheart."

"I was glad to help. Everybody was. We have great friends."

He released her hand to open the screen

door. "Yes, we definitely do."

Shannon stepped inside and he followed her, setting the empty picnic basket Hope had forgotten on top of her dryer. "I'd like music," she said, walking toward the front room. "What are you in the mood to hear, Daniel?"

He thought of the Jerry Jeff Walker tune whose lyrics spoke of listening to country when one was in pain. "Not country. How about—"

Her startled scream cut him off.

Daniel's heart dropped. The baby! He was moving toward the doorway before the sound died away. He burst into the living room to see her standing frozen, her complexion bleached white, her hands steepled over her mouth.

Her round-eyed, horror-filled gaze was fastened on a cloud of stuffing lying strewn across the hardwood of her living room floor. Daniel gazed from her to the stuffing, then back to her. "Jeeze, honey. You scared me. I thought something bad had happened."

She clutched at the back of a nearby chair, her knuckles white, and shifted her wild-eyed gaze toward the window as if seeking for signs of an intruder. The cop in Daniel went on full alert even as Soupy poked her head around the bedroom door, the body of the teddy bear he'd brought back to Shannon after his trip dangling from her mouth. "Bad dog," Daniel scolded, before returning his attention to Shannon.

"It's all right, honey. I can replace it with the exact same thing. It won't be any problem to call the shop and have it shipped."

A series of emotions flashed across her face. First bafflement replaced the fear, then slow-dawning realization, and finally, relief. "Soupy. It was Soupy."

Who did you think it was? "I'm sorry. I shouldn't have left her in the house. She was a terrible chewer as a puppy, but I thought she would have grown out of that."

"Soupy," she repeated.

She closed her eyes for a moment, then offered him a bright, fake smile. "No problem. That's good. A new bear would be nice."

Daniel watched her closely, reminded of crime victims in the wake of an attack. He hadn't missed her hand moving to cover her belly, a mother's protective gesture as old as time.

This wasn't about the bear. What was he missing here? "Shannon, what did you think—"

"Excuse me," she interrupted. "I need to run to the bathroom. Growing baby, you know." Then she dashed for the bathroom, leaving a frowning Daniel in her wake. What the heck was that all about? Her reaction had been totally out of proportion to the event.

Daniel stared at the closed bathroom door. This wasn't the first time she'd reacted peculiarly, either. His mind returned to Mallory Square during their Key West visit. She'd blanched then, too. "When somebody called her by a different name," he murmured softly.

Well, crap. He didn't need a visit from his Gypsy sixth sense to figure this out. Shannon was afraid. Of something. Someone. He'd shaken it off then, but he couldn't —wouldn't—do that this time. She had thought this blizzard of stuffed-animal polyfill was something other than what it was. The pieces to this particular puzzle fit together nicely and presented a clear and disturbing picture.

Shannon was afraid of someone.

Or, maybe he should say Chelsea was afraid of someone.

Seriously afraid. And she hadn't told him. After he'd laid open his soul to her, she'd continued to keep secrets? Why?

She doesn't trust me.

Why not? Because he failed his family once before? She's afraid history would repeat itself?

The idea was a knife to his heart, and harsh words formed on Daniel's tongue. Then the words Celeste had spoken to him that morning echoed through his mind.

"About Shannon."

"Shannon?"

"The dear girl still has a little work to do." Celeste patted him on the arm. **"Remember that, Daniel. Don't let hurt block you from the truth."**

He repeated those words to himself now and added, **Slow down. Don't assume. Get the facts and keep the focus on what's important.**

Something had the woman he loved frightened to death. He needed to find out what that something was.

Damned if he'd lose this second chance.

He turned on his heel and went into the kitchen where he removed a glass from the cabinet and filled it with water from the tap. He drained it, refilled it, and drank half of it down again. At the sound of Shannon's return, he set down his glass and filled a second glass with water and faced her. She still looked pale.

"Are you all right?" He handed her the glass.

"I'm fine." She sipped the water.

"In that case, why don't you tell me what's going on, Chelsea?"

Shannon couldn't hold back a little whimper. He'd put the clues together. No big surprise, of course. The man was a detective.

Facing her moment of truth and the steady demand in his crystal-blue eyes, she briefly considered attempting to bluff her way through it, though better sense prevailed. Daniel didn't deserve more lies, and something in his expression—patience, maybe?—suggested that everything would be okay. Hadn't she decided while washing her face not two minutes ago that if the moment presented itself, she'd come clean with him? **Here's your moment.**

"I planned to tell you, Daniel."

He folded his arms and waited without speaking.

"I thought it best to hold off until after today." She dragged her fingers through her hair and crossed to the stove. "I need some tea. Do you want some tea? I'm going to make some tea."

She noisily filled a kettle with water—banging the sink, rattling the lid, and setting it clumsily on the burner. She was shaking badly. Without saying a word, Daniel walked over and put his arms around her and held her. It was exactly what she'd needed, and relief washed through her.

Turning to face him, she took a deep breath and said, "I'm being stalked. The bottom line is that I'm hiding from him. Eternity Springs is my refuge."

Daniel lifted his hand and rubbed the back of his neck. "Sit down, Chelsea, and tell me your story from the beginning."

I'm not that woman anymore. "Shannon. I'm Shannon. She's who I am now."

"Okay." He pulled a chair away from the kitchen table. "Sit down, Shannon."

His easy acceptance of name choice had tears pooling suddenly in her eyes. Her knees a little weak, she sank into the chair.

"The beginning," he encouraged.

"You have to promise me if I tell you, you'll leave it alone. You can't fight him. He will win. He wins every time."

"Just talk to me, okay? From the beginning."

"No. You have to promise. I want your word, Daniel, otherwise I will sit here until doomsday, and I won't say a word."

"Honey. That's not—"

"Your word, Daniel!"

His lips went flat and he sighed. "All right. One question first. Are you wanted by the authorities?"

She blinked, totally taken off guard. "No. Not at all. I haven't done anything wrong. I haven't even had a traffic ticket in ten years."

"Okay, then. You have my word."

"Good. All right. Whew." She exhaled a

heavy breath and began. "Okay. I grew up in the Midwest. My parents divorced when I was a teenager and my mother remarried a nice guy from California. My father moved to Argentina with his girl-friend. I haven't seen him since. My step-dad was a great guy and my mom was happy, so it was all good. I did my under-grad at Stanford. I started dating a boy—Ted Colby—who was a computer engin-eering student. We fell in love and got engaged. It took me way too long to figure out that Teddy and his circle of friends—all idealistic computer nerds—had become involved in computer hacking. Serious hacking. Government databases and stuff.

"That **is** serious."

"I told Ted he had to stop. We almost broke up over it, but he eventually agreed that the thrill wasn't worth the risk. He told his friends he was quitting and that started a big brouhaha with the guys. The leader of the group was charming and friendly and very good-looking. He came to my apartment to plead their case, but he couldn't change my mind. He seemed to give in graciously. Yet, from then on, something about him made me uncomfortable.

"The summer before our final semester, Ted did an internship in Chicago. I worked a summer job, so I stayed busy, but I was alone. A few times the guys invited me to hang out with them, and I did. It was all friendly and innocent—until the night Russell followed me home and wouldn't leave." She paused for a long moment, working up the nerve. "He raped me."

Daniel swore beneath his breath and the gentle encouragement in his eyes evaporated in a flash of fury. "God, Shannon. No. Did the cops—"

"I didn't report it."

"But—"

"No. Let me get this out. I didn't report it because when I told him I was going to, he laughed in my face. No one would believe me. I was a little nobody from Kansas. He was somebody. Well, the son of somebody. He came from money. His father was a politician."

"Who?" Daniel demanded.

Shannon held her hand up, palm out, closed her eyes, and shook her head.

"Sorry," he murmured. "Go on."

"I didn't tell Ted until he came home. August fifteenth. I told him August fifteenth." She drew in a shuddering breath. "They all shared a house. An older place. Two stories. All the bedrooms were upstairs. Ted went home to confront Russell. The official story is Russell wasn't home. Ted somehow tripped down the stairs and broke his neck. Just an accident, everyone said. I even believed it. In fact, I blamed myself. He'd been so angry and I thought he must have been distracted and that's why he fell. I cannot tell you how horrible I felt."

"What made you suspect Russell?"

"His smirk at the funeral when he looked across Ted's casket toward me. I will remember it until my dying day. We were leaving the cemetery and he sidled up beside me and said, 'I told you to keep your mouth shut.'"

Daniel muttered a curse.

"Even then, I told myself my suspicions were crazy. Being a rapist didn't make someone a killer. It wasn't until later, after the second…incident…that suspicion escalated to belief."

"So he's your stalker."

"As always with Russell, I can't prove it, but I know he is. I didn't enroll that semester. I was a basket case and I left school. I moved home, rented a duplex near my mom's house, and took an admin job at the local high school. I came home one afternoon and found a Ken doll on my front doorstep. His head was separated from his body. I didn't think much about it at first. I thought a neighborhood kid had been playing on my porch. The next time, though, was creepy. He came into my house and left the first teddy bear on my bed. The bear had a big red bow tied way too tight around his neck."

"Teddy bear. Ted," Daniel murmured, making the connection. The kettle began to whistle, and he poured hot water into a mug and set it in front of her.

She chose a tea bag from the caddy on the table. "I think so. Since then, it's always been teddy bears, and the frequency with which they appeared escalated. I moved four times. He always found me. When the bears began showing up without arms and legs and the missing limbs turned up at Mom's house, I really began to get scared."

"What did the cops do?"

Her lips twisted with bitterness. "Nothing. They didn't believe me. I got labeled a crackpot and that was that."

"You're kidding me."

"Nope. I'm still the little nobody from Kansas. He's still the senator's son."

"Senator? United States senator? Who the hell is this guy?"

Shannon winced. She hadn't meant for that to slip out. Although she didn't know what difference it made because Daniel could probably learn on his own in less than ten minutes based on the little she'd given him so far. She took a sip of her tea, then spoke the name. "Wilbarger. Russell Wilbarger."

"Holy crap, Shannon. They're not Kennedy fame and fortune, but they're not far behind."

"It's a no-win situation for me."

"So how did you choose Eternity Springs?"

"I was living in Denver waiting tables while I tried to figure out what to do with my life.

I'd lost my parents the previous year within six weeks of each other, Mom from complications from diabetes and my stepdad of a heart attack, and they'd left me enough money to buy some time. Or so I thought. The day I came home from the gym one afternoon and found stuffing scattered all over my apartment and a teddy bear carcass pinned to my bed with a butcher knife, I knew I needed to do something drastic. My guardian angel must have been looking out for me because that night I overheard a particularly interesting conversation between one of my customers and her friend. She said that a distant relative had died and left her a pub in a middle-of-nowhere town, and she didn't know what she was going to do with it—especially with her upcoming wedding. She was flying to Japan to marry her fiancé who worked there with the Foreign Service."

"Shannon O'Toole?" Daniel asked.

"Yes."

"Handy."

"I thought so at the time. Now I think it was meant to be."

"You may be right. The one thing I can tell

you is that Russell Wilbarger needs to be in jail." With that, Daniel's questions became all business. "Did you have a security system?"

"By the third incident, yes. He always wore something that shielded him—hats and sunglasses. One winter he even wore a ski mask."

Daniel reached into his pocket and removed the small spiral notebook and pen that he carried constantly. For the next ten minutes he quizzed her like a math professor, drawing out every detail she could recall about the stalking incidents and the day Ted died. "Tell me about the roommate, the one in his room. Was that the guy in Key West?"

"No. The Key West guy's name is Alden Ramer. Alden had already graduated at that point. The guy in his room was Larry Dennard. Larry was the nerdiest of the group. Smartest, too, I think. He founded a firm that does some sort of computer security thing. He's been wildly successful. You've probably used his equipment."

"So this Larry didn't see what happened?"

"That's what he claimed at the time. He

said he heard Ted cry out, and thuds and bumps as he fell. He said Ted's voice cut off abruptly about halfway through the fall."

"You didn't believe him?"

"I did at first."

"He said Wilbarger wasn't there?"

Shannon nodded slowly. "He told everyone he was alone in the house."

"You don't believe him."

"I did then. After the funeral, I wondered."

"Why is that? If he was in his room, he wouldn't necessarily have seen anything."

She pursed her lips and tried to put her feelings into words. "It was subtle and something I only noticed in reflection. Larry had all but worshipped at Russell's feet. He was like a puppy dog, always begging for the treat of attention. But at the funeral..."

Shannon pursed her lips and thought back to that horrible event. She'd been in shock. Her mom and stepdad had come, and her mother had held Shannon's hand throughout the service, her lifeline. Ted's mother sobbed quietly throughout. His father stood like a stone. "Larry and Russell were both pallbearers, as were two of their other roommates."

"Names?"

She told him and he jotted them down. "They were both in class when it happened. They had a big exam. They were both obviously devastated at the funeral. Larry was...different. He was pale and withdrawn and uncomfortable around me. I don't think he ever met my eyes. The biggest deal was that he stood apart from Russell."

"Did you ever ask him why?"

She shook her head. "I never saw him again. I left school."

Daniel made more notes in his book, then fired off a few more questions about the funeral. He did not pursue further questions about the rape, thank goodness, because Shannon couldn't go there. Talking about Ted's death left her raw enough.

Finally, she said, "Stop. I cannot think about him anymore. He's my past and I've truly begun to believe"—superstitiously, she knocked on the kitchen table—"that he's going to stay there."

"He needs to be stopped."

"Maybe someday, someone will do it. It won't be us."

"But—"

"You promised me you'd leave it alone," she said. "You gave me your word."

He shoved to his feet and paced the kitchen, raking his fingers through his hair. "We're going to have to figure a way to get through this, Shannon. I gave you my word as it pertained to a stalker. I did not, however, say I'd let a murderer go free. That's something different."

"Exactly," she protested. "It's even more reason for you to leave it alone."

"Shannon." He chastised her with both his tone and the chiding look in his eyes. "You know me better than that. Let's have some honesty here. You had to know what my reaction would be when you told me the entire truth."

"But—"

"Shannon?"

"Oh, all right." She sighed heavily. "I guess I knew you wouldn't be happy."

"Not happy? Sunshine, the fact that all this happened to you—that the guy has gotten away with it until now—just pisses me off so bad that I...hell...it makes me feel...impotent."

That startled a laugh from her. "You?

Impotent? You're a walking erection, Daniel."

He frowned at her. "I don't know if that's a compliment or an insult. Look. Your safety and that of the baby's is my highest priority. I understand evil. I have a lot of up close and personal experience with evil. Put aside the fact that seeing Wilbarger pay for his sins is the right thing to do, we as a family can't live with this sword hanging above our necks. We have to deal with this. You need to trust my experience here. I won't let Russell Wilbarger be a threat to you any longer. You're not alone any longer, Shannon. You need to trust me."

We as a family. She took the words into her heart and hugged them.

"I need some time, Daniel. I need to think about it."

"Fair enough."

She knew the man well enough to be certain her reprieve wouldn't last for long. However, now free of the burden of her secrets, she experienced a wave of sudden giddiness. She rose from the table and went to him, her joy reflected in the lightness of her step and velocity of her smile.

"Now, about that question?"

His expression went wary. "What question?"

"Compliment or insult? Why don't we take it into the bedroom and see if we can't come up with an answer?"

A slow smile spread across his lips. Shannon pulled his face down to hers and gave him her hottest of kisses. Later, as she lay snuggled against him, warm and naked and sated, she reflected on the day. All in all, it had turned out better than expected.

Daniel trailed his thumb slowly up and down her back, and they lay together accompanied by only the sound of Soupy's snore coming from her bed beside the fireplace.

Until his deep voice rumbled, "Chelsea Abbott. It's a pretty name. Sure you don't want to—"

"I'm sure," she interrupted, sorry that her reprieve appeared to be over. She closed her eyes. "Chelsea Abbott no longer exists."

"Sure she does." Daniel kissed the top of her head. "She still has a Social Security number. Still pays taxes out of a trust account. Unless you've finagled a death certificate since we returned from Key West, that is."

She went still. "You investigated me, didn't you?"

"I checked out the name."

She rolled onto her back. "I really wish you wouldn't have done that, but I guess I always knew you would. It's why I haven't stopped looking over my shoulder or shaking at the sight of strange cars, and why every time I see a number I don't recognize on caller ID, I break out in a cold sweat. So much for peace and tranquility."

"Now, Shannon."

"He'll find out, Daniel. He always does. I think he must have hacked into the NSA network or something."

He shifted onto his side and came up on his elbow. "I may not have a computer science degree, but when it comes to investigation, I'm no slouch myself. I'll find what we need to neutralize any threat to you and our child."

"You don't understand Russell."

"And you underestimate me. I will protect you, Shannon. You are my light and I won't let darkness win. Not again. Trust me."

Yearning welled within her. "I'm scared. Aren't you scared?"

"Honestly, for the first time in a decade, no, I'm not. I'm determined. You are my beacon, Shannon. You've led me out of the darkness. Let me return the favor." He leaned down and sweetly kissed her lips and repeated, "Trust me."

Dare she? Of course. She already trusted him. She wouldn't have told him about her past otherwise. Conceding to that reality, she licked her lips and said, "Okay. I will. I do."

"And, marry me."

"Okay. I...wait—what?" Her heart leaped and she sat up abruptly.

He laughed and pulled her back down and rolled above her. His sapphire eyes glowed with love as he locked his gaze with hers. "Marry me. Not because of the baby—though she is a bonus—but because I'm desperately in love with you and I can't live without you. Say yes, my love."

"Yes, my love." Her smile bloomed like a Rocky Mountain meadow in springtime. "Yes, I'll marry you."

The joy that filled Daniel's eyes was beautiful to behold.

"And to think the tourists believe summertime provides the best scenery around Eternity Springs," Rose remarked one week later as she helped Shannon work the tap in Murphy's Pub, filling another round for the local men who'd joined Daniel for a strategizing session—Jack Davenport, Gabe Callahan, Zach Turner, and Lucca Romano. "So much beefcake here I don't know if my little old heart can handle it."

Shannon grinned. "Better not let Cicero hear you say things like that. He'll get jealous."

Rose's smile went sly. "Yeah. Then he'll do the branding-me-as-his-own thing again. He does this thing with his tongue that—"

"TMI, Mrs. Cicero. TMI."

Both women laughed as the pub's front door opened and another man sauntered in. "Holy cow," Shannon murmured. "Hard to imagine but the scenery just got even better. Who is **that**?"

The man was younger than the others, but no less tall, dark, and handsome. He had vivid eyes the color of the forest in springtime and shoulders that rivaled the span of Daniel's. Something about him looked familiar, but she couldn't place him. "That's Brick Callahan. Gabe's nephew."

"Brick?"

"A nickname that stuck, I believe. He's Mark's son by his first wife."

"Wow, those Callahan men are pretty, aren't they?"

"Genes are hard to beat."

"So is the way they look in jeans."

Shannon and Rose shared a look and a laugh, then delivered the drinks. After Gabe introduced his nephew to Shannon, Rose retreated upstairs for what Jack Davenport had termed the "hen party"—right before his wife, Cat, socked him on the shoulder.

Shannon had closed Murphy's tonight in order to accommodate the meeting that Daniel had finally talked her into convening. She'd been a bundle of nerves in the hours leading up to it, worried how her friends would react to her confession. She need not have worried. To a man—and woman—they supported her.

I am so blessed. What was that Celeste-ism about friends? Something about friends being the air that put the lift beneath wings? After the gift of their support tonight, she seriously felt as if she could fly.

Daniel had told the story for her—just the basics, not the gory details—while standing behind her, his hands resting on her shoulders. Out of everyone, only Rose, her best friend, threw her a less-than-sympathetic frown. Shannon read the message in her expression. **You could have told me. You should have told me.**

I'm sorry, Shannon had silently telegraphed back. **I was afraid.**

Rose had nodded once, and that had been that.

Daniel had finished his summation of their situation, then asked Shannon, "Would you like to share our other bit of news?"

"I would. Daniel and I are getting married on December 28. We hope you'll join us."

They'd chosen to keep an announcement about the baby for a later date, though not too much later since the fact would become apparent in another month and obvious by their wedding day.

Their friends' reaction to word of the pending nuptials was all that Shannon could have hoped for. Rose squealed and hugged her. Hope burst into tears and threw her arms around Daniel. The men started ribbing him in the way men did, until Celeste announced that she thought the women should reconvene upstairs where they could commence wedding planning in peace.

Celeste pulled a notebook from her tote bag. "We've much to do in a little over a month. How many guests do you expect, Shannon?"

"We're going to try to keep it small. I'm alone, but Daniel said his whole family will attend. He has three brothers—two of them unmarried—and his parents are still alive."

"Two unmarried brothers?" Celeste's voice hummed with interest and she made a note.

"Younger brothers."

"Even better."

"Speaking of brothers, Daniel has accepted a job working with Gabe's family's security firm. He'll do consulting, but mainly teaching. He really enjoyed that, and he needs a break from the other."

"That's wonderful news," Hope said. "I'm so glad for him. Thrilled for you both."

Nic said, "The whole Callahan clan is planning to spend Christmas here, so they'll swell your numbers."

"Speaking of Callahans...what's the dish on the dish?"

"Brick?" Nic's eyes twinkled. "I think like so many other Texans this time of year, he's come to Colorado hunting. Only not deer or elk. Veterinarians."

"He's trying to steal you away from his uncle?" Savannah Turner asked.

Nic laughed. "He hasn't admitted it, but I think he has his eye on Lori. She did a summer internship on the Callahan ranch. I think sparks flew."

"I thought she was dating some guy from Denver?" Ali Timberlake asked.

"The girl changes boyfriends as often as her shoes."

"Except for Chase," Ali replied, a wistful note in her voice. "Once upon a time, I thought those two would marry."

Celeste patted Ali's hand. "There, there, dear. It will be all right. You know that, don't you?"

Ali responded with only a sickly smile. Shannon recalled the woman Chase Timberlake had with him at Murphy's a couple months ago. She was athletic and outgoing and gorgeous. Shannon could see why she'd succeeded as a television star.

"When is his wedding?" Cat Davenport asked.

"Valentine's Day," Ali said. "But that's enough about that wedding. We're here to talk about Daniel and Shannon's. Are you thinking a church wedding or Angel's Rest?"

"We booked St. Stephen's yesterday."

"What about a dress?"

"I have one. My grandmother saved hers for me." She didn't share that she hadn't wanted to wear it for her wedding to Ted. Now she believed she knew why. This wedding, to this man, while wearing the gown her grandmother had worn when she married Shannon's grandfather, had been meant to be.

Their wedding planning took longer than Daniel's strategizing about how to save her life, and when the men began calling up the stairs for their "women" to come fix them "samiches" like "good little wives," Celeste shut her notebook and said, "I think we've made an excellent start on the planning. Better get downstairs before one of the Neanderthals goes too far and comes to me needing to rent a room for the night. Angel's Rest is completely booked. A quilters' retreat."

"Would serve them all right," Cat grumbled.

"Wait a minute," Shannon began. "Before you go, there's something I want to say, I need to say." She gazed around the table and her heart filled and overflowed. "I can't thank you enough for your friendship and understanding and support. I found my home in Eternity Springs. I found a life here."

Celeste rose and gave her a hug. "We are so glad you did. In fact, to mark this occasion I have a little gift for you."

She removed an Angel's Rest blazon from her bag, and seeing it, Shannon knew that she had, indeed, found a home.

Now if she could only stay alive to enjoy it.

Chapter Fifteen

Daniel lowered his cell phone and told himself there was no need to fret. Russell Wilbarger was in Washington, D.C., under surveillance by Mark Callahan, and Shannon was tucked away at Jack Davenport's estate, Eagle's Rest, where the security system surpassed anything Daniel had ever seen. She would be safe until he got home.

He missed her. He'd been on the road crisscrossing the country for weeks now, making it home to Eternity Springs only long enough to pick up Shannon and take her to Boston to meet his family at Thanksgiving. They'd loved her, of course, and the holiday had been his happiest in a decade.

He'd hoped to be home before now, but so far, his search for dirt on the dirtbag had turned up infuriatingly little. He'd interviewed over a dozen people. Spent hours upon hours poring over databases and researching newspaper archives. Experience had taught Daniel that the criminal who committed one vile act invariably had others waiting to be uncovered. So far, he'd come up dry, but it was only a matter of time until he found it. If he was going to have this threat eliminated by the wedding day—his goal—then he needed to find the so-far-elusive evidence PDQ.

He had his hopes up for today's meeting. He'd wanted to interview Larry Dennard right off the bat, but the man and his wife had been out of the country on an extended business trip to Asia, and today was his first available appointment. Daniel checked his phone for the time. Ten minutes to the hour and a five-minute walk through downtown Austin from his hotel. Might as well get going.

He exited the elevator in the high-rise office building at precisely ten o'clock. "Daniel Garrett to see Mr. Dennard," he said to the pretty blond receptionist.

"Good morning, Mr. Garrett. If you'll have a seat I'll let Mr. Dennard know you're here."

"Thank you."

The man kept him waiting ten minutes.

He assumed it was a power play until Dennard walked another man out, shook his hand, and thanked him for coming in. "Appreciate the special trip, Ryan. Next time I'll come to you. You have my word on it."

"Hey, no problem, man. I love doing business with you. Never had such a conscientious consultant."

When the visitor exited the office lobby, the receptionist said, "Mr. Dennard, Mr. Garrett is here for your ten o'clock."

Honest delight lit the man's expression. "Garrett. You're the consultant with Callahan Security, correct? Pleasure to meet you, sir."

"Thanks for giving me your time, Mr. Dennard."

"Call me Larry, please." The two men shook hands, then Dennard continued, "Follow me back to my office. Can we get you a cup of coffee or a soft drink?"

"Water would be nice."

Larry led him down a hallway to a corner office. While the businessman poured two glasses of water, Daniel perused the framed certificates hanging on the wall:

Boy Scouts' volunteer award, certificate of appreciation from a church youth group, Citizen of the Year from the city. Guy was a do-gooder. Excellent.

Larry handed Daniel one of the glasses of water, then instead of taking a seat behind his large mahogany desk, he sat in one of a pair of easy chairs placed in front of the floor-to-ceiling windows and motioned for Daniel to take the other. "What can I do for the Callahans?"

"Answer some questions," Daniel replied.

"About our product line? Our service plan?"

"Russell Wilbarger."

Every drop of color drained from the man's face. He sat back heavily in his chair. Daniel's heartbeat quickened, and he leaned forward, his detective's nose sniffing the scent of the trail.

"I haven't seen Russell since college," Dennard said, making an ineffective stab at deflection.

"It's his college years that interest me at this point. You lived with him then. You were a member of AnonyBytes."

Dennard winced and closed his eyes. "I

was young and stupid and idealistic."

"Actually, I was told you are extremely smart."

"Not then, I wasn't." Dennard rose and crossed his office to a wet bar. He poured a glass of water from a pitcher and downed it like a tumbler full of scotch. "I did some very stupid things, and I learned the cost of inadvisable friendships. It's a lesson I've tried to teach my own children. I've spent the years since trying to make up for my mistakes.

"Mr. Garrett, let me give you a piece of advice. You are obviously very good at what you do. You wouldn't be working with the Callahans otherwise. But you don't want to tangle with Russell Wilbarger. He was bad news in college, and like the saying goes, leopards don't change their spots. Now that he's following in his father's footsteps in politics, I can't imagine that his character has changed for the better."

"You are right about that." Daniel decided to cut to the chase. "Do you remember Chelsea Abbott?"

Dennard's gaze shifted out the window.

"Of course. Really sweet girl. I haven't seen her since college, either."

"She's a wonderful woman and she needs your help. She's being terrorized by Russell Wilbarger, and I'm looking for leverage to shut him down. You were in the house on the day Ted Colby died. I need you to tell me about it, in as much detail as you can recall."

Larry crossed to the window and stood with his hands shoved into his pockets, gazing out at the cityscape, contemplating or reflecting or making some sort of decision. Daniel knew the value of patience, so he allowed the moment to drag out.

When the man finally spoke, Daniel almost wished he hadn't.

"Ted Colby was a great guy, a fabulous friend, just an all-around fine human being. He was head-over-heels in love with Chelsea. Shoot, we were all a little in love with her. She was so sweet and kind and funny. A beautiful girl who didn't act like she knew it. I was overweight and already losing my hair and awkward. Never had a girlfriend in my life. Chelsea never once treated me like a loser. Neither did Ted. He was a true friend. I could see that in hindsight. At the time, I was blinded by Russell's charisma. By the time those blinders came off, it was too late. At least, that's what I've tried to convince myself ever since."

Daniel waited, and a full minute passed before Larry spoke again. "I told myself I was helping a friend, but that's a lie. I let my real friends down. Ted and Chelsea were my real friends. You said Russell's been terrorizing Chelsea. Tell me what he has done to her."

Daniel had no intention of telling anyone about the rape, but he detailed a handful of the stalking incidents, finishing with, "She's expecting her first child. She needs to neutralize the threat to her."

Larry glanced over his shoulder. "A baby! That's wonderful news for her. Tell her I'm very happy for her."

"If you're happy for her, then help her. Give me something on Wilbarger."

Again, another long pause. "I never wanted my wife and children to know. It may well ruin me."

He's close, but not quite there yet. "He hurt her, Larry. He physically hurt her. I don't doubt that she's not the only woman he's hurt. Was he there the day Ted died?"

"Yes." Larry turned to face Daniel. "I didn't hear anything. I was in my room wearing headphones. I didn't see the fight. But..."

"But?"

Larry exhaled heavily, then nodded once. He walked to his desk and pushed an intercom button. "Mary, get Louise Burnett on the phone, would you please?"

But? Daniel sensed the man had something big to offer. But what? Keeping his impatience in check proved to be an exercise in discipline.

"Louise. Good morning. I need you to bring an investigator onto our legal team so I can provide him some information that's going to leave me open to legal charges." He paused while the lawyer talked. "Yes. Yes. No. We'll need to negotiate. Yes. No. I have full confidence in you. Yes. Daniel Garrett—" He glanced at Daniel. "Is that one **t** or two **ts**?"

"Two."

"Two **ts**. With Callahan Security. Yes. Yes. Gotcha. Will do. Yes, right now, please. So, what did you think of the woodworking project that Landry brought home from the den meeting last week? Pretty cool, wasn't it?"

Larry and the woman Daniel deduced to be his attorney spoke for another two minutes until a knock sounded on the office door and the secretary walked into the room carrying a printed sheet of paper. Larry called, "Come in. Mary has it now. Thank you. Will do. See you at the next den meeting."

He ended the call and handed Daniel a paper to sign. An employment agreement. "It's time I own up to my personal failings. Give me your John Hancock, and I'll give you Russell Wilbarger."

"I'd give you my left nut for him."

"I'm tempted to take it because my own are in full retreat. The idea of taking on Russell chills like jumping into a glacier lake. However, you're gonna need yours if you're going after him."

"Oh, I'm going after him, all right." Daniel scratched his name across the contract.

"Thank you." Larry stared down at the contract, then when he lifted his gaze toward Daniel, a haunted look had entered his eyes. "Russell was there when Ted died, and I knew it."

"He knew you knew it?"

"Yes." He closed his eyes for a moment, then announced in a voice ripe with shame, "He offered me fifty thousand dollars to lie about it, and I took the money."

Bingo. It was all Daniel could do not to pump his fist.

What Larry said next had his mouth dropping open in shock.

"I didn't realize until two months after Ted's funeral that I had evidence showing Larry pushed him down the stairs. By then, I'd already sunk the money into start-up costs for my business."

"Evidence? You had evidence?"

"Somebody was stealing my candy. I wanted to find out who. I set up a nanny cam to identify the culprit. It automatically backed up online. It was searchable. Caught the argument between Ted and Larry and had a clear picture of the fall."

Daniel took a step forward. "You're telling me you had video showing Russell Wilbarger kill Ted Colby?"

"Yes."

"Please tell me you still have it."

"Yes, it's in a safe-deposit box."

Daniel could hardly believe what he'd just heard. The man had proof? And he'd kept it hidden all this time? Left a murdering rapist to go free and continue to terrorize?

"In addition to the video, I have a file filled with some very interesting financial records. After Ted died, I walked away from Anony-Bytes. Russell did not. Nor did he discover the back door I built into our little network, so when he took hacking to a new level I was able to watch—and document. He's stolen a significant amount of money and has it stashed offshore."

Daniel didn't try to hide his shock at this. "You've been watching him all these years?"

"I always knew this day would come. I'm ashamed to say I didn't have the courage to make it happen myself. I've very glad you came to see me, Detective Garrett. Glad, but at the same time, scared to death."

"This is it. We have him. This is icing on the cake."

"Not necessarily. He's a wealthy, powerful member of a wealthy, powerful family. He has dangerous friends."

Daniel thought of the many law enforcement professionals with whom he'd worked over the course of his career. Add to that the friendships he'd developed as a result of his connection to Eternity Springs—Jack Davenport and the Callahans. Zach Turner was no slouch, either. A slow smile dawned across Daniel's face. Dangerous friends? "Don't worry, Larry. So do I."

Events happened quickly over the next two weeks. After viewing and copying Larry Dennard's video and financial files, Daniel returned to Eternity Springs and consulted with his experts over the regular poker game at Cam Murphy's place. Over a two-dollar ante pot, the team developed a plan. The following day, they put the plan into action. It was a glorious thing to watch.

Amazing how quickly the government could move when motivated. His team did motivation very well. Daniel watched the developments from afar, his own job being the most important of all—acting as personal bodyguard to the woman who'd brought him back into the light.

A week before Christmas, the hammer went down.

Shannon sat snuggled up against Daniel on the sofa in Heartsong Cottage watching cable news. "I guess the political paparazzi are everywhere now," she observed. "I must say it's gratifying to see his perp walk on national TV."

Matt Callahan's wife, Torie, had been the one to suggest tipping off the camera hounds. A former paparazzo herself, she'd known just who to call with the tip. "The news sharks are in a feeding frenzy," Daniel observed, watching with smug satisfaction as a throng of microphones and cameras surrounded Russell and the men taking him into custody. "I love it."

In the background, reporters droned on, but Daniel didn't really listen to them. He was busy being captivated by the change he spotted in this new, relaxed version of the woman he loved. She glowed with a quiet confidence and inner joy that either never previously existed or had burned with a mere glimmer of a flame before now.

"We shouldn't get ahead of ourselves," she murmured. "He'll make bail."

"I wouldn't count on it, if I were him. He's a definite flight risk. Prosecutors will ask for him to be denied bail, but even if the judge lets him out, he'll make him wear a bracelet. You don't need to worry about Russell Wilbarger any longer. You're safe, darling."

She tugged her gaze away from the TV. "I know I said this before, but it bears repeating. Thank you, Daniel. You've given me back my life."

"Right back at you, babe. I am totally in your debt."

She gave him a little impish grin and said, "In that case, begin to pay it down and tell me where you're taking me on our honeymoon."

"Not a chance." He leaned down and nipped her bottom lip. "You said to surprise you. It's going to be a surprise."

"But I'm worried about what to pack."

"Now, that's just silly since I intend to keep you naked all the time." She rolled her eyes and he rolled her backward. They ended up on the floor—laughing and happy and naked—with all thought of Russell Wilbarger banished from their minds. So it was later, much later, after they'd showered together and dressed to go out to dinner at Ali Timberlake's Yellow Kitchen restaurant that the presence of the news truck parked down the street caught them unawares. Before he knew what was happening, a swarm of reporters surrounded them, cameras whirring and clicking.

"Detective Garrett! Detective Garrett! Tell us what put you on the trail of Russell Wilbarger. Detective Garrett, you specialize in finding children. Is Russell Wilbarger a suspect in a missing-child case? Is he a pedophile? Detective Garrett! Did you interview Senator Wilbarger?"

Oh, holy hell. Daniel shot Shannon a sidelong glance, concerned about her reaction. She didn't appear pleased, but neither did she look frightened. He gave her hand a squeeze, then addressed the reporters' questions, managing to say little more than "no comment" with skill born of experience. Finally, though, he decided he'd fed them enough. "That's it. I have no further comment. You all have a nice day."

He placed his hand at the small of Shannon's back and guided her up the street away from Heartsong Cottage. Shannon said, "That was a skillful bit of deflection. You are good at that."

"Practice, I'm afraid. That's another thing I won't miss going forward."

"You're excited about consulting."

"Yes, I am. I'm excited about life, and it's all because of you." He brought her hand up to his mouth and kissed it. They shared a warm smile until a stranger's voice interrupted the moment.

"Detective Garrett, may I have a moment of your time?"

He sighed and tore his gaze away from Shannon. The pretty blond woman looked vaguely familiar. "I have no further comment."

Ignoring the statement, she quickly said, "I'm Amanda Carstairs with WBPA in Boston. I covered your son's kidnapping and murder a decade ago, and some of the missing-children cases you've worked since then."

Daniel remembered this reporter. "You've been very helpful in the past, Amanda. I appreciate it."

"I attempted to contact you last fall about

a documentary I've done about lost children who've come home. I wasn't able to reach you."

Last fall. Probably when he'd been hidden away here with Linda and Benny.

"The program is finished and set to air on Christmas Day, but I need to replace one of the segments. One of the teenagers we featured attempted suicide last week."

"Oh, no," Shannon murmured as Daniel grimaced.

The reporter continued. "It's heartbreaking for her family, and they've asked me to pull her segment. I had already contacted Mrs. Romano about adding Holly's story when news about Russell Wilbarger broke. We're taping with Holly tomorrow morning."

"Hope and Holly's father agreed to this?" Daniel was surprised. Hope had always been careful about the media exposure her family allowed—something Daniel advised as a primary safety measure.

"Yes. Mrs. Romano has very strict—and smart—requirements, but I showed her a clip from the show. It is heartwarming and hopeful. I'm very proud of it. Holly is excited to be part of it, but her story won't be complete without your input. Please say you'll do it?"

Daniel glanced at Shannon. She encouraged him with a nod.

"Okay."

Amanda Carstairs broke into a happy smile. "Wonderful. Thank you so much. I'll make the process as painless for you as possible, I promise. We are filming at Angel's Rest. If you'll be there tomorrow morning at ten, that will fabulous."

They shook hands, then the reporter strode away, whistling. Her cheeks rosy from the air's winter chill and her doe eyes warm with affection, Shannon said, "How fun. I always dreamed of being married to a TV star."

"I promised to make your dreams come true, didn't I?"

"You did. You have. I love you, Daniel."

He kissed her once, hard. "I love you, too."

She insisted on going with him to the taping the following day, and delighted him by getting a little teary-eyed when Holly gushed about her role as a flower girl at their wedding.

"I'm so happy for Daniel and Ms. Shannon and their baby," Holly told Amanda. Then realizing what she'd said, her eyes widened and she clapped her hands over her mouth. "Oh, no. I'm not supposed to tell. It's a secret!"

Daniel immediately whipped his head around to meet Shannon's gaze. He held up his hands. "Hey, I didn't spill."

"I didn't, either."

"So it's true?" Hope asked, excitement lighting her eyes despite the wince of embarrassment etched across her face. "We didn't know, honestly. One of the Cicero children told Holly he overheard his parents talking about it, but we didn't want to be nosy and ask."

Her eyes dancing, the reporter asked, "Do we need to edit that out, Detective?"

Daniel spoke to Shannon. "Honey?"

"Are you positively certain they'll be thrilled?"

"I am."

"In that case..." She shrugged. "Leave it in. Everyone can count, and doing it this way lets everyone know at once. Your family will all be here Christmas Day. If we watch the program together and let that be our big reveal, it could be fun."

He considered the idea, nodded slowly. "Yeah."

"So I'm not in trouble?" Holly piped up.

"Not one little bit, Little Bit," Daniel leaned down and pressed a kiss against her forehead.

The TV people used that moment for the closing shot for the interview. The producers called it the most heartwarming moment in television since Lassie saved Timmy.

From Daniel's perspective, watching his mother melt into a mushy, teary puddle of joy as comprehension bloomed would top it by a mile.

Chapter Sixteen

Shannon awoke on her wedding day with a song in her heart.

For a few moments, she reflected on the miracle of the day. After Ted's death, she'd wondered if she'd ever find another love. Once Russell began his nasty little tricks, she hadn't dared to even dream about getting married. She never would have guessed she'd find her hero in a little mountain town halfway to nowhere.

But found him, she had. Now at five o'clock this evening, she'd have that church wedding complete with an ivory satin gown trimmed in antique lace, three brides-maids, a sweetheart of a flower girl, and a reception at the community center where it all began.

Could she be any more blessed?

Now she just had to brave the chill of the winter morning and make coffee for herself since Daniel wasn't here to bring it to her in bed. How quickly she'd grown accustomed to that little perk, not to mention sharing a mattress with the blast furnace of a man who kept her toasty warm on these cold winter nights.

She stretched and yawned and wished she'd taken the time to set up the coffee-maker last night before she'd gone to bed. But she'd been floating on a cloud of happiness after the rehearsal. She'd been too lazy to do it.

On the bedside table, her phone vibrated. She identified the number and smiled. "Happy wedding day."

"Are you all right?" Daniel snapped.

The worry in his voice cued her that this was not an idle question. "I'm fine. Why? What's the matter?"

When he didn't immediately reply, she sat up. "Daniel? What's wrong, honey?"

"Nothing. I guess. I just...I woke up with a bad feeling. You sure everything is fine?"

"Yes, Daniel. I just woke up myself. I'm still in bed. Even Soupy is sleeping in. She's all cuddled up in her bed."

"Maybe I should come over and check on things."

"Don't be silly. I'm fine. Everything is fine. It's our wedding day!" What was the matter with the man? He seemed just fine yesterday. Could men get bridal jitters? Groomal nerves? She wanted to giggle at the silly, nonexistent word that had popped into her brain. Instead, she put a pout in her voice as she asked, "Aren't you excited? I am."

"This is a stupid tradition. I should be there with you."

"No, you shouldn't. It's a fine tradition, and frankly, I don't have time for you today. My day is packed from beginning to end."

"What's first on the agenda?"

Shannon rolled her eyes. "Why do you want to know? If I tell you are you going to 'coincidentally' show up?"

His long pause answered the question for her. "Daniel, you're just nervous about the ceremony. You told me last night you had lost-ring anxiety."

"Yes, but—"

"I'm fine. You need to find something to do to keep yourself busy. Take your brothers to Refresh and play with some of Cam's toys. I heard he has some new crossbows that have the hunters in town all agog."

"Agog?" Daniel muttered. "That's a ridiculous word."

Shannon decided not to argue any more, but to let him work his way around to her way of thinking. He repeated, "Where are you going to be today?"

"If I tell you will you promise not to show up?"

"Yes."

"Or send one of your brothers around to check on me?"

"I don't think there's any tradition about brothers, but no, I won't send them to check on you." He waited a beat, then added, "I was thinking of one of the Callahans."

Shannon rolled her eyes, then recited her schedule. "If you feel better having Brick Callahan standing around watching me get a pedicure then by all means, send him on over to the Angel's Rest spa. At least he's pretty to look at."

"That's a helluva thing to say to your groom on your wedding day," he grumbled.

"I love you, Daniel."

"I love you, too, Shannon."

"Today is going to be wonderful. Don't fret. Get your brothers and go play with Cam's toys. Just don't play too hard. You need to save some energy for tonight. Wait until you see my nightgown. It's soft and silky and clings like a second skin. And, it's your favorite color."

"I don't have a favorite color."

"You will after tonight."

With that, she managed to get a groan out of him, and then a laugh—the perfect way to end the call.

Laughing herself, she threw back the covers and climbed out of bed. She slipped her feet into her house shoes, pulled on her robe, and hurried to the kitchen. The new coffeemaker they'd received as a wedding gift ground the beans in addition to brewing the coffee, and the aroma was to die for. She closed her eyes, inhaled the delicious scent, and dreamed about the day to come. Mrs. Garrett. Shannon Garrett.

She'd never imagined she could be this happy.

When the coffee was ready, she filled a mug to take into the bathroom while she showered. She turned around.

And screamed.

In the creekside cabin Shannon had rented for him for the night at Angel's Rest, Daniel stared down at the phone and tried to tell himself that the dread churning through his gut was a result of his usual nightmare. Sure, he hadn't had it in weeks, but then he didn't always remember his dreams, did he? It wasn't surprising that his subconscious would churn up the old memories on the eve of his day of beginning again. Shoot, it would be more surprising if he'd not had the dream.

He threw back the covers and minutes later stood beneath a steaming shower. Speaking with Shannon had eased his mind, he insisted to himself. She was right. He was being ridiculous. This was Eternity Springs and Russell Wilbarger was under house arrest in Virginia, wearing a bracelet, and being surveilled by members of Callahan's security team. Shannon was in no danger from him.

Yet, as he switched off the water and grabbed a fluffy white towel, his stomach continued to churn.

Wilbarger could have hired someone to do his dirty work. What about the senior senator himself? Everyone said he was a fine person, that he and his wife were devastated by their son's criminality. But Daniel hadn't met an honest politician yet.

He should have planned today better. He hadn't anticipated that she'd kick him out of Heartsong Cottage last night before midnight, so he hadn't arranged extra security. He should have argued with her more, but he'd been in a mellow mood after all the toasts his brothers and friends had offered last night at the rehearsal dinner. And to be perfectly honest, he liked holding to traditions, himself.

"This is Eternity Springs," he muttered as he pulled on his jeans. "The Mayberry of Colorado. She's fine. She's safe."

And the last time your intuition screamed at you this way a predator tortured and murdered your son.

He muttered a curse and called Brick Callahan.

"Sure, I'll head over there right now," the young owner of the region's newest tourist attraction, a "glam" camp, said after Daniel explained the situation to him.

"Thank you. I know it's probably unnecessary, but having you with her will ease my mind."

"Glad to be of assistance."

Daniel finished dressing and went up to the main house for breakfast. The restaurant was filled with family in town for his wedding, and for a time, they proved to be a fine distraction.

And yet, the unease continued to slither through him.

Shannon couldn't take her gaze off the pieces of shattered coffee mug scattered across the kitchen floor. As long as she didn't shift her stare, she wouldn't see the blood staining the tile. Brick's blood.

She prayed his head was as hard as his uncle Gabe claimed, and that no permanent damage had been done by the frying pan the stranger had hit him with after forcing Shannon to call out for Brick to enter Heartsong Cottage. Head cuts always bled a lot, didn't they? And he wouldn't still be bleeding if he were dead, right? Surely the reason why he hadn't regained consciousness was due to whatever had been in the syringe the doctor had stuck him with.

The doctor. Judging from his rambling

rants, she surmised he was a doctor, anyway. He'd arrived with a black leather doctor's bag and handled a scalpel like an extension of himself. She'd never seen the man before in her life.

He had nothing to do with Russell Wilbarger. He wasn't her enemy, at all. He was here because of Daniel.

He said Daniel's name with absolute loathing in his voice.

Another wave of fear crashed over her. She tugged ineffectively at the zip ties he'd fastened around her wrists and ankles.

He paced the cottage like a tiger, muttering and periodically snapping the rubber band he wore around his wrist. "We wanted another child for so long. When I discovered that Linda is finally pregnant again, I bought a stuffed lamb for her. So soft and cuddly. Benny loves cuddly. I know Megan will, too. It plays 'Jesus Loves Me.'" He laughed bitterly. "What a crock."

Linda. Benny. A pregnancy. Shannon realized just who had invaded her home. This was the man from whom Linda and her son had been hiding when Daniel served as their bodyguard. How did he get out of jail?

He whirled toward her, his red-rimmed hazel-colored eyes glowing with a haunted fury. "People talk like he's a god, you know. Your Daniel. I saw it on the news. On Christmas Day. He's such a fraud. A liar and a fraud."

Shannon wanted to speak up and defend Daniel. She wanted to reason with this man, but she'd tried that already. It hadn't helped; he'd acted even more deranged, pointing at her with the scalpel, bringing it to within an inch of her face.

"So he thinks he gets to be a new daddy, does he? He can by God think again. He stole my family from me. Next Christmas, he can be the one with presents under the tree that will never be opened. He can be the one whose milk and cookies for Santa sit and go sour and stale."

The stranger paced as he ranted, and Shannon watched for an opening of some sort, any sort, her mind racing. She had to do something, but what? Soupy was napping as usual in her bed in the bedroom. Should Shannon call for her and command her to attack?

Yeah, right. If the doctor were allergic to dog slobber from being licked repeatedly, perhaps. Soupy didn't even have a tail to whip him with. Her little nub might wiggle nonstop, but it was no weapon.

"It can't be allowed to happen, of course," the doctor declared. "My mother cried all Christmas Day. Cried and cried and cried. Meanwhile, Garrett sat there looking so happy. That other family was so happy. No. No. No. That just can't be."

Shannon breathed a tiny bit easier when he set down his scalpel. Then he reached into his bag and pulled out another syringe and a little bottle. "No. No. No. He shouldn't have been happy. I lost my babies."

He stared at Shannon, a maniacal glint in his eyes. "He needs to lose his, too."

Daddy! Daddy! Daddy!

The voice echoed in his mind as clear as the wind chimes hanging on Angel's Rest's front porch and a black tidal wave of dread roared over Daniel. In the process of stirring cream into his third cup of coffee, the silver spoon rattled against the china coffee cup.

Something is very wrong.

Brick hadn't called him. He'd had plenty of time to arrive at Heartsong Cottage. He should have called by now.

Something is very, very wrong.

Without conscious thought, he abruptly shoved to his feet. "I've got to go," he said to his brothers.

"Now there's one nervous bridegroom," Nick Garrett said.

Daniel didn't waste time on an explanation. He didn't have one to give. All he knew for certain was that he had to get to Shannon fast.

He grabbed his jacket from the hall tree on his way past it and hit the front door at a fast walk. When he descended the front steps, he broke into a run.

Daddy! Daddy! Daddy!

The last time he'd had a sick feeling like this he'd lost his family. "God, please."

Overnight, more than a foot of new snow had blanketed the valley, and he ran the path by memory, forging his own way to the footbridge spanning Angel Creek. He yanked his phone from his pocket and hit the speed dial for Shannon.

Ring. Ring. Ring. Ring. Ring. Voice mail. He hit end and as he pounded across dialed Brick's number. **Ring. Ring. Ring. Ring. Ring. Voice mail.**

No. No, no, no. He kicked his pace up a gear, running as fast as he could manage through the snow. There was a reason neither one of them answered. Maybe she was already at the salon and she couldn't hear the phone ring over the roar of blow-dryers.

Daddy. Daddy. Daddy.

Let this be nothing more than paranoia. Let Shannon answer the door and fuss and fume at me for spoiling the whole tradition thing.

He dialed her number again. Still no answer. He ran up Cottonwood to Fifth Street, then over to Pinion and turned south. Urgency dogged his steps. With every second that passed, the certainty that Shannon needed him strengthened.

Finally, he passed the intersection of Pinion and Third. In the middle of the block light glowed in the windows of Heartsong Cottage.

As Shannon watched the stranger fill the hypodermic with a clear fluid, panic washed through her and she felt the flutter in her womb that was her baby. A voice like that of a child rang clearly in her mind. **"Talk to him. Ask him about his family. Give Daddy time to get here to save Sister."**

With that, she knew what to do.

She knew Daniel would come to save them. She needed to keep herself and their child safe until he got here.

Praying she chose the right path, she asked, "Tell me about Megan. It's a lovely name."

At her question, the man went still. He closed his eyes and shuddered. "Megan Elizabeth. My choice. Linda thinks she can name her something else."

Shannon swallowed hard. "Megan Elizabeth. That's beautiful. I'll bet she'll be a beautiful child."

"She'll be an angel. My angel. I never would hurt her. Never! Just like I'd never hurt Benny. I'd cut off my right arm first. It was all a mistake. I didn't mean to do it. Linda…she just freaked out. She shouldn't have freaked out."

You shouldn't have hit her.

"They say I'm a sex offender. It's not true. It's a lie. It's a horrible label. It was a mistake. That's all. A mistake. I'd had too much to drink, and I was online and surfing around. I clicked something I shouldn't have clicked. I'm not even sure how I got there."

Shannon bit back the caustic comment she would have made under different circumstances—**gee, maybe using the search term "child porn"?**—and said instead, "I've done some ill-advised things when under the influence."

"Then you understand! She didn't. She wouldn't listen. I didn't know what they did on that island, either. It was all a mistake. Linda wouldn't listen, and now they've given me that horrible label and taken my children away. And he helped them do it. Daniel Garrett. He took what was mine…so now I'll take his."

He advanced on her, and Shannon recognized that she'd run out of time. She prepared to use the final weapons in her limited arsenal—a bloodcurdling scream and launching herself at the intruder's knees—when movement in the the kitchen doorway caught her attention.

Her groom had come to ruin the wedding-day tradition.

Thank God.

Having stealthily entered the kitchen, Daniel heard the stranger's declaration and immediately identified him. Dr. Mason Tate. Benny's father, Linda's soon-to-be ex-husband. Daniel's blood ran cold, then immediately fired hot. **No, you won't take my family. You damned well won't.**

Time slowed to a crawl as he swiftly considered the handful of different actions available to him. Attempt to reason or attack? Be bold or sneaky? Use a weapon or only his martial arts training?

No sense trying reason. The guy had tracked him down to Eternity Springs, attacked Brick—out, but breathing regu-larly—and was threatening Shannon. He's obviously insane.

Daniel lifted Soupy's leash from its hook beside the back door and moved swiftly as the doctor advanced on Shannon, the hypodermic gripped and raised like a knife in his right hand. Two long strides took Daniel up behind him. Hearing him,

Tate started to turn, but Daniel was on him before he could mount a defense.

Daniel did a low sweeping kick with his left leg, hitting the doctor at the ankles and dropping him to his left. The sweeping kick spun Daniel to his right and all the way around.

As Tate hit the ground, he kept hold of the syringe with his right arm up, successfully avoiding pricking his own skin. As Daniel completed his turn, he shifted his weight onto his left foot and performed a side kick into the doctor's right elbow. The crack of bone was audible as the arm broke. Tate screamed and dropped the syringe.

Daniel reached down and grabbed the broken arm and pulled it above the doctor's head, forcing him onto his stomach. Daniel then planted a knee in the bastard's back and tied him with Soupy's leash.

It had taken only seconds. Daniel focused all of his attention on Shannon. "Are you okay?"

"I'm fine. I'm fine. But we need to call Rose. He gave Brick a shot of some sort. The bottle is on the desk."

Daniel rose and dragged the moaning doctor farther away from Shannon before looking at the bottle and removing a pair of scissors from the desk drawer. "It's a sedative."

Daniel quickly snipped the ties binding Shannon's wrists and ankles, then moved to stand over the doctor. He yanked his head up by his hair. "How much did you give him?"

The doctor blubbered a response. Daniel looked to Shannon. "Call Rose. I'll call Zach."

In less than ten minutes, Eternity Springs' sheriff, physician, and half of the Callahan clan crowded into Shannon's living room.

After relaying their story to the interested parties, and with both Brick and the assailant in good hands, Daniel led Shannon into their bedroom and shut the door. He took her into his arms and hugged her tight, burying his face in her hair. Shaking like a tree in a gale, he breathed his first easy breath all day.

"Ah, jeeze, Shannon. Ah, jeeze."

"I know. I know." She gave a shaky little laugh and asked, "What took you so long to get here?"

"I didn't want to spoil the whole tradition thing."

"Traditions are overrated."

Grinning, he pressed a kiss against her hair. "Glad to hear you've come around to my way of thinking."

He paused, then drew back just a little bit. "Sweetheart, I'm so sorry. This happened because of my job—"

"No." She lifted her hand and placed her index finger against his lips. "You know better. It's all on him. You saved us, Daniel. I'm safe. Your baby is safe."

He swallowed hard against a stewpot of emotion. Residual fear, relief, joy, anger— and one he'd never expected to experience —**redemption.**

Her finger slid from his lip down to the angel's wings pendant hanging around his neck. "I have something to tell you. It's going to sound weird, but it's important that you hear it."

"Okay."

"While we were waiting for you to come and save us, I could tell that he was about to act. I didn't know what to do. I knew I needed to do something, but I was so afraid that my mind was frozen. Then suddenly, just as clearly as the bells of St. Stephen's on Sunday morning, I heard a voice whisper through my mind. It was a child's voice."

She repeated the words she'd heard and Daniel went still for a full ten seconds. He cleared his throat. "Say that again?"

"'**Talk to him. Ask him about his family. Give Daddy time to get here to save Sister.**'"

Oh, God.

Shannon's eyes filled with tears. "Celeste says that our guardian angels are always with us if we only will open our hearts to hear them."

"I didn't think I had a guardian angel. But maybe he's been with me for…well…for the past decade."

"I'm a believer. Especially after today."

Daniel's arms wrapped around her once again for another fierce hug. "You know what this means, don't you?"

"What's that?"

"We're going to have a girl."

Daniel was a believer, too.

The wedding itself went off without a hitch. Not one of the many babies present cried during the ceremony, and the numerous adults who teared up managed to do so silently. Daniel's brother didn't drop the ring on the best man–to-groom handover. And when Shannon felt the flutter of their baby as Daniel tipped her chin to kiss her for the first time as her husband, she silently declared the moment totally perfect.

The reception was deemed the party of the season. Brick Callahan had a grand time showing off his new stitches and everyone wondered why Chase Timberlake was there without his fiancée. Rumor had it that Sarah Murphy was nosy enough to ask Ali Timberlake if there was trouble in Paradise, and Ali had replied, "Not exactly." Shannon looked forward to learning the scoop about that—at a later date.

Now the time had arrived for the bride and groom to take their leave from the Eternity Springs community center. As arranged, a car waited for them, but when it turned onto Pinion Street and their destination came into view, Shannon squeezed his hand. "Let's walk from here."

"Are you sure?"

"Positive. It's snowing. Big, fat, beautiful snowflakes. I want to walk in the snow."

Daniel directed their driver to pull over.

"You're not going to want to do snow angels in the front yard or anything, are you?" he asked as he helped her from the car.

She laughed, a joyous sound that rose through the winter night like a song.

Daniel grinned and held her hand as they walked toward the little white house with red trim where a curl of smoke rose from the chimney and warm yellow lights glowed in the windows. He told himself that the moisture stinging his eyes was the result of the chill in the air—though he knew better.

He opened the front gate for Shannon, then placed his hand at the small of her back, and together they approached the front door.

And Daniel began to sing to the tune of Etta James's "At Last."

My heart,
was broken and alone.
I had given up all hope,
but then Shannon came along.
My love,
led me back into the light.
She has filled my life with song.
And brought me home
to Heartsong Cottage.